THE
TERRORIST'S
HOLIDAY

THE
TERRORIST'S
HOLIDAY

WITHDRAWN

ANDREW
NEIDERMAN

OPEN ROAD
INTEGRATED MEDIA
NEW YORK

978-1-4976-9395-1

Published in 2015 by Open Road Integrated Media, Inc.
345 Hudson Street
New York, NY 10014
www.openroadmedia.com

For my wife, Diane,
who has never taken a holiday from our love.

THE
TERRORIST'S
HOLIDAY

PREFACE

The two figures hidden in the darkness of the alley remained stone still and silent with an air of expectation, their bodies frozen in movement, caught on pause. It had rained, and the street glittered with the reflected light of an occasional car headlight. Minute particles making up the heavy mist could be seen dancing in the beams like fireflies brought to life by the illumination. Suddenly, the door to the basement of the synagogue across the street cracked open with a sound resembling a gunshot, echoing into the alley. Words and laughter followed, triggering the two dark figures to stand erect. Both raised their shoulders and were hunched up like hawks, perched and studying their prey.

Three young men, all under the age of twenty, emerged from the synagogue basement. They spoke quickly and fluently in Hebrew. One of them laughed, and then the other two joined in. All three still wore yarmulkes.

It was the end of March. They were on Wallace Avenue in the

Bronx. They had just emerged from a meeting with the other members of the JDL, the Jewish Defense League.

"Soviet Jews will sing praises in your name forever. Daniel, son of Hymie and Sylvia Goldstein," one of the young men said and laughed.

"Since he was in the Middle East his name sends cold fear down the spines of Arabs," the other one said.

"Laugh, you two, but Kaufman agrees with me."

They grew serious.

"Then you'll go with him back to Israel in the fall?"

"I don't know yet. I'm going to talk to my parents about it."

"Good."

They all stood facing each other for a moment. Then Daniel reached out, and the three took hands.

"Never again," he said.

"Never again," they repeated.

"Shalom," Daniel said.

"Shalom."

"Shalom, Daniel."

The two others started up the street. Daniel stood there for a moment watching them. Then he turned to go in the opposite direction.

He hesitated at the street corner. It was certainly cold and damp out. He would have preferred snow. There was something neater about snow until it melted and became rain, he thought. He wiped his face with his handkerchief and then looked at his watch. It was nearly midnight. His parents would have many questions again—his father genuinely interested and desiring to know, but his mother, sitting with worry, holding her breath. She had given up trying to hold him back.

Recently she had said, "This is what comes of sending you to Israel? You come home, believing yourself to be a soldier?"

"Every man, woman, and child is a soldier in Israel," he had replied. His father nodded, smiling. *Yes* was written over his face.

"The boy's got a feeling for something," he said. "He's got pride and deep belief. You want him to be like the lost youth roaming America?"

"I don't want him to go find wars. There'll be plenty who'll do that for him. Plenty. Do you have to be in the protests and the demonstrations? A policeman will hit you over the head with his club and make you a vegetable."

"Leave him alone. You want him to be a coward like that Grossfield boy?"

"A valedictorian you call a coward? He'll be a success, rich and safe."

"No Jew is safe if one Jew is in danger because he is a Jew," Daniel said. "That's what Rabbi Kaufman says."

His father had smiled again. Daniel remembered that smile now. It made him swell with pride. He took a deep breath and started across the street.

The two figures in the darkness stepped forward in such synchronized unison, it was as if they were attached to each other. When Daniel reached the sidewalk, the taller figure stepped farther out and took a position against the far wall. Daniel began to walk past the alley. The other figure waited, frozen in a ridiculous posture—bending over, his arms hanging forward, his head tilted to the left. Just as

Daniel was in front of the alley, he stepped out in front of him. Daniel stopped abruptly and stepped back.

"Shalom, Jew," the figure said.

Daniel raised his hands quickly and took a karate stance. The second and taller figure came out of the darkness behind him. He raised his right hand high. He had an ice pick grasped within his fist. It came down on Daniel silently and swiftly, punching a small hole where his brain met his spinal column. A little spurt of blood came up around the shiny pick. Daniel didn't even utter a cry. He grimaced and raised his shoulders like someone who had just caught a chill. The man with the ice pick pulled it up in the same quick motion with which he had brought it down. Daniel's body folded beneath him like a suit of clothes sliding off a hanger. The first figure stepped back and watched him collapse to the sidewalk.

The two assailants looked at each other for a moment, and then they heard the door of the synagogue basement open again. Instantly, they moved back into the darkness of the alley and disappeared down the corridor of shadows. When they were safely away, they spoke.

"It was easy, Joseph, easy," the first figure said. He spoke with hot excitement.

"Call me Yusuf. Now and forever."

They stopped to rest, leaning against the stone wall of a corner apartment house. Both of their faces shone with the wetness that had settled on their cheeks and foreheads. The boy's face, although lighter in tone, was spotted with dark blotches from some skin ailment. He looked younger than his sixteen years. Even standing still he was animated, driven by that nervous energy of adolescence. His eyes darted about as he continually searched the neighborhood, and he shifted weight from foot to foot rhythmically. The young man with him had dark, Semitic skin and a rather long, thin nose. His lips curled downward at the corners, giving him a habitual sneer. He closed his eyes and took deep breaths as he rested.

"Even in public? Call you Yusuf, even in public?"

"Of course in public." Yusuf squeezed his arms against himself as if to hold in the excitement, but his voice was high pitched. He cursed himself for not having his brother's coolness. It was important to master one's body if one wanted to master others.

"But isn't that dangerous? Hassil said . . ."

"Hassil is too cautious. He is a sheep among horses, a sparrow flying with a flock of hawks. We must be stronger," Yusuf said and put both his hands on the boy's shoulders. The boy smiled and straightened his body.

"And what will you call me?"

"The name of your father. Abu. Now and forever."

"Now and forever," the newly baptized boy said.

They grasped hands. The boy's lips were burning. He ran his tongue over them. It seemed to him that his whole body was hot with excitement. He was a torch. It was as if he could light up an entire street.

"It was easy," Abu whispered. "Easy. Just as you said it would be."

"It won't always be as easy, but it will always be as good."

"Yes. It's good."

"Let's go. We better not be seen on any of these streets now."

They started walking away, keeping to the shadows, hugging the protection of the darkness. They feared the touch of streetlights.

"Now what? Can I tell my father?"

"No. We wait."

"They'll recognize us now, see our true value and count us in when the time comes?"

"Yes, they'll recognize us."

"Do you think . . . maybe something big?"

"Of course big. Nessim is respected. My brother is the best. Wherever they send him, we will all go. You, your father, Nessim, and I. It will be big."

"Big enough to make a difference? A real difference?"

"Yes," Yusuf said, but at the time he had no idea just how big it would be.

1

Abe Rothberg folded the newspaper and put it down on his desk. He shook his head and stood up to walk over to the window that looked out over Sixth Avenue, clasping his hands behind his back. *It is getting to be too much,* he thought, *too much.* He had turned forty-three just last week, but he felt much older and very tired. He saw it in his mirrored reflection—the graying temples and thinning hair, the deeper creases in his brow, the drooping of his eyelids, the paleness in his cheeks and lips. At times he even caught himself slouching when he stood talking to people. It depressed him because he let it happen. His life was shrinking inside him.

On the other hand, Lillian grew softer and more beautiful every day. She was radiant and alive. Her energy made him feel insecure. She never seemed to stop. She was into everything she could possibly get into—an officer in Hadassah, president of their chapter of B'nai B'rith, a leading fund-raiser for the United Jewish Appeal, active in the PTO. The list went on and on.

Here he was, the president and owner of one of the biggest wholesale paper goods outfits in the city, and she seemed busier and more important than he did. It was unnerving at times to be so overshadowed by his wife.

Of course, it was difficult to attach a great importance and significance to paper goods in light of her battles for justice, education, and a free and secure Israel. At parties and dinners, the conversation rarely turned to his work. What could he say—toilet paper had gone up in quality?

Even his sixteen- and fourteen-year-old daughters, Denise and Lori, looked at him as if he were an oddball in the house sometimes. He was the provider of dresses, cars, cosmetics, stereos, televisions—a machine to make possible the consumption of consumer goods. They loved him in an offhanded sort of way, he was sure, but did they really respect and understand him? What's more, did they care?

He was worrying about them the way he would worry about a finished paper goods product. Increasingly, he had come to consider his children as products. They were, after all, created and molded at home. Denise, especially concerned him. She took more and more for granted each day. He hated to use the word *spoiled*, and Lillian never seemed to know what he was talking about when he talked about Denise's attitudes. She had no respect for money, never yet having had to earn a penny, and she used the credit cards as if they were tickets admitting her to a world of dreams. It struck him that a good many people in America had that attitude about credit cards. They had long since lost their original purpose, or perhaps, the originators knew right from the start just what a temptation they had turned loose on the population. No, his daughter was a big problem. She had become a Jewish American Princess, and he was afraid there was little he could do about it now.

The ringing of the phone snapped him out of his depression. It was Lillian, bubbling over the wires as usual.

"It's a coup, a real coup. Everyone's been trying to put something like this together for years. I told you. All it takes is real effort."

"Slow down. What are you talking about?"

"What I described at breakfast." Her voice dropped like a deflated balloon. "Weren't you listening?"

"You mean that business on Passover?" He had picked up key words. Over the years he had learned how to converse with Lillian; how to nod at the right times and go "uh-huh" at the pauses in her diatribes.

"Of course. You did make the reservations, Abe. I left that up to you."

"Yes," he said lying, "I did."

"Well, the fund-raiser will be held at the New Prospect. We've got Chaim Eban for the third night. That's when we'll have the rally. We did it," she said, her voiced filled with special excitement.

Chaim Eban was the Israeli general whose military strategy was held to be chiefly responsible for keeping the Syrians from retaking control of the Golan Heights during the '73 war. Now he was moving into the political arena as one of the leading advocates of a hard line with the Arabs.

"This is a hundred percent?"

"Practically. His exact words were 'Barring any unforeseen circumstances.'"

"Oh."

"Whaddaya mean, oh?"

"Tell me a day when Israel doesn't experience unforeseen circumstances."

"Thanks for your optimism," she said. "Be a little more cheery at supper, will you, Abe? Denise, especially, is looking forward to this family holiday."

"Family? She said that?"

"Well . . ."

"The Marx boy will be there too, I assume."

"Of course."

"A matchmaker at thirty-nine, Lillian?"

"My mother taught me well."

"Damn right," he said. "Okay, I'll see you later. My intercom is buzzing." He hung up. He hated using deceptions like that, but Lillian could tie him up with her projects for hours. He pressed the intercom and waited for Mrs. Green to pick up.

"Yes, Mr. Rothberg?"

"Call the New Prospect and make reservations for me and my family for Passover, Mrs. Green. Tell them the same accommodations for the same length of time."

"Certainly."

He hung up the receiver and opened the paper again. He had circled the headline: "Eighteen-Year-Old Boy Murdered on Wallace Avenue."

Daniel Goldstein. He read the name again. Poor Hymie and Sylvia. He was surprised Lillian didn't know yet. When she found out, she would call him and bawl him out for not telling her. She knew he read the paper thoroughly every morning in the office. But he couldn't do it; he never could do it. There was something about being the bearer of tragedy, something that made him feel closer to it, almost a part of it. It was easier to sit back and let others tell the horrible news—easier to just react with everyone else.

The article had mentioned a JDL meeting too. Abe had just recently had a pretty heated discussion with Hymie about that. Sylvia sided with him, not Hymie.

"I wouldn't want my boy to toss bombs and indiscriminately kill people, no," Hymie said, "but we must begin to go on the offensive. It's the only message anti-Semites understand. Act like sheep and they'll act like wolves."

"So you encourage your son?"

"I don't encourage him. He's got a mind of his own. I don't discourage him, either."

"Same thing."

"I tell him it's no good," Sylvia said. "I tell him there are other ways, more peaceful ways."

"They do no good."

"Who says they do no good? What have you won so far with your wolves, Mr. Samson?"

"You're not realistic," Hymie said.

"I am realistic," she snapped. "Abe's right. The actions are stupid. They're insignificant in the light of what's happening, and they only bring negative feelings and comments. They feed the anti-Semites, give them something to point to and talk about."

"So we should go hide in a synagogue somewhere?"

"I didn't say that."

"Neither did I," Abe said.

He relived the entire conversation. Daniel Goldstein. He could have had a son nearly Daniel's age. Perhaps he would have been out there too, meeting secretly in synagogue basements or back rooms, planning revenge for the massacre at the Olympics. Is it better to have daughters?

He thought about Denise—how she had blossomed into a beautiful young lady, taking on Lillian's good features—small and dainty curves, gentle blue eyes, rich and thick dark brown hair. She knew she was attractive, and she took advantage of it. He had fallen in love with his own daughter the way a father falls in love with images of his wife and images of himself. She was a bright girl, despite the problems he saw developing in her character. Her grades in school were always in the A range, and Lillian had already picked out Skidmore, mainly because the Solomons had sent their daughter there.

"I want her to mix with best. Touch only good things. Realize what she can become."

"The wife of a rich businessman, like Bernard Marx, who will inherit his father's position with a chain of department stores, maybe?"

"Why not? There's something bad about that prospect?"

People were prospects to Lillian—prospective donors for her charities, prospective speakers for her meetings, prospective workers for her causes, and prospective husbands for her daughters. To her everything existed for its potential. *Maybe nothing's wrong with that*, he thought. The phone rang.

"Abe, Bill Marcus. You heard about the Goldstein boy?"

"I read it in the paper."

"It's not just a mugging you know."

"Seems not."

"All this is a result of that damnable resolution in the U.N."

"I don't know."

"Now, more than ever before, we've got to get behind Tel Aviv. We have no one but ourselves, just the way it was before the Second World War."

"Maybe so," he said. He hated arguing with Bill Marcus. The man was so dramatic and often twisted words. It was better to speak in short, impotent sentences.

"This affair in the Catskills is beginning to take on a lot more significance. I'm glad our wives are deeply involved. You heard about Chaim Eban?"

"Lillian called."

"I'm working on Stanley Plotnik. He never leaves that practice of his for more than a week."

"Doctors are always in demand."

"Bullshit. He can't stand the thought of losing the money. But between Toby and your wife and me, I think we've got Beverly convinced she should work harder on him too. He could give a few thousand just like that. You'll try too if you see him soon?"

"Yes, I will."

"Good. When will you sit shiva with the Goldsteins?"

"Tomorrow," he said.

"There's no easy time to say Kaddish for an eighteen-year-old."

"I realize that."

"OK," Marcus said but paused for a long moment. "We'll talk then."

"Good-bye."

When he hung up the phone, Abe sat back and thought again. He didn't mind going up to the Catskills for Passover. They had been doing it for years and years now, ever since his mother passed away and his father went into the home; but he liked to think of it as a vacation, as a time to relax. Didn't he earn it, work hard enough to deserve it?

Sometimes, when the weather was good up there, he could get in a little golf. The New Prospect was a dream resort. He wanted to lower himself into the recreations like someone easing himself into a warm bath. The card games, the indoor pool, the nightclub, and the good meals were all designed to make you relax and forget the hard, cold, real world. Now, his wife and many of his friends were going to make it a time of intense Zionistic activities. All the guests, upwards of twenty-five hundred, would feel an obligation to be serious and talk politics. How could he think about gin rummy when the Arabs were planning on attacking a kibbutz full of children?

Unlike many of the people he knew, being a Jew had never been a burden to him. Most of them carried the weight of great suffering in their faces and in their talk. He had always been well protected and pleasantly unaware of the havoc that rattled outside the walls of his fine home, his fine education, and his fine possessions. He was a practicing member of a reformed synagogue, but he didn't consider himself a religious person. He knew that some of his Conservative and Orthodox friends called the Reform Synagogue religion with convenience, and he tended to agree with them. But that didn't matter. None of it did.

As he sat there thinking, it seemed to him that nothing in his life worked him up—not his Jewishness, not his business, not even his family. *I really need this vacation,* he thought. *I need a renewal, a reincarnation, a revival. The hell with it all. I'm going to have a good time.* He was so determined about it that he deliberately left for lunch a half hour early just to be extravagant with his leisure time.

2

Yusuf was having the dream again. People were kneeling before him and pleading for their lives. They were all ages and sizes, and they were all naked. The mass of them was very similar to those pictures of the Nazi concentration camps. Now he was walking among them. They were still on their knees. Most were afraid to look up at him. Some did, and some tried to reach out to have him touch them with mercy. He was smiling. A Jewess, perhaps in her late teens, offered her body to him. She had her hands under her breasts and lifted them as an offering. He swung out and whipped her across the tops, near the nipples. She screeched in pain and cowered back. There was a group on their stomachs. He stood on the buttocks of an old male and surveyed the people. Suddenly he was naked too, and he had a terrible erection. It began to swell and pulsate. The people began to laugh. He was shouting at them, and they were laughing harder and harder. His neck strained with the effort to shut them up, his veins visible just below the skin. They wouldn't stop. It was horrible. He woke with a start.

As usual he was sweating, and he did have an erection. It frightened him and he sat up quickly. There was barely enough light in the room to make out the outlines of chairs and a dresser. He had the window covered with a dark shade. He rubbed his cheeks vigorously to take the numbness out of his face and then swung his feet out over the side of the bed. He thought for a moment. The picture of the hawk and the sword was a dark blur on the mirror, but it comforted him nevertheless.

He stood up to go to the bathroom. He had to walk through the living room, which served as a bedroom for Nessim and Clea. They had a pullout couch. There was a little more light out there and it was easy to find his way across the room without bumping into a table or dresser, but he still had to walk close to their bed. Clea was turned away, facing the windows, also shaded; Nessim was on his back. Clea's long black hair traveled over Nessim's right arm. Yusuf hesitated a moment. Her naked back was exposed, the cover drawn up over her breasts and angled down across the small of her back.

He had seen Clea naked before, and although it excited him, he always felt guilty. She was his brother's woman. They had met her in Athens. She was stuck there en route to France because her mother had suffered a stroke. Her mother was from France, but her father had been a Palestinian. He was killed in the shelling, and Clea and her mother had decided to leave the endless bloodbath known as "the Middle Eastern Situation."

Nessim and Yusuf were part of the organization's force to be stationed in America. As far as Hezbollah was concerned, there were two battlegrounds on which to wage the war against Israel and the Zionist imperialists—the Middle East and America. Without America, there would be no strong Israel with which to contend. Therefore, to defeat Israel on the home ground, she first had to be defeated in the States. The government and the people of America had to be influenced and persuaded. Privately, the leadership was happy with some of the results that the oil embargo had created, but they were unhappy with the tempo of change. Also, they were aware of the strong and effective Jewish organization in America. Ways had to be found to get at them and weaken them. For that purpose, units were to be sent to the States. Nessim and Yusuf were on the first leg of their journey when they met up with Clea.

Nessim had fallen in love with her almost immediately and she saw strength and hope in him. He was nearly eleven years older than she was, and seemed beyond defeat, drawing up pictures of a new world for her. But she had been reluctant to leave the West Bank. As terrible as the situation had become, it was still her home, and France was a far-off uncertainty. Nessim radiated optimism, the positive belief of a man who had full faith in his cause. Caught in a world of turmoil with everything she knew disintegrating around her, Clea was eager to become involved with someone as dynamic and promising as Nessim.

Yusuf, who loved his brother with an idolization close to religious zeal, sat with them in Athens and listened to Nessim's soft, convincing optimism. Clea sat with smiling eyes and drifted in and out of his words, moving to the undulating rhythms of his statements. She accepted him as a leader of causes with all the romance it involved and desperately tried to ignore the truth of what that meant he would become and would do. Someday it would all be over, and they would return to the West Bank, live on a quiet farm, and raise beautiful children, like her parents had hoped to do.

When her mother died, Clea turned to Nessim completely and without question, changed the direction of her travel plans, and accepted his destiny as her own. They were all off to America to work some kind of magic and help bring an honorable peace to the Middle East. As a symbolic gesture to the dream, Nessim did not propose marriage to her.

"We shall do that ceremony when we can enjoy some relative peace," he had said, and she had accepted the temporary relationship he proposed.

Yusuf knew that Nessim had great difficulty getting the organization to permit him to take Clea along, but together, the three of them moved on and came into the United States to be part of the illegal alien movement Hezbollah and its allies had managed.

The command had created an overall battle plan that called for different units to integrate themselves into a community and be ready to act when they were called on to act. Up to this point, Nessim had only performed small acts of sabotage, but he was waiting. The big order was coming soon. It had been promised. They knew his great value. He had been trained by Russian demolition experts, and the command considered him one of its most important fifth columnists. He had built himself a significant reputation in the Middle East, and it was only because of the new importance the organization had placed on the American front that he was shipped out at all.

"What is it?" Nessim now whispered to Yusuf, raising his head off the pillow.

"I had a nightmare. I've got to splash cold water on my face." Yusuf moved on and went into the bathroom.

When he had come home after the assassination of the young

JDL member that night, he had gone right to his bedroom and fallen asleep. Nessim and Clea were over at Hassil's, and they didn't get back until very early in the morning. He was eager to tell Nessim what he had accomplished, but he didn't want to say anything in front of Clea. He would wait until the morning when they were alone. Clea worked as a waitress in an Armenian restaurant on Thirty-First and Madison. She went in at ten and worked until eleven at night, six days a week.

Yusuf turned on the bathroom light and looked at his face in the mirror. He thought he could see the great changes in his features that had come about these past few months. It was as if something inside was eating away at him, bringing down his youth and casting the pallor of age and death over him. His eyes had grown dull, and his facial muscles drooped. He looked like a man who was perpetually angry. Even Nessim had commented.

"You must permit yourself to forget for a little while. Hatred is a small parasite. It feeds like a parasite lives on a host, eating away at your soul. We are driven by it, but we must not let it suck the life out of us."

Yusuf splashed cold water over his cheeks and began patting his forehead. Suddenly he noticed blood on the inside of his fingers, where he had held the ice pick. It frightened and nauseated him. The Jew had been with him all this time—a part of him had followed. He shoved his hands into the water and scrubbed them madly with a bar of soap. Before he was finished and dried, the bathroom door opened and Nessim stepped inside. He brought his finger to his lips to indicate silence and then closed the door behind him.

"What is it?"

"Just a dream. I told you."

"You're too intense. Animals catch their prey best when they pretend to ignore them and the prey becomes relaxed and confident. Then the animals strike and succeed."

"We wait too much and strike too little."

Nessim studied his brother for a long moment. He knew him with the sensitive touch a blind man uses to know the world around him.

Yusuf was smaller and thinner than he was, taking more after their mother than their father. Nessim stood six feet two and had broad shoulders. He had thick forearms and big hands. Yusuf's hands were big, but the fingers weren't as powerful or as thick.

There was also a difference in their faces—Nessim's contained a controlled intensity. He could direct his eyes and manipulate his facial muscles to remain still and exhibit great concentration. He had energy, but it wasn't in any way an anxious energy. It was the face of a man with great inner strength, a man who had a fine domination over his nervous system. He moved with the sleek silence of a cat and spoke with the softness of a transcendental guru. On the surface, he appeared to be a man at great peace with the world. This superficial cover made his thrust and blow that much more effective. He could strike out with the swiftness of a snake and quickly retreat to the peacefulness of a turtle's shell. Nessim was a man of great extremes. Only someone who had been through the eye of a hurricane could understand the ominous silence in his eyes.

"Why do you choose to wash up now?"

"I went right to bed."

"Where were you?"

"With Abu, the son of Abu."

"You don't use those names in public?"

"When we're alone," Yusuf said, but he was obvious about his unhappiness over it.

"You must be careful. We can't afford suspicions. Not now."

"Have you heard something new?"

Nessim turned to the toilet and began to urinate. "A message might come tomorrow."

"Tomorrow. Finally." Yusuf slapped his hands together.

"Quiet."

"How will the message come?"

"In the classified section. It'll tell us where to go for the meeting."

The command used the Lost and Found column. The heading was always, "Lost, a pair of Siamese cats, one with a red ribbon, and one with a blue."

"I don't know why they do that."

"They do it to be careful. We must always be careful. Always. You don't understand that yet. We are always around our enemies."

"I know that," Yusuf said, his eyes firing up.

"You know that too well. They can learn it from you. That's a weakness."

"I'm careful. You'll see. You'll be proud of us when you . . ."

"What?" Nessim turned quickly. He knew that expression on Yusuf's face. "What else were you going to say?"

"Nothing."

Nessim grasped Yusuf's arm and squeezed it tightly. Yusuf felt the power of his fingers. His forearm began to ache.

"What?"

"I struck out for the hawk."

Nessim's eyes widened. He turned Yusuf's body completely around and pressed him against the wall.

"How?"

"Abu and I. We took one of them down. A JDL demonstrator."

"Where? How?"

"Nessim," Clea called.

"*Shh.*" He opened the door a crack. "What is it?"

"I heard talking."

"Yusuf and I. Go to sleep. It's all right."

"Nothing's wrong?"

"Nothing."

She was quiet so he closed the door. Then he leaned back.

His face suddenly exhibited a new control. His body relaxed, and he spoke softer.

"Tell me everything. Quickly."

"We went up to Wallace Avenue, to that JDL hangout, and we waited for an opportunity. We've been going up there periodically, waiting for the chance. Tonight we had it."

"Had what?"

"We caught one of them alone, near an alley. I drove an ice pick into his neck." He added, "The way you once showed me." His face distorted as he re-experienced it.

Nessim took a deep breath. "You did this and got away clean?"

"Clean. And Abu was great. He played the decoy. He's ready to do big things."

Nessim stared for a moment. "You might have done great damage to the general plan."

"How? We've struck out and driven fear into their hearts," Yusuf said, a look of disappointment moving quickly over his face.

"You've also placed them on their guard and you've brought down the house. Idiot, this will bring on intense investigations. You took one life. A meaningless act."

"Meaningless?"

"Timing-wise. I told you the plan was imminent. You think I came all the way over here to kill one Jew?"

"But . . ."

"But nothing. Why did you do this without checking with me?"

"To prove our value."

"This was no way to do that. You might have proven not only your lack of value, but mine as well because you're with me."

"I did it for us . . ." Yusuf's face showed a new fear. He looked away.

"Go to sleep. I can't think about it now. In the morning we'll talk some more. In the meantime we'll wait to see what the command does—how they react to this."

"If they don't like it, we won't own up to it."

"Lying to the command is not the way for us to present a unified strike. We can't divide ourselves now. I want you to get Abu over here tomorrow. He must understand everything. You've baptized him in blood, and he must understand the significance of the new religion."

"I only meant to help you, Nessim."

"I know that," Nessim said. There was great fatigue in his voice. "Let's go to sleep."

He stepped out of the bathroom. Yusuf hesitated a moment. He felt terribly depressed. The bloodstained water remained in the sink. It began to sicken him, and he felt a weakness in his stomach. Quickly, he pulled out the drain and let it disappear. The residue remained. He washed it away, fighting back a dry heave as he did so. Then he shut off the light and moved across the living room. Nessim was turned away. His arm was draped loosely over Clea's hip. When Yusuf shut the door to his room, he stood in the darkness, cursing wildly to himself. He didn't know whom to strike out at.

Those damn Jews, he thought. *They defeat me even in their deaths.* He raged on in the darkness until he grew tired again and drifted back to sleep.

3

Hassil called right after he saw the morning papers. As a legal American citizen, he served Hezbollah by performing his role as a section commander to oversee the illegal aliens whom the organization sent over from the Middle East. Those in his section checked with him periodically, the way parolees check in with a parole officer. He was a 250-pound, five-foot-eight-inch man with heavy hips and a face of thick, large features. At first glance, he looked to be a man suffering from elephantiasis. The insides of his thighs brushed against each other when he walked, making him waddle. The smallest physical activity was a major exertion for him. In every room in his apartment, there was some kind of sweet or rich food to nibble. Nessim had often made the comment that Hassil experienced sexual pleasure by masticating while others reached it by masturbating.

"He looks at food the way you and I would look at a woman," he told Yusuf. Nessim knew that Yusuf detested their visits to Hassil's, and he left his brother behind whenever he could. He now wished he had not done that the last time.

At fifty-eight, Hassil apparently had only two interests in life besides working for the cause, eating and selling his antiques. His small apartment was crowded with his collection. Even though he had a shop in the Village, he did a lot of buying and storing outside the shop. Customers often came up to his apartment to look over something "extra special." He laughed about the fact that he had no sexual interests.

"I once had a prostitute come up to visit me," he told Nessim and Clea one night, "but when she finally discovered my prick hidden under all this fat"—he shook his lower stomach with his hands—"she found I had already had an orgasm." He laughed—small convulsions of soundless facial movement, his jowls shaking. "Even I have trouble finding it sometimes, so when I urinate, I sit down like a woman; just to play it safe." He laughed again.

Because of his obese form, he spoke in a low, whizzing sound, breathing heavy all the time. He was always sweating and wiping his face with a gray handkerchief. When he spoke over the phone, it sounded like a man trying to disguise his voice. If anyone had tapped his phone, he would surely think he was on the right track.

"Have you seen this news item in today's paper about the murder of a JDL member last night? It wasn't far from your apartment," he said when Nessim called that morning.

Nessim knew he was testing and seeking information. He leaned on his elbow and wiped his eyes. Clea was apparently still asleep beside him. He thought for a moment, recalling the scene between him and Yusuf in the bathroom.

"I know about it. Let's talk later."

"Have you looked in the classifieds today?" Hassil said.

"No."

"Do that. There are some interesting items."

"I will."

"We'll talk again," Hassil said and hung up.

Nessim held the receiver for a moment, thinking. Hassil would report that Nessim had something to do with the murder of the JDL boy. There would be problems. Clea turned on her back, and he hung up the phone. He studied her face for a moment.

He loved her dark eyes and the way her small chin turned up, revealing the smooth lines of her neck. She moved her lips together and twitched her nose. It made him smile. There had always been something refreshing about waking up beside her. Her black hair, longer than shoulder length now, ran along both sides of her body. He stroked it first and she looked at him—still wearing that look of morning grogginess. He leaned over and kissed her gently on the forehead. She smiled and reached up to run her fingers along his lips.

"Who called?"

"Hassil."

"Another meeting?"

"We'll be busy today."

"Should I go to work?"

"Yes, definitely."

She stared at him for a few moments, as if she was considering whether or not to ask the next question.

"Was there something wrong with Yusuf last night?"

"His nightmares."

She nodded and turned away. "I can understand." She closed her eyes hard as if to chase away memories. He leaned over and kissed her shoulder.

"We must keep each other from suffering," he said.

She smiled and reached up to stroke back the strands of hair that had fallen over Nessim's forehead. He had thick, dark brown hair, and although he kept it well groomed during the day, it was always wild in the morning. She laughed about it and pressed her pelvis against his leg.

"I know how we can do that," she said coquettishly.

"Wait," he said.

He got up and went into Yusuf's room. Yusuf lay on his back, breathing through his opened mouth. Nessim was instantly reminded of their father lying dead on the road, still and crumpled, his arms twisted around, his legs on their sides, and his mouth opened as if he were about to shout. The memory sent a chill through his body, and he felt suddenly very cold standing naked. He shook the bed, a little more vigorously than was required. Yusuf woke with a start, sitting up quickly.

"What is it?"

"Hassil just called. It's in the paper already. Your deed for the cause."

Yusuf wiped his face and stared at Nessim, looking for some clue in his expression, but as always Nessim was neutral, unemotional.

"And?"

"We'll see about that later. Couldn't talk on the phone. But the message is in today's classified section. Get dressed and go get a paper."

"Right away," Yusuf said. He got out of bed quickly and started to put his pants on. "What will you tell Hassil later?"

"We'll tell the truth. I told you."

"He's a worm. He won't support us. He'll . . ."

Nessim reached out and grabbed his shoulder. Yusuf stood still. One look into Nessim's eyes silenced him. Nessim turned and left the room to go back to Clea. She was lying with her arms behind her head. He winked at her and she smiled. He sat on the edge of the bed and lit a cigarette. Yusuf came out, hopping on one foot as he struggled to put the other shoe on. Clea laughed.

"I'll be right back," he said.

"Don't hurry," Nessim replied. Yusuf stopped and checked his brother's expression. This time he knew the look and nodded slightly, without revealing his understanding to Clea. Then he left the apartment.

Nessim turned toward Clea. She had dropped the cover, exposing her firm breasts, only a shade or two lighter than the rest of her body. He always found that interesting. Her nipples were as dark as the nipples of a black woman. The French blood in her was responsible for her facial features, but the color of her skin and the color of her hair was Arabic. She had a funny little clipped accent, too.

He remembered the first time he had seen her, standing near the railing of an open-air café looking out at the port in Athens. The breeze played with strands of her hair. She wore a brightly colored dress that was tapered to her hips. She struck him as being statuesque, someone caught in time. There was a great stillness in her face. The sight of her touched him deeply. He had been yearning for something soft and peaceful. A string of violent memories had followed him out of Palestine. Only a week before, he had successfully blown two Israeli border guards to kingdom come. Their bodies had heaved into the air like cloth puppets.

Clea turned and her breasts moved together, forming a cleavage. He ran his fingers gently between them, separating them and then stroking her nipple with his thumb. She smiled and put her hand between his thighs. Instantly, a warmth traveled down to his loins. He felt his penis nudge against his thigh as the blood rushed into it. It climbed away from his body and he smiled to himself, thinking of an artillery piece being tilted upward for trajectory. *My military experience invades everything*, he thought.

She brought his head closer to hers and they kissed, her tongue forcing its way between his lips and pushing his back. Her hands ran down the sides of his body, grasping his buttocks and pulling them forward, pushing him into place. She was a natural lovemaker—someone who appeared to have the instincts for exquisite sensations. Every one of her movements, every touch, was designed to carry him slowly into the pitch of excitement. There was no rushing, no mad, wild passion but a careful, controlled manipulation of bodies for mutual satisfaction. At times, he thought her to be a fine artist, molding their bodies. She played upon him as one would play upon a musical instrument, and he loved it.

Their lovemaking gave him a zest for living that sometimes conflicted with his fanaticism and devotion to the cause. He had always believed himself dedicated and ready to lay down his life when the time came. And he had never questioned or doubted the fact that the time would come, could come at any moment. It might have even started today, in the message hidden among the classified advertisements. When he was with her, though, he wanted to live, to go on forever. Despite the cause, he wanted life and that made him feel weak. He had been warned. Sardin, his immediate superior, had told him in Greece.

"She'll weigh you down. She'll make you hesitate. If you care that much about her, you'll think of her at the wrong moments. We who sacrifice for the cause must not think of our lives in the present, but only what our actions will do for the future. We live in the future."

"Nevertheless, we have needs now, for the time being. You're sending me to America to be hidden among them. I must not wear the face of a fanatic. I must look like someone struggling for everyday happiness. She'll make that possible," he argued. Sardin saw some merit in that. "I have never failed the cause," Nessim added. In the end, Sardin relented.

And now, here they were, making love again, like millions of Americans, at peace in their beds.

"Don't worry, Yusuf won't hurry back," he said.

"I know."

He moved into her slowly and then they began a careful, quiet rhythm, building it into climax after climax and returning to a slow movement that had the makings of a ballet. She threw her arms over her head to indicate that she was reaching a great climax, and he grew excited by the power he had to make her feel such ecstasy. It drove him into a frenzy, and he worked his body deeper and deeper into her until she moaned and bit her lower lip. Then he exploded inside her, the heat of him pouring out. She savored it, grinding slowly to a halt, turning her head from side to side, her breathing slowing down, and her breasts relaxing. They lay there, still entwined for a few quiet moments. She kissed his neck and he rolled over. Only then did they hear the sounds of the city outside their window.

"We're good together," she said. "We always will be."

Whenever she suggested the future, he felt an anger build inside himself. It made him turn off, and he grew deeply silent. The future was a promise he could only dream of making. Perhaps Sardin was right. He should have never taken her with him. He was on his way to oblivion and he had stopped to enjoy life. What a fool. Someday he'd pay for this; it would hurt his effort. He was sure of it, but he couldn't turn her away.

"What's the matter? You look like a man being threatened, not a man being loved."

"There's something very big about to happen," he said. She touched his arm; he recognized the gesture as one of great fear. "You always knew it would come. I never fooled you about it."

"That doesn't make me any less afraid."

"Nevertheless, we knew it was to happen."

"When?"

"It starts today."

She got up and pulled a T-shirt over herself. Then she slipped into the jeans that were draped over a chair.

"I'll make some coffee and get breakfast going," she said.

He didn't reply. He lay back and waited for Yusuf to come with the paper.

4

Toby Marcus stepped out of Fitness Delight and sucked in the roundness her stomach still possessed. She could wear a panty girdle and hide it as far as the public was concerned, but she wasn't concerned with the public. She had to work it away for private encounters—especially one in particular that was coming up shortly. They were going to the Catskills again, and she'd have a chance to spend some time with Bruno. Just thinking about him drove her silly with excitement. He had come into the city twice this year, and they had met at the West End Hotel. Despite the fact that she saw him so rarely, he was sure of what she would do when he came into town and called. He didn't even pretend to court her anymore.

If he got her on the phone, it was, "I'm here. You wanna make it?"

Very crude with animal directness—that was Bruno, but that was also what she wanted. She hated herself for being so easy, but what the hell? She got just as much out of it as he did. Maybe more. *Oh, let it not be more,* she thought. If it came to that, he wouldn't call at all and he wouldn't pay any attention to her when they went up to the New Prospect.

So she acted like his sex slave, ready to jump at his beck and call. So what?

The main thing was to keep in decent shape. She had hit forty this year, and there were parts of her body that wanted to retire, slip back, sag, and drift into jellylike texture. Well, she wasn't going to let that happen, not now, maybe not ever. She dreamed of being ravishing at sixty years of age. Look at Maggie Levy—sixty-four years old with the figure of a thirty-five-year-old woman. She'd had her face lifted four times and had even had corrective cosmetic surgery done on her breasts. Why, Bill often remarked about her attractive figure, and no one who didn't know her believed that she was in her sixties. Sure it was possible. Toby could have the same things done. Maybe she wouldn't look exactly like she did when she was in her twenties, but she'd be a damn good piece of ass if she could help it.

It had gotten to the point where she had grown jealous of her daughter's trim, buxom figure. Dorothy was nearly fifteen, but she looked like a fully grown mature woman. She had a thirty-six bust, for Christ sakes. All of Bill's friends looked at her lustfully when they came to the house. It was getting so that few ever noticed her anymore if the kid was in the same room.

And she didn't like the way Dorothy returned those stares. Was it always just accidental or coincidental that she stretched and nearly popped her blouse buttons when Bill's friends were around? Just how innocent was she—if she was at all? She never came to her for any advice about sex or asked her questions about her body. She seemed to know everything she had to know. Toby mentioned that once to Bill, but he said it must be because the school ran health and sex courses nowadays. He was so oblivious. Kids today were more sophisticated in some ways, but that didn't mean they were necessarily better off.

Her daughter was a puzzle to her in more ways than one. She was a loner, content with staying in her room, playing her records and talking on her phone. Bill was always too busy to care, and anyway, he had this incredible faith and belief that nothing terrible would happen to his family without his becoming aware long beforehand.

The whole situation was annoying, but she couldn't let it get her down the way it did to so many of the women who fretted and worried wrinkles and gray hair onto themselves. They frowned and creased their foreheads. They ate all sorts of garbage foods out of nervousness and grew old before their time. This was not going to happen to her.

She crossed the street quickly and headed up the block for Ceil's Boutique. There was a bathing suit she had planned to buy for the holiday if she could trim down five pounds. She had nearly done it. She always enjoyed the indoor pool at the New Prospect. Bill hated it, so it made for a good place to meet with Bruno after he was finished with work in the dining room. It was really a silly affair. She knew the hotel workers looked for women like her—eager to have a sexual encounter that went no further than the weekend or the holiday period. It wasn't that she was stupid or naive about it.

But Bruno was something special. He had that Latin face and those dancing green eyes. The combination turned her on the moment she set eyes on him. He had come out of the kitchen that first night, carrying a tray of soups for her table, moving with ease and grace, broad shouldered and tall. The moment she saw him and he saw the way she looked at him, they both knew. Thereafter, it was just a matter of arrangements, working out the timing. Once, she claimed a headache and stayed up in the room while Bill took Dorothy to a gymnastics show in the field house. Bruno came up and they made love so passionately and desperately that she really did look like someone suffering from a headache when Bill returned.

After that, she searched for opportunities to get herself up to the New Prospect. When Lillian Rothberg suggested the rally for Israel on Passover, she worked hard with her to make it happen. Now Bill was hooked on it as much as Lillian or anyone in the organization. It wasn't that she didn't care about Israel and all that. She cared, of course, but why not combine a lot of pleasure with a lot of good work?

Actually, she felt very clever about it. Bruno knew she was coming. His attention flattered her. She realized he could be chasing young girls—and probably had a good share of them during the year—but when she arrived, he sought her out as something special. She had managed to hold on to that. It made her feel eternally young. In her mind, she had come to believe that as long as this kind of thing went on, she could hold on to that intangible thing called youth. It would radiate in her face and move over her body.

Too bad she didn't feel that way because of Bill; the fire had long since gone out between them. He was once a handsome man and quite sexy, too; however, he had let himself go badly. A potbelly, a lack of concern about his clothes, and a general degeneration in his facial features all combined to literally take the sex out of him. They made love now as though it were part of some marriage routine. Just like you had to take out the garbage, you had to turn over in bed and do it.

She had mentioned that in a session with her psychiatrist once. She had called it, "Flushing out the reproductive system." It was like a sexual laxative. The doctor liked that a lot—a young-looking Jewish fella who called himself Ross even though she knew his surname was Rosenfield. He suggested she be more open about it all and discuss the situation with Bill, but all that did was make him angry. There was no way to correct the situation. Her husband had become merely someone with whom she shared orange juice in the morning and joined names on a mortgage document.

So she joined the organizations, worked on the causes, and hung out with "Dynamite Lillian Rothberg," as everyone called her because of her seemingly endless energy. Together they were out to create some excitement in their lives. Of course, Lillian had purer motives. She was actually caught up in the causes and the projects. At times, Toby was sickened by her dedication. There were many occasions when they confronted good-looking men, men who could easily develop interest, but "Dynamite Lil" just went right on talking about the damn Community Chest, boring the hell out of them. Now there was a woman who had lost track of her sex instinct. Toby imagined Abe and Lillian made love only occasionally, and when they did, Dynamite Lil probably proofread charity advertisements while he experienced orgasm. *God forbid I ever get like her*, Toby thought.

As she walked up the street, she repeated the things that she was going to have to do as if they were all part of a prayer: *I will cut down another five hundred calories; I will begin the morning with 75 sit-ups; I will jog a mile; I will rub in vitamin E cream every night; I will get my teeth cleaned; I will* . . .

She stopped before the boutique door and pulled in her stomach again, this time in preparation for the trying on of the new bathing suit.

5

Nessim and Yusuf walked to the corner of Ninety-Third and York as soon as they got off the bus.

"This is the block," Nessim said, studying the numbers. The entry in the classifieds under Lost and Found had given the address and they set out immediately to get there. Nessim was uncharacteristically quiet during their ride downtown, and this increased Yusuf's nervousness.

"I still don't understand the reason for the roundabout way to tell you where to meet them," he said. "Why couldn't they just phone?"

"Phones are tapped. You see what's going on in America. Everyone's bugging everyone. It's become the national pastime here."

"But just to give a meeting . . ."

"You've got to learn to respect caution; otherwise, you will be worthless to the organization. Somehow you've come to believe caution is weakness. Caution is strength."

"I still think we could have brought Abu along. He needs to be in on everything."

"The fewer who know everything, the better and more secure things are for those who do. We can tell him what he has to know when the time comes. If we need him, that is."

"Whaddaya mean, if we need him? I've been working with him ever since his father arrived in New York."

"We'll see," Nessim said. "It's not for us to decide."

He was in no mood to argue now. They were at the address. He had waited months for this rendezvous. Although he didn't betray his feelings, he was excited and anxious. Apartment 4D. He pressed the button under the slot assigned to that apartment. There was no name in the slot. They waited in the small entranceway. A long moment of silence worried Nessim, but the buzz came, permitting them to open the otherwise locked front door. They entered and took the small winding stairway up.

When they got to 4D, they found the door slightly opened. Nessim hesitated and pushed Yusuf back against the hallway wall. He gestured for complete silence. Yusuf's heart began beating madly. The cautious way his brother moved terrified him, but he could see now that Nessim was right. Every doorway, every phone call, every stranger on the corner presented potential danger to men like them. They lived on the brink of death. It was the currency of their lives now. The relatively quiet months spent in America were months of deception.

Nessim fingered the .25-caliber pistol in his jacket pocket and approached the door. He pushed at it with his foot. It opened to an apparently empty room.

"Go on in, Nessim," a familiar voice said. Nessim spun around to face Hamid Zeid, a friend he had left back in Jordan. Hamid stood down the corridor in the doorway of another apartment.

"You!" Nessim stood back to look at his old friend. Yusuf stepped forward, smiling. "You see what I mean by caution," Nessim said to Yusuf.

Yusuf nodded quickly as Hamid approached them. Nessim and he embraced, laughing.

"What was it you said when we parted on the banks of the Jordan? Good-bye forever?" Hamid laughed.

"You devil. How long have been with the organization?

"Since the day you left."

Nessim turned to Yusuf.

"Eh?" he said.

"He's bigger, much more mature. The traveling aged him."

"I'm a man ready to do a man's work for the cause."

"Good," Hamid said, his face growing serious. He placed his hands on Yusuf's shoulders. "There is much that has to be done and much that will be done."

Hamid was only a year younger than Nessim, but he had a much older and worn look. His hair had grayed considerably, and his face and limbs were thinner. He looked tired and somewhat defeated. It brought a surge of anger into Nessim and he nodded. Hamid turned to him.

"My cousin, Abdul, is dead. He was shot in the old city during a demonstration."

"Abdul?" Yusuf said.

"It started peacefully, but someone threw a grenade into an Israeli jeep and they opened fire. They carried his body through the streets in protest."

"What was he, fourteen?" Nessim said.

"Closer to twelve. Come, let's meet El Yacoub," he said proudly and indicated the apartment.

"The Claw. He is here?" Yusuf said, eyes lighting up.

"He is here," Hamid said.

Nessim touched his brother's shoulder to indicate containment. He himself had only met the Claw once. He had stopped on his journey from Libya. In the bureaucracy of the organization, El Yacoub was equivalent to a CIA director. Few had access to him. He remained in the shadows, even to the members of the organization. To be incognito was always an advantage. He could infiltrate anywhere and everywhere. Nessim knew that El Yacoub's showing of himself now indicated that this was going to be a very big assignment.

When they looked back into the living room, the Claw was sitting in an easy chair in the corner. Nessim found it impossible to recall the man's physical features. When he had come into Lebanon that night, the Claw had stayed in the shadows talking to other men. Nessim had tried to get a better look at him, but didn't want to simply intrude on the conversations. When El Yacoub left, he turned and waved at the whole group. The light from their campfire danced around his face, distorting the features. All Nessim could really remember was that he was not a very tall man.

When he looked at him now, he was surprised at how old El Yacoub was. Somehow, he had believed that a man who moved about with ease and had the reputation the Claw had would have to be a young, vibrant man. El Yacoub appeared to be in his late sixties. His hair was quite thin and all gray. Heavy wrinkles permeated his forehead, cheeks, and neck. He had the face of a man who came from the desert. His skin was very dark and leathery in texture. He peered at them with small eyes, open slightly like those of a snake.

To Nessim, the man's face registered tremendous insecurity and caution. Everything threatened. He looked and sat as though he could crawl under a rock at the least provocation. He was, after all, a hit-and-run soldier. All his strategies, and those of all who worked under him, were built on that premise. To stand and fight was a luxury only rich armies could afford. His was an army of scorpions, snakes, and lizards. His weapons were the darkness, the unknown, the momentary advantage.

It suddenly struck Nessim that at another time in history, he, Hamid, El Yacoub, all of them, would be considered cowardly soldiers. But the nature of their battle and the forces that they were up against made any other kind of warfare impossible. Someday, he wanted to fight in an open field, face-to-face with the man he called the enemy. The dark-skinned boys of Semitic heritage who sang songs and loved around campfires sometimes seemed strikingly similar to him. Many of them spoke his language well. Perhaps this was a deeper reason why they had to fight in the fashion men like El Yacoub, the Claw, designed. As long as the enemy was a generalized Them, it was easy to be lethal and ruthless. These men whom he called his leaders were experts in the delivery of massive and indiscriminate death. And he had become one of their best soldiers.

A tall, stout young man was sitting at El Yacoub's right. He had a bull-like neck and gross facial features. Sitting at the edge of his seat, he appeared prepared to jump up instantly and strangle any foe to death in moments. Yusuf, especially, was unnerved by the way the man stared into his face.

Nessim was more intrigued by the woman to El Yacoub's left. She looked to be in her forties and very American. Her light brown hair was cut just below the ears and came down straight in the back. She wore a tight blouse opened at the collar and a long, dark blue skirt. There was something altogether pleasing about the peacefulness in her eyes and the slight, almost angelic smile she wore on her face. Her pierced ears were filled with little gold dots. On a street in New York, in any restaurant, almost anywhere in this city, she would be as unobtrusive and as ordinary as could be, but sitting next to the Claw, in the midst of all this intrigue, she was mysterious.

"Sit, Nessim," El Yacoub said and made a small gesture toward the couch and chairs. Then, nodding at Yusuf, he asked, "This is your brother?"

"Yusuf," Nessim said.

"Hamid has told me many personal details about both of you. I, of course, know you in a more professional sense. This is my personal bodyguard, Amaril; and this is a very dear friend, Miss Brenda Casewell. Her grandfather was a man I idolized," he said, smiling. She patted his hand. "She is loyal to his memory," he added. It was his way of explaining her presence.

Nessim only nodded. He and Yusuf sat on the couch. Hamid remained standing near the doorway.

"We're honored to meet you, El Yacoub," Nessim said. "Your name and reputation drives courage and dedication into all our hearts."

El Yacoub nodded and smiled; then he sat forward.

"You're still living with this woman you met in Athens?"

"Yes." Nessim was about to add that it had presented no problems, but El Yacoub immediately said, "Good. It will be necessary for you to have a woman with you for this assignment."

"Necessary?"

"Yes, but first, let me ask you about the killing of a Jew boy in your neighborhood. He was a member of the JDL."

Nessim sat back and took a breath.

"It was my brother's work."

Yusuf sat forward, ready to relate the whole incident.

"You were told big orders would be coming, were you not?"

"Yes," Nessim said. He knew what was to follow.

"Why such a foolish risk now, over the life of one JDL member? We brought you here for important work."

"I didn't authorize nor participate in the killing. My . . . my brother took that action on his own. He was anxious to prove himself."

"This does not prove your value," the Claw said, looking directly at Yusuf. "It makes you a liability to us. We must move as one no matter how eager we might be to strike out for the cause." He turned to Nessim. "Does he understand this now?" Nessim nodded. Then the Claw asked Yusuf, "Did you do it alone?"

"There was a boy," Yusuf said, surprised at how weak his voice sounded.

"What boy?" the Claw looked up at Hamid.

"Abu Munze. I've been training him," Yusuf said.

"The blind leading the blind," the Claw said.

Brenda Casewell smiled and nodded. For the first time, Nessim noticed something cold in her eyes. Her look of quiet was deceptive. She was a calculating woman. Her type disconcerted him. Such women were impossible to read because they changed moods and expressions so quickly.

"My brother has great enthusiasm," Nessim said.

"But it's misplaced, wasted if it cannot be channeled correctly. We are in a war, not a series of skirmishes."

"It won't happen again," Nessim said.

"It can't. What did you do with the weapon?" he asked, turning to Yusuf again.

"The weapon?" Yusuf looked confused.

"The ice pick," Nessim said quickly.

"I . . . It must have fallen when we ran."

"It wasn't mentioned in the news story," Nessim said.

"If they find it," El Yacoub said, "can it be traced to you?"

"Where did you get it?" Nessim asked.

"Pelham Fish Market. I work there part-time," Yusuf explained to the Claw.

"Are there markings on it?"

"Yes," Yusuf said weakly. He looked down.

"You fool," Nessim said.

"I am glad we have decided to move you today," El Yacoub said. "At this moment, some of our people are helping your woman gather necessary things together. You are to be moved out of that apartment. You will be taken to a house in Monroe, New York. That is on the way upstate. We can't afford to take the chance of the police investigating you. Not now."

"Why upstate?"

"It's on the way to the Seder Project."

"Seder Project?"

"That's our code name for this assignment," the Claw said. He smiled again at the woman. "Brenda made that contribution."

"It seems so appropriate and so poetically just. I'm sure you know the word *seder* refers to the Jewish Passover meals," she said.

"Yes, but . . ."

"You know," the Claw said, growing serious again, "that the main thrust of our work in the United States is designed to hurt the Jewish power structure that influences the American government so much and sends such direct aid to Israel. We will have an opportunity, a golden one at that, to strike a double blow for the cause." He added, "And you have been chosen to do it."

"Very good," Nessim said. "In Monroe?"

"Oh no. Give me that brochure," the Claw said to Brenda. She took a folder out of her pocketbook and handed it to him.

Nessim reached forward to take the advertisement from El Yacoub.

"A Catskill Mountains hotel? The New Prospect?"

"You've heard of it?"

"I think so, but what does it have to do with the Seder Project?"

"Hamid will explain many of the details on your trip to Monroe. I'll join you there before you go off for your Passover holiday."

"Holiday?" Yusuf said.

"Oh yes," Brenda said, smiling, "but instead of a holiday for the Jews, it'll be a holiday for us."

The Claw laughed.

"See," he said, "she has a very good sense of humor."

Nessim looked up at Hamid and saw that his face was filled with excitement. He had the eyes of one who could see great death.

6

Lieutenant Barry Wintraub had just completed his final bar mitzvah rehearsal in the dream again and his uncle Morris was holding up the keys to the go-cart, waving them like a proud dog owner waving a bone before his show dog, when the phone rang and blew the redundant nightmare to bits. He was relieved, but his wife, Shirley, was poking him in the rib with that damn pointed elbow of hers and going, "Barry, Barry, answer the phone. For God sakes, Barry . . ."

"All right, all right. Stop it, will ya. I'll develop a cancer in that spot, for Christ sakes." He rubbed his side and lifted the receiver. "Wintraub."

"Come and get it, motherfucker. It's Baker."

"What? What?" he whined. It was twelve thirty.

"Homicide on Wallace Avenue. You're walking distance. Might be near your synagogue, come to think of it."

"I'm Reformed. Reformed, I told you. I musta told you a thousand times, you black bastard."

"Barry, what is it? Who is it?" Shirley said, half asleep.

"Just a minute, Shirl," Barry said. Then to Baker, "Where should I meet ya?"

"I'll pick ya up in fifteen minutes," Baker said. "And Wintraub, brush your teeth, will ya? I know you had onions for supper. It's Wednesday."

"Drop dead."

He hung up the phone and groaned as he lay back against the pillow.

"What was it, Barry?" Shirley kept her face right in the pillow.

"Homicide on Wallace Avenue."

"Our Wallace Avenue?" she said, turning quickly and sitting up.

"Wallace Avenue, Wallace Avenue. Whaddaya mean, 'our' Wallace Avenue? What, do we own the avenue?"

"It's our neighborhood practically."

"So? Homicides occur all over the city. That's why I'm a homicide detective."

"My mother thought you were going to be a narcotics detective. I thought you were going to be a narcotics detective."

"So they have it better?"

"You know what my mother thought."

"Your mother. She had a brother who was a corrupt narcotics detective with two homes, a boat, three cars, and two-hundred-and-fifty-dollar suits; and she figured that was the whole story."

"She read *Serpico*."

"Leave me alone, Shirl. I don't want to get into that. I'm trying to wake myself up so I can go investigate a homicide," he said and stood up.

"Who was killed?"

"I don't know."

"You don't even know who was killed?"

"You heard the whole conversation practically, didn't ya? I'm going out to investigate."

"All I heard was a lot of stupid cursing. I meant to talk to you about that, Barry. I know it comes with the job, but Jason and Keith are starting to use dirty language. You've got to watch your mouth around them—eight- and seven-year-olds are very alert nowadays."

"Right, Shirl."

"You comin' back for breakfast?"

"For Christ sakes, Shirl," he said, slipping into his pants, "how the hell do I know? I'm just getting started."

"Maybe you shoulda gone on to be a rabbi," she said, turning over. "At least then we would have had some semblance of a regular life."

"Thanks for tellin' me now."

Barry finished getting dressed and rushed for the door. Then he remembered that he did have onions for supper and went back to brush his teeth quickly.

I wonder if I coulda been a rabbi, he thought as he started out of the apartment again. *I wonder if I would have been successful at it. People tell me I talk to people well. Maybe I woulda been successful. I had the right upbringing, that's for sure.*

He had been brought up by his aunt and uncle in a kosher home after his parents had been in a fatal car accident. At the age of seven, what did he know and what could he object to? Vaguely, in the beginning, he resented the strict observance of the Sabbath. Saturday had always been a day of joy and play. Now it was quiet meditation. Even today, it seemed odd to work and live normally on the Sabbath.

He had been a very good student in school and a very polite boy. The first time that cost him was when Bobby Dennis tripped him in front of some girls and he excused himself. They started calling him the "Jolly Yellow Giant." It got to him, and when Dennis tripped him again, he let go with a left jab that folded the creep up like a loosened paper poster.

Barry grew up quickly. He was five feet eleven in the tenth grade and weighed over one hundred and eighty pounds. For some reason, his physical size seemed incongruous with the vocation of a rabbi and when he told his teachers his plans, they looked at him with restrained disbelief. They knew he came from a religious home and they knew he followed the law, but he looked like a potential football player, not a potential rabbi.

He began his first year at Yeshiva University and met Shirley Feinberg on the steps of the New York Public Library. She was struggling to hold on to her pile of books. A rabbi could marry, of course, and sex was not the original sin, but Shirley was a middle-class Jewish girl who ate ham and eggs and went to synagogue only when she was invited to a bar mitzvah.

She liked him from the start, but her mother was very discouraging. After all, what kind of a living does a rabbi make? But there was something immediately enticing about Shirley. He liked the way she curled her lip up at the end and drove her tongue into his mouth when they kissed. Her lovemaking was fast and furious, and when he undid her bra in the living room of her house at one thirty in the morning, he was surprised at the bountiful bosom that came pouring out.

"My mother makes me wear these tight bras," she said in explanation.

"Don't apologize. I like a well-kept secret."

She won him over with her sarcastic humor and general good nature. Actually, he had developed an increasing indifference to the vocation of rabbi, but his aunt and uncle had become his mother and father, and they lived for the day he would conduct services in a synagogue. To them it would be visible proof that they had fulfilled their great responsibility to the memory of his parents. Barry broke their hearts. He left Yeshiva a week after the second semester had begun.

Ironically, it was Shirley's mother who suggested police work to him. She was always talking about the "success" of her brother, a detective in narcotics. Any other Jewish mother would have liked to see her daughter marry a doctor, but Shirley's mother wished only that Shirley would marry a narcotics detective, or some detective. It was all the same.

Barry enrolled in the police academy that summer. Although he was bright, big, and quite capable, he would have never made detective as fast as he did if there wasn't pressure to promote some token Jews. B'nai B'rith had financed an investigation of the police department and concluded that it was laden with subtle anti-Semitism. Public pressure began to mount, and the commissioner sought out good Jewish candidates. Barry fit the bill. Shirley's mother was temporarily satisfied and Barry and Shirley got married.

Although there were other Jewish men in his precinct, Barry Wintraub became the standard-bearer of the religion as far as they were concerned. It wasn't by choice. He didn't wear his religion on his sleeve. But because he was so well versed in the precepts of his faith, he inevitably corrected the others when they voiced their misconceptions and misinformation about Jews. Finally, the men jokingly referred to him as "the Rabbi." He laughed to himself, because none of them knew how close he had come, but he voiced no objections nor acted in any way offended. Few would want to tangle with him if he did become angry.

Now, at forty-two, he was still in fine physical shape. He stood six feet four and weighed over two hundred and ten pounds. Workouts in the gym with weights and calisthenics had provided him with powerful, thick arms and round shoulders. He was barrel chested and small waisted. When he was in his gym shorts, the muscles in his legs jumped with every step. He was the only one in the precinct who could hold a captain's chair straight out with one hand, chewing gum and smiling as he did it. Everyone respected his strength—especially his partner, Bob Baker.

"You don't think there was anything deliberate about puttin' a Jew and a black together, do you?" Baker once asked him. Barry thought about it and concluded there probably wasn't.

"But it looks like there was," he admitted. "Some probably hope we won't get along."

"We'll get along just as long as you keep your place, kike," Baker said, and the relationship fastened itself on a foundation of sick humor. The partners developed great respect for each other.

"Do you think we deliberately like each other to prove the bigots wrong?" Wintraub once asked. Baker thought about it and concluded they didn't.

"But it looks like we do," he admitted. Wintraub laughed.

*   *   *

"Get in," Baker shouted as soon as he pulled up to the curb.

"What's the fuckin' rush?"

"Chief just got me on the radio. He thinks there might be some kind of religious war 'bout to break out 'round here."

"Why? Who was the victim?"

"A member of the JDL. One of your boys."

"Who took the call?"

"Jacobi and Doyle."

They sped two blocks down, three blocks over, and two more blocks down. The black-and-white was parked by the sidewalk. Several JDL members were still gathered in front of the synagogue. Patrolman Jacobi stood on the sidewalk talking to a young man wearing a small black yarmulke, a thin dark jacket, and jeans. Danny Goldstein's body was covered with a police blanket, but his feet stuck out and the fingers of his right hand were visible.

"Whaddaya got?" Wintraub asked, stepping out of the car.

"Eighteen-year-old, white male. Name's Danny Goldstein."

"How?" Baker asked.

"Some blood on the back of his neck. Can't tell what kind of wound. Hafta wait for an autopsy, I guess."

"How long you gonna leave him out here, for God sakes?" Barry said.

"Figured we'd hold the call till you guys saw it all. The chief said . . ."

"Yeah, yeah, we know what the chief said," Baker said. "Who's this?"

"My name's Mark Lederman," the young man with Jacobi said. "I found him. He left the meeting only a little while before I did."

"By himself?"

"No, with two others."

"What two others?" Barry said.

"Martin Feldman and Larry Griff."

"Get their addresses, Baker."

"They'll be here soon," Lederman said. "We already called them."

"Who's we?"

"We," Lederman said. His eyes were glassy and filled with the mixture of anger and sorrow. Wintraub studied him for a moment, ultimately letting the boy's repetitive response go for the moment. Then he lifted the blanket off Goldstein's body and studied it. Baker joined him.

"Anything missing?" Barry asked, looking at Jacobi and Lederman.

"Wallet's still on him and his watch."

"Nothing's missing but his life," Lederman said.

Barry dropped the blanket back over the body and approached Lederman again.

"You have some ideas about this?"

"No," he said quickly and looked to the group across the street.

Barry followed his gaze and studied the scene.

"Who leads this army?"

"Their leader's a Rabbi Kaufman," Jacobi said. "He went to tell the Goldsteins. I got his address here for you."

"Thanks," Barry said, taking it.

"Someone in the alley took him from behind," Baker said.

"Of course behind," Lederman said. "Daniel was a black belt."

"Black belt? You mean karate?"

Lederman nodded and looked down again.

"Listen," Baker said, "if you guys have some known enemies, it would help us get a start on this to know of them."

"Are you kiddin'?" Lederman said. "Known enemies? We're Jews."

"I'm black."

"Congratulations."

"Now listen . . ."

"Here comes Feldman and Griff," Lederman said.

Two more young men stepped out of a taxi and started toward them. Barry pulled Baker aside.

"All right," he said, "we'll question these two guys and some of the others. Then we'll follow the body to autopsy. In the morning, we'll go see this Rabbi Kaufman. My guess is these guys are not going to be very cooperative unless their leader gives them the green light."

"You Jews aren't a very trusting bunch, are ya?"

"Reminds you of when we go into Harlem and question the brothers about a crime, don't it, Baker?"

"Tryin' to say somethin', Wintraub?"

"Yeah. You get Jacobi's flashlight and give the alley another going over and I'll talk to these two."

"Givin' me the dirt work again, honky?"

Barry smiled. Before they split up, Jacobi approached them and took them farther aside.

"I just got a thought," he said.

"Go on."

"Maybe they're all acting like this because one of them is responsible. Why else would they be so tight-lipped about it? They lost one of their own."

"Maybe they've been burned before," Baker said.

"When?" Jacobi asked, some indignation visible in his face.

"Here and there over the last two thousand years," Wintraub said.

7

"'A round puncture wound in the back of the neck, made by a sharp cylindrical metal stem, an ice pick, for example.' This description of the point of impact and body damage makes it sound as if a surgeon committed the murder," Wintraub said. He put the autopsy report down and looked out the window of the car. He and Baker were on their way to interview Rabbi Kaufman.

"Coulda been a lucky stroke or coulda been someone who's learned his craft well."

"From what we've learned so far, anything's possible."

"According to Jacobi, this Rabbi Kaufman doesn't work in a synagogue. He's kind of controversial. Leads the young JDL members and conducts services for them like their personal rabbi. He's been arrested a number of times for demonstrations. A hard guy."

"I think I heard of him, now that you mention all that."

"He's a real militant. Was even asked to leave Israel once by the Israeli government."

"Um."

"This is gonna be one helluva waste of time," Baker said as they turned onto Kaufman's block. "Never a fuckin' place to park."

"You'll hafta go in front of the fire hydrant. It's this brownstone."

"Settin' a bad example for the citizens."

Ignoring him, Barry said, "What was it, 1B? I'll go on in alone."

Baker studied him. "You're not kiddin', are you?"

"No. I've been thinking about this. I want to put it on terms of a brother dealing with a brother. Isn't that a good way to put it?"

"Right on," Baker said. "I always believed you people were clannish."

Barry stepped out of the car and looked around. The street was deserted. He felt a bump in his jacket pocket and reached in to pull out one of Jason's toy metal cars. The kid was always stuffing his things into Barry's clothes. Barry analyzed it and came up with the theory that the kid was trying to tell him he should be spending more time with him. *The kid's right,* he thought and started up the stone steps.

"Mazel tov," Baker called out.

Barry gave him the finger and walked on.

It was an old apartment building, and the entrance opened without any security buzz. The first floor was terribly cluttered. There was a baby carriage against the far wall, cartons piled against the door of another apartment, and a collection of rusted metal toy trucks and cars scattered against the side wall a ways down the corridor. Someone had left a mop sticking out of a dirty pail of water nearly smack in the middle of the corridor.

He walked to 1B, unzipped his jacket, and knocked softly. A few quiet moments passed. He brushed back his loose, thick brown hair and knocked again. The sound of small footsteps was heard. The handle turned slowly, and the door opened against a chain lock. A little boy, about nine or ten years old, peered through the crack. He wore a yarmulke and a very loose white shirt.

"Yes, please," he said.

"I want to see Rabbi Kaufman. My name's Wintraub. I'm a policeman," Barry said and flipped open his identification.

The boy stared at the gold shield and then closed the door. A few moments later, it was opened again.

Rabbi Kaufman was not an imposing man physically, especially in relation to Wintraub, but his demeanor and his strong, handsome face with dark eyes, sharp cut chin, and straight, almost Romanesque nose gave him the appearance of a gladiator. Everything about him—his posture, his slow careful movements, his way of studying people— suggested a soldier. He wore his yarmulke far back, almost completely off the top of his head. It was pinned to his cropped dark brown hair.

"You're here about the Goldstein boy," Kaufman said. It was completely a declarative sentence, registering no doubt whatsoever. Barry nodded. The rabbi went on, "I gave all the information I had to the patrolman who came immediately."

"I know that."

"What do you want?"

"Just to talk, Rabbi."

"We're sitting shiva."

"Not at the boy's home?"

"This is the boy's home. We are all of the House of David," he said. His eyes burned with anger.

63

"So am I of the House of David," Barry said.

"Do you come as a Jew or as a city policeman?"

"As a Jewish city policeman," Barry said.

The first sign of relaxation in Rabbi Kaufman's face occurred around his eyes. He stepped back to let Wintraub enter. The little boy stood behind the rabbi, in the doorway to another room. He leaned against the wall and ran his arm up the side of the door frame. Barry smiled at him and wondered how his boys would look with a yarmulke on them all the time.

"What is it you wish to know?" The rabbi gestured for Barry to take a seat in the living room that was off to the left. It consisted of a small couch, an easy chair, one round table, and a wooden rocker against the window. There was one standing lamp next to the rocker. On the far wall was a picture of an old Jewish man leaning over to touch a small boy's shoulder. The boy looked as though he had been crying.

"Was there any special reason why the Goldstein boy was chosen out of the group?"

"He was alone, an easier mark—and he was a Jew." Kaufman remained standing.

"You seem absolutely positive that this was not an attempted mugging."

"That isn't a serious statement. Nothing was taken from the boy, not his watch, not his wallet, nothing."

"Maybe the mugger was frightened off. Goldstein was found very shortly after the attack."

"Hardly. Muggers are thieves who kill when they are resisted. They don't assassinate and then rob. There was no sign of resistance. Goldstein was surprised and murdered. He would have resisted otherwise. He was trained in self-defense and he was a brave boy. But you know all this, Lieutenant. What is it you're after?"

"I want to know what you know. I can do something about it."

"Can you?" Rabbi Kaufman sat on the couch. "What can you do? Hunt down the killer and take him in so that the lawyers and judges can make a nice comfortable settlement because the court calendar is so crowded?"

"If you and your organization do anything on your own, we'd only have to hunt you down."

"The difference is we're used to being hunted down. Throughout time, we have been the prey. We can't be threatened with a condition that marks all our history. Try a different argument."

Barry wiped a hand over his face and sat back. He thought for a few moments and contemplated the man sitting across from him. Rabbi Kaufman had a slim build, but there was a hardness evident in his forearms and shoulders. He remembered how people found it incongruous for he himself to be a rabbi because of his physical presence. A rabbi was not necessarily a soft-spoken, quiet man with gentle eyes any longer. He didn't wear old suits or have a pale face with a heavily outlined beard and mustache.

"Will you be able to get to the murderer?"

"Perhaps," Kaufman said.

"Will you be able to prevent it from happening again?"

"I strongly doubt it."

"You believe this murderer acted on orders then?"

"Most probably we are dealing with an organized movement. Yes, I believe that."

"Then you might only scratch the tip of the iceberg. Revenge that is committed quickly and at the height of passion is usually unsatisfactory in the long run. You don't have the capabilities we have. We can make a more significant dent in them."

"Like you've done in Russia, or on the borders of Israel?"

"I didn't say we could end anti-Semitism or persecution. I just said we can get at the true heart of any organized group of killers," Barry replied, the veins in his forehead straining.

"You are apparently an emotional man. For a policeman that's a disadvantage, is it not?"

"I became a policeman ass backwards," Barry said. "Backed into it."

Kaufman expressed a look of confusion.

"I had intentions of becoming a rabbi myself," he added. *Why not take advantage of it?* he thought. For once, maybe, he could use his Jewish background as a tool. It was always being used against him, making him the butt of jokes, or the object of some ridicule.

"A rabbi? And you became a policeman?"

"One polices the soul, the other the streets. Besides, you're a rabbi and you became a soldier," Barry countered. Kaufman nearly laughed. He leaned forward.

"How much pressure is coming down to solve this case?"

"Oh, the usual ton."

"I see." Kaufman thought for a moment. "How good a Jew are you now, Lieutenant?"

"Not very, I'm afraid. I barely practice anymore."

"Does it bother you at all that a Jewish boy was killed because he believed in his people?"

Barry thought for a moment.

"Although I don't like the fact that it does, it does. I'd rather it bothered me that a human being was killed. I would hope that it bothers me equally when any boy, or any person, is killed."

"It's a fair reply." Kaufman studied Barry for a moment. "Perhaps you would like something to drink?"

"Cold glass of milk, maybe. I think I'm developing an ulcer."

"Cold milk? Good. Avrum," he called, and the boy approached. "Go get a glass of cold milk, please." The boy nodded and hurried out.

"Your son?"

"Yes. I have three. He is the youngest. The other two are over at the Goldsteins with my wife. I will be going there later," he added, seeing the question in Barry's face.

"I don't particularly support what you do," Barry said, sensing the sincere and honest approach was the best with this man. He seemed not only able to take it, but to expect it. "As a policeman I can't condone illegal acts."

"But as a Jew?"

"As a Jew, I'm confused. I confess I don't follow political events as closely as I should."

"I disagree with your definition of what is legal and illegal. When you're in a war, acts that would be illegal in peacetime suddenly become good, even great. We are in a continuous war. It's as simple as that."

"Nothing's that simple. Perhaps we're not opposing the battling so much as the battlefields you choose, such as the streets of New York."

"For a Jew, the world is one continuous battlefield. Even the heart of Israel."

"I understand you had some difficulties over there."

Kaufman smiled. "You do follow some headlines."

Avrum brought in a tray with a glass of milk in the middle of it. He carried it very carefully, not taking his eyes off the glass as he walked. When he got to the center of the room, Rabbi Kaufman did not lean over to take the tray. He let the boy finish the job.

"Thank you, Avrum."

He backed away slowly, staring at Barry, and then disappeared around the corner of the doorway.

"Perhaps you find me too cynical, Lieutenant, but it keeps me alive. David Goldstein should have been a little more cynical."

Barry took a long swallow of milk and then rubbed his stomach.

"I may have been cynical, but I don't think I'm as paranoid," Barry said.

"That's because you've chosen to assimilate."

"Maybe that's why I have this damn bar mitzvah nightmare all the time," Barry said. Kaufman smiled. "Look, Rabbi, what can you tell me about this situation?"

"You are aware, I am sure, that there are illegal Arab aliens here."

"Of course."

"We have reason to believe one of them was responsible for David Goldstein's death. But not alone."

"How do you know this?"

Kaufman leaned forward. "What if I told you we have found the murder weapon and can trace it to a certain individual?"

"If that's true, you're withholding evidence."

"And if you feel that way, I will not tell you that."

"Okay," Wintraub said, smiling. "Let's talk off the record."

"Off the record? From now on?"

"From now."

"Just a moment then," Kaufman said. He got up and walked out of the room. When he returned, he carried an ice pick in his right hand.

8

Daniel Goldstein's death reached the New Prospect in the form of his relatives' canceled reservations. Mrs. Gladys Aldelman, the head clerk and receptionist, crossed the rooms off the main sheet quickly and put them back on availability. She did not know the reason for the cancellations, and she did not care. Reservations had been coming in at a phenomenal pace since the Obermans agreed to sponsor the Israeli rally on the third night of Passover. A first-class suite of rooms was being held for Chaim Eban and his party. It was all very exciting and added a rhythm of importance and a serious mood of business to everything she and her assistants did.

Mrs. Aldelman had been with the Obermans for twenty-two years and was a most efficient worker. Other hotel owners had tried to steal her away year after year, but her dedication to the "family" was too strong. A thin, now completely gray-haired woman, she seemed to have ink smears on her fingers, and often on her face, constantly. Regardless of her long experience as a hotel receptionist, she was always nervous and ended up doing things like putting a ballpoint pen in her mouth, wrong side in. There was often a small, blue dot on the tip of her tongue.

She stood at the corner of her long L-shaped main desk and peered out over the luxurious soft carpeting of the New Prospect main lobby. Occasionally, she would strut back and forth in the small area between the desk and the bookkeeper's office, looking like the captain of a ship overseeing the sailors. She guarded the plush furniture and shiny gold-tinted fixtures, chastising children, and sometimes even adults, who abused them. She snapped orders at bellhops; directed guests to services and recreations; and reassured elderly people as to the hotel's ability to cater to their needs and wishes. For some frequent guests, Mrs. Aldelman was something of a hotel fixture herself.

To the Obermans, Mrs. Aldelman really had become family. Even though she had children of her own, she treated David Oberman as if he were one of her own sons, and he never resisted her matronly affection—affection that increased considerably after the death of David's mother. He stood patiently and obediently as she buttoned his shirts, straightened his collars, or fixed the wave in his hair. Now, as the president and general manager of the hotel, David found it difficult, if not impossible, to treat Mrs. Aldelman as one of his hired help. He could only speak to her in one tone of voice. She was professional enough to maintain an employee-employer relationship, but she still fixed his collars or straightened his hair on occasion. Gloria, David's wife, teased him about it.

At thirty-seven years old, David Oberman was one of the youngest men to run a major Catskill resort. The New Prospect had been in the family from its beginning as a farmhouse that took in tourists. His grandfather had come from Russia in the early 1900s to escape the Russo-Japanese War, when Jews were being conscripted into service with too great an efficiency. There was a great history here in the Catskills, tied to the development of the old O & W Railroad that stimulated its own business by advertising the up-and-coming resorts in its publication, *Summer Homes.*

Every summer made more and more demands on the Obermans' resort facilities, and they were constantly in the process of expansion, but it wasn't until David's father, Solomon, began his dealings with major financiers that the New Prospect took on the lush and luxury that was to become so characteristic of the Catskills by the middle of the 1940s; it lasted through the early 1950s and the late 1960s. It was the period of "megahotels," theirs being the most complicated and involved of all. The New Prospect had become a little city in itself and survived all the economic downturns.

David's grandfather never lived to see the construction of indoor pools, skating rinks, tennis courts, and health clubs with sauna baths and elaborate gymnastic equipment. There was a separate sports building that housed a regulation prizefighting ring. Major contenders came to the New Prospect to train. His grandfather never saw the elaborate nightclub, said to be one of the biggest in the world, able to seat a little over three thousand people at once. He never played a round of golf on the grand golf course, already named "the Par Killer," and the site of two major tournaments. The hotel now had its own landing strip for small-engine planes and a string of stores off the lobby of the main building—luncheonettes, barbershops, beauty parlors, clothes and jewelry shops. It employed over twenty-five hundred people and it required as much power and service as did many of the villages and towns surrounding it.

With the combined effects of the Passover holiday and the rally for Israel, the New Prospect would have a population of over three thousand people during the coming vacation period. David wasn't particularly overwhelmed by all this. He'd dealt with full capacity and slightly over capacity, booking often during the course of the time he had been running the hotel. However, with a major political event scheduled to occur at his hotel, he was concerned that everything run in its normally smooth way. Astute at public relations, he saw the great value in helping to sponsor such an affair.

"I wouldn't want to go ahead and make these kinds of arrangements without your complete agreement and cooperation, Mr. Oberman," Lillian Rothberg had told him over the phone. She waited, testing the air.

"We'd be delighted to host such an activity. I'm sure you know the New Prospect has been at the center of many charitable affairs in its time."

"Yes, of course."

"I'll have my secretary call the Israeli ambassador's office and inform him that Chaim Eban and his party will have accommodations at our expense."

"Wonderful."

"Just let me know how you want the schedule arranged, and we'll work things out."

"I certainly will. Thank you ever so much."

He smiled, remembering "Dynamite Lillian Rothberg." When she was up at the hotel, she dragged her poor husband around like a dog on a leash. He went from one activity to another, always wearing a look of pitiful longing for a chaise longue or soft chair. She was the type of guest who took complete control of things in the early days—organizing games and sing-alongs. "If you ever need a job," he told her, "come and see me."

David Oberman stepped out of his office and started across the lobby to the reservations desk, behind which his seven-year-old daughter, Lisa Sue, was barely visible. He smiled and shook his head. His son, Bobby, stood on the side near the water fountain and took on the posture of a waiting bellhop. He wore a bellhop's cap and folded his arms over his chest. He was surprisingly tall for ten years old. David attributed that to Gloria's side of the family. She was barely an inch shorter than he at five feet ten. Her hazel green eyes turned him into jelly. Even now, it was fascinating for him to stand back and watch her, unobserved.

When she turned away from a guest at the main desk, Gloria saw him standing there. He waited as she came across the lobby.

"We're eating with Pop tonight, remember, so don't make any other arrangements. I've got a roast going over there."

"He let you work in his kitchen?"

"He did supervise. I hate to see him eating alone in that big house so often."

David nodded. It was that softness, that sincere warmth for other people that had attracted him to Gloria when she came up as a model to do a spread for *Stunning* magazine.

"You think you might get him over here for the First Seder?"

"I mentioned it to him, but he said you never asked."

"I must've said it a hundred times this last week."

He shook his head. His father, something of a recluse now at the age of seventy, used the entire first floor of the old main house. It was a three-story wooden structure with a large porch that wrapped around the front of the building. His father lived in what had mainly been the first tourist house. The hotel had grown around it, all the modern additions constructed some distance from the lawn and landscaping around the building. It was as if it maintained an aura of religious protection, a temple built for the god of vacations. Nothing on it was replaced. It was always repaired—even to the extent of getting workmen to glue and paste broken pieces of window shutters. If they went over capacity, they utilized the second and third floor. When he told his father that guests resented that, he bit into the stem of his pipe and cursed them for their lack of appreciation.

"These spoiled modern tourists would rather have plastic and neon than good solid wood and thick heavy walls. They don't know what real quality workmanship means. You can keep this generation."

David laughed and shook his head, but secretly he appreciated his father's love for all things antique.

From time to time, David got a call from Solomon, telling him about some problem he had spotted, workers who were goofing off, cars that were parked incorrectly, guests who misused hotel equipment. Most of it was trivial stuff, but David listened and was sure to have the problem corrected, because if he didn't, his father would let him know.

"Did you mention anything about Chaim Eban?"

"He said he'll believe it when he sees him."

"That means he'll be over here that night for sure," David said. "To either congratulate us or tell us he told us so." He added, "Thank goodness for that." But if David were aware of the conversation going on in a car heading toward Monroe, New York, at that moment, he'd have wished his father, along with his wife and children, would stay in the old main house the whole holiday.

9

Clea sat in the corner of the backseat of the black Lincoln town car and clutched her small purse to her body. When Nessim opened the door, he was struck by the look of fear on her face. Yusuf waited beside him, and Hamid stood talking with El Yacoub. There were two men in the front, neither of whom Nessim had seen before.

"Are you all right?"

"Yes," she said. He started to get in. She went on, "They said you knew all about this; yet, you hadn't mentioned anything this morning and you didn't call. I didn't know what to think."

"However, you agreed to go along. You're learning blind loyalty," Nessim said, smiling. He patted her on the forearm, and she relaxed some. "It was apparently a decision of the moment."

He decided not to mention anything about the killing of the JDL member. Yusuf got in beside him, and Hamid shook hands with El Yacoub and got in the front beside the two men. The Claw came to the window.

"So this is the beautiful woman from Palestine," he said, smiling.

"El Yacoub," Nessim said to Clea as a form of introduction. Clea leaned forward and smiled.

"Welcome to the cause," El Yacoub said.

"Thank you, but this morning the cause took things into its own hands," she said. The Claw laughed.

"Such is our life." He turned to Nessim and grew serious. "I'll see you in Monroe. There will be time to talk and make final preparations. In the meantime, Hamid knows everything you need to know for now."

"Good," Nessim said, looking at Hamid. He nodded.

"And you, Sword of Damascus," the Claw said, touching Yusuf's shoulder. "Sit and listen. Speak only when necessary and move with the organization, not alongside it, and especially not in front of it. Understand?"

"Yes." Yusuf was practically whispering.

El Yacoub backed away and they started off.

"This is Ali el-Bunit and his cousin Zvi Monar," Hamid said, introducing the driver and the man beside him. They nodded back at Nessim. "They'll be with us as long as necessary."

"And this is Clea," Nessim said. "She'll be with us forever." Hamid laughed, and Clea squeezed Nessim's hand.

"What was that stuff with Yusuf?" she whispered.

"Later," Nessim said. He turned back to Hamid. "Before you begin, you must tell me when and why you became part of the organization. When we parted, you had other ideas."

"I've come to realize that the Middle East no longer belongs to either the Israelis or the Arabs. The future is in hands that are elsewhere. We're pawns, being moved around at will by bigger and stronger powers. There will be no settlement there until it first comes here."

"And when I told you those things?"

"I was younger and dreamed of glorious victories on the battlefield—not younger so much in years as in understanding."

"Your sister?"

"Safe. On the West Bank, in Israeli-held territory."

"Tell me about this Seder Project."

Hamid turned around completely.

"You know about the Catskills. They used to call it the Borscht Belt—this playground for Jews up in the mountains."

"Certainly."

"There used to be many rich resorts up there, big hotels. They've basically died away except for a few where wealthy Jews frolic in the sunshine on their grounds, especially on Passover."

"So?"

"This Passover, something special is to occur in one of these remaining big hotels."

"The New Prospect? That brochure in the apartment?"

"Yes. There's to be a rally for Israel. Chaim Eban will be there to speak."

"Eban!"

"Himself." Hamid smiled, but it was the smile of a cat. "Many of the most affluent Jewish businessmen and their families will be there to participate and listen. These are the people who raise the large sums for Israel, sums that can be turned into arms, bullets, and bombs to be used against us. These are people who finance political candidates, candidates who vote pro-Israel because they are in such debt to the Jews."

Hamid lowered his voice automatically. Yusuf sat forward, great excitement showing on his face. This was going to be it—the big event, perhaps the biggest, and he would be there. Would be in on it!

Clea had listened to every word, but she was frozen in her position, terrified of what was soon to be said.

"Go on," Nessim said.

"They will all be together, in one room, for nearly an hour or more. They're coming from all over. Not just New York. It presents us with a golden opportunity, don't you see?"

"Yes," Nessim said.

Hamid said no more. Yusuf was disappointed.

Clea stared at Nessim, shocked suddenly by the realization that he understood and knew the unspoken words between him and Hamid. She knew them too, in her most wild and most horrible imaginings. Nessim's stoical expression frightened her. She understood that he was capable of inflicting great death. She always knew he had the skill and the technology, but things had been soft between them. It had been hard to think of him as anything other than her lover these past months. She was fully aware of the fact that he had gone off to do some work for the organization, but from what she was told it was mostly sabotage of machines, sabotage of instruments, strikes against things.

The abrupt way in which she had been jarred out of their little apartment, scooped up and out of the life they had created for a while, and placed in this automobile heading north with the men of hard faces, sent chills through her body. Her hands were cold and sweaty. It was like some button was pressed, and they were missiles heading for target. The metaphor was not as far-fetched as it might seem to her at the moment.

Just about the time Nessim, Yusuf, and Clea were being driven north by the organization, Barry Wintraub slipped into the front seat of his police car. Baker turned in anticipation and waited.

"Well?"

Wintraub put the ice pick on the seat beside them.

"Head for Pelham Fish Market, 218 White Plains Road," he said.

"I guess you Hebs do stick together," Baker said with a smirk.

"I guess we do," Wintraub replied.

Pelham Fish Market was run by a tall Hungarian named Gitleman. He had a pencil-thin mustache and long, gray hair that hung in loose strands down the back of his head and into the collar of his white shirt. His apron was stained with blood. It was a rather large shop, running in a rectangular frame down to the back freezer. Two women worked behind the counter, and Gitleman and another man trimmed and brought up stock from the back. The stench of fish began just outside the door to the shop. Baker and Wintraub got Gitleman off to the side and showed him the ice pick.

"Yeah, that's mine," he said, reading the handle. Pelham Fish was engraved on the end. "So?"

"We think it might have been used as a murder weapon last night."

"A murder weapon?" He looked around to be sure that none of his customers were in earshot. Instinctively, he knew it would be bad for business.

"All your employees are here now?"

"All my full-time ones. Actually, that's my wife and my sister. Her boyfriend works with me in the back."

"How many part-time employees do you have?"

"Right now, only one. A young man comes in to clean up."

"Is he here now?"

"No, and he was supposed to be here more than two hours ago."

"What's his name?"

"Joseph Mandel."

"Can you describe him for us?"

"Do you have his address?" Baker asked.

"What first?"

"Give us a description," Wintraub said, eyeing Baker. He smiled and stepped to the side.

"A description?" Gitleman wiped his face with the dirty apron. The odor was beginning to turn Wintraub's stomach, but he held on. "Tall, about an inch taller than you, dark, black hair. Not too thin, but not fat, either. He's never smiling. Always unhappy about something, but he does his work. Doesn't talk much. He's got a gold tooth, all the way back here," Gitleman said and pulled his mouth to the side and pointed.

"Any sores or markings on the face?"

"No. Wait, yes. A chicken pox hole in his forehead, near the temple."

"Uh-huh."

"He'd be a better-looking boy if he smiled more. Says he's twenty-two years old, but he looks much younger to me."

"How do you mean?"

"Apparently doesn't shave much. Skin's so smooth. Hairless. Some savings."

"Savings?"

"On blades. You know what a pack of single-edge blades sells for nowadays?"

"What about his address?" Wintraub said, looking at Baker. Baker smiled.

"I paid him in cash," Gitleman said. "He wanted it that way," he added quickly. "But I kept track on the books. Always kept track. Maybe my wife knows his address."

"No," she said, coming around the side when he called to her and asked. "He never gave me his address. He never talked much or answered questions about his home."

"How did you reach him?"

"We have his phone number," she said.

"Can I have that?" Wintraub said. Giving them a card, he added, "And if he should come in anytime, please call this number."

"He did something wrong? Murdered someone?"

"We don't know. We'd like to question him."

"I didn't even realize the ice pick was missing," Gitleman said as they started out.

"We've got to hold on to it," Wintraub said. He saw the way Gitleman looked at it.

"I understand. He never stole anything from me. I can tell you that."

"Except this ice pick," Baker said.

"Possibly," Wintraub added.

"Yeah, possibly."

"Well, he was never near the register. Just comes in and does his work and goes." Then he thought a moment. "If he only smiled more." They left him standing in the doorway.

They called the phone number back to headquarters and received an address only a few blocks from Pelham Fish a short while afterward. As they started away, neither Wintraub nor Baker noticed the brown Gremlin parked a block behind them. Four members of David Goldstein's section of the JDL sat quietly within, watching and waiting. The driver started the engine, and without saying a word, pulled out slowly to follow the police car.

About ten minutes later, Baker and Wintraub stood before the doorway to Nessim and Clea's apartment. It had been only a few hours since she was ushered out of it with only their necessary belongings. Barry knocked and waited. Calling on suspects had proven potentially fatal only once before in his career. He had gone to question a man who reportedly shot his brother. These family arguments that broke out in violence were most common. He had read a study once that claimed more than ninety percent of the murders committed in the country were committed by members of families against each other as a result of passionate controversies. The murderers weren't psychotic killers, and in most cases were normal, gentle people in all other respects. A policeman didn't feel as threatened when he approached the situation.

Was Barry surprised! When the door of that apartment opened, he was staring head-on into the barrel of a .45-caliber automatic. The disheveled man holding the pistol was shaking and foaming at the mouth. He still believed he was in the process of arguing with his brother and he saw Wintraub as his brother. Barry recalled the way his heart hesitated and then began beating madly. He felt the curl of cold fingers on the back of his neck. At that point, he wished to God he had gone on to become a rabbi.

Perhaps it was because of his feel for conversation and the ability to get to people—abilities a candidate for the rabbinical order would have to develop—that he was able to talk himself out of that potentially fatal situation. He took on the role of the man's brother and apologized in general. It calmed the man enough for Barry to move in quickly and disarm him.

Despite his size, Barry was an agile guy with excellent reflexes. He was the only one in the precinct who could line up a hundred pennies in ten stacks of ten on the underside of his arm while touching his shoulder and then flip them so quickly he could catch all of them in the air. It was one of the silly games the detectives played while killing time.

Baker knocked again and then put his ear to the door.

"I don't hear a thing in there."

"Try the handle."

It turned and the door opened. None of El Yacoub's men had taken the time to lock it. They saw no reason to care. The Claw's orders were "get her out of there as fast as you can." The apartment was still in its morning lived-in state. The couch was still opened and the blanket pulled back. A pair of pants was draped over a chair, and a blouse hung on a makeshift clothesline hung from the kitchen doorway into the living room. The sink was still filled with the breakfast dishes. An old refrigerator hummed with the irregular sound of a worn drive belt.

Both the detectives moved cautiously through the apartment, their guns drawn. Wintraub pushed opened the door to Yusuf's room and stared inside. The bed there was not made either; and shirts, underwear, and pants were folded and draped on chairs and over the dresser. He saw an interesting drawing on the dresser mirror, taped up in the corner. It consisted of a hawk with a sword through it. The hawk seemed unconcerned about the sword. It was as if it were part of the hawk's body. Barry studied it for a moment. Interpreting art had always been a mystery to him. The bottom drawer of the dresser was still open. He could see that it had been nearly emptied. It was the same way with some of the drawers in the dresser in the living room.

"They're here and they ain't," Baker said. "Whaddaya make of it?"

"I don't know. From the looks of things, someone left in a big hurry and yet didn't leave."

"Yeah, the milk is still out on the table and the butter too."

"Could be just lousy housekeepers. Go down and see if you can locate the super to this building. I'll keep looking around here."

"Right," Baker said.

Wintraub moved back over the apartment slowly. It was always interesting to him to come into another person's living quarters and try, from the ingredients he saw within, to picture the individual both physically and mentally. Gitleman, the fish man, had given them a very general description. They could begin with it, but they needed more. Barry realized, of course, that a woman lived here too. He lifted the blouse off the dresser and held it up, gathering a mental picture of her bust and shoulders. Then he brought the blouse to his face and smelled it. Shirley was always putting some kind of scent in with the clothes—usually a bar of sweet-smelling soap. It wasn't really a bad idea, but he would have never thought of doing it himself.

There was a scent in this blouse. It wasn't sweet or sour. It didn't particularly smell like clothing bleach, either. It was unusual, like the odor of some incense. He dropped it and began going through the drawers. He found two different sizes of men's clothes in the apartment, one size indicating a man somewhat taller and broader than the other. Just before Baker returned without a superintendent of the building, Barry picked up a newspaper that was still lying on the kitchen table. It was turned to the classified section. One of the small squares was circled. It read, "Lost, two Siamese cats. One with a red ribbon, one with a blue. Reward. Write to Apartment 4D, 498 East 93rd St." *Odd*, he thought. *Wouldn't the individual want you to call?*

Walking back into the apartment, Baker said, "No super. They call a number when they have troubles. I got it from a tenant on the first floor. I called and asked about this apartment."

"And?"

"Been rented to a Mandel, all right. Mrs. Clea Mandel. As far as managers of this building know, the Mandels are still living here. Rent's paid up through the next three weeks anyway. What's that?"

"An address with an ad for lost cats."

"So what about it?"

"They don't ask you to call. They ask you to write. And we're pretty far away from East Ninety-Third Street. What did these cats do, take a bus?"

"I got a cat," Baker said, looking around. "And there's usually a bowl on the floor most all the time for food or milk."

"I doubt that they found cats, but they appear interested in this."

"So what's that got to do with anything?" Baker said.

"I don't know, but let's take a ride to East Ninety-Third anyway."

10

This time Wintraub and Baker went to the super first and inquired about the occupant of apartment 4D. The super was a tall, middle-aged man with a Charles de Gaulle face. His stomach protruded like a volleyball just above the groin, and he slouched so terribly that he appeared to have a hunchback.

"4D?"

"Yes, sir, 4D," Wintraub said.

The super scratched his face and stepped out of the lower-level apartment.

"4D's been unoccupied for two weeks. The man got caught up in one of those city layoffs and left the area. It's for rent. There's been a few people looking at it, but no one's taken it yet."

"Are you sure?" Wintraub said. "Because there was this ad in the papers." He showed the super the circled block in the classified section.

"Well, that must've been some kind of mistake, misprint."

"He could be right," Baker said.

"Look, we'd like to take a look around apartment 4D, okay?" Wintraub said. He was bothered by all this and held on to the vague suspicions teasing his mind.

"Sure, if it'll make you happy. No problem. Let me get my keys." He went back inside.

"What's the point, Barry?"

"Maybe someone's been using the place right under this guy's nose, or maybe he's full of shit."

"The JDLs got you thinkin' everybody's part of a conspiracy against the Jews, huh?" Baker said, smiling.

"No harm in checking things out completely. If you want, wait in the car."

"Don't get so touchy. Okay, okay, we'll check it out."

They followed the super up the flight of stairs and waited while he found the key on his key chain.

"It's a furnished apartment," Barry said on entering.

"Yep."

"Has it been cleaned up since the other party left?"

"Sure. We do that right away. Can't show a dirty apartment to new tenants, can we?"

Wintraub walked in slowly. He didn't know what he was looking for, but he felt he should give the place his usual once-over. Why were the occupants of the Mandel apartment so concerned about this address? He looked about the living room while Baker stood by the entrance staring indifferently.

"When you're finished," the super said, "just close the door. It's set to lock."

"Thanks."

Barry pulled out a dresser drawer and looked. Baker wandered into the bathroom. He opened the medicine cabinet and then came back out.

"Looks like he was telling the truth."

"Yeah."

"What now, Sherlock?"

"I guess we'll get an APB out on Joseph Mandel and stake out the Mandel apartment."

"Right. We'll pick him up when he returns."

"If he returns," Barry said, sitting on the couch. "You agreed you got the impression someone left in a hurry."

"Yeah, but they left stuff there. Maybe the other occupants will return."

"Maybe." Barry's eyes drifted down to the easy chair before him and then to the small table beside it. There was a colorful brochure lying there. Seemed like a travel folder. "Some cleanup," he said, bending over. It was an advertisement from the New Prospect.

"What's that about?" Baker asked.

"Catskills. Big resort," Barry said, tossing the pamphlet onto the easy chair. "I wish I was there now."

"Let's go," Baker said. Barry nodded and stood up. When they got outside, he stopped and looked up the sidewalk.

"Get the car and meet me up at that corner phone booth," Barry said.

"What now?"

"Just do it."

Baker shook his head and started away. He noticed the brown

Gremlin parked across the street, but the four men in it seemed involved in their own conversation. He did not see that they all wore small yarmulkes.

When Baker got up to the corner, he waited a few moments. Then Wintraub stepped out of the booth and got into the car, a look of deep thought on his face.

"So?

"I just called the paper and asked about this ad."

"And?"

"There was no mistake. It's the address whoever placed it wanted."

"Who paid for it?"

"The person used a money order."

"So what?" Baker said, a look of real annoyance on his face.

"I don't know," Barry said. "But it bothers me." He thought about Rabbi Kaufman's intense eyes.

A group of nearly thirty people had gathered at the Goldstein house to sit shiva, but other friends and relatives were dropping in and out all day. Most of the people stayed in the living room and the kitchen, talking in soft, low voices, shaking their heads with dramatic emphasis and greeting one another with gentle handshakes. The women kissed cheeks. Everyone was comforting one another. There was the impression that all this regret and condolence would touch the Goldsteins. Everyone behaved as though he was the immediate family. All were a direct part of the tragedy. All shared the great sorrow.

Mrs. Goldstein remained upstairs in her bedroom, under sedation. Mr. Goldstein sat in the living room, his head resting on the palm of his right hand propped up by the elbow. His face was pale, and there were lines of darkness around his eyes, over his chin, and across his cheeks where he did not shave. He was a small man, made much smaller by his terrible grief. After each had entered and approached to shake his hand, the mourners looked at him through sideward glances. The women kissed and hugged him and then backed away, holding handkerchiefs to their faces. He looked up with red, glassy eyes. He was a man caught in a daze. None of it seemed real. He had the feeling that in a few moments all these people would disappear and he'd be seated, reading a book. It had all been a momentary daydream. He was lost in a fantasy. He hoped that was somehow true. David had been their only child. They had placed all their hope in him. He was to carry them into the future. Now they had no one but themselves. It was too much, too much to believe.

Bill and Toby Marcus stood up when Abe and Lillian Rothberg entered the house. They greeted one another first, the women kissing, the two men shaking hands. Lillian squeezed Bill's hand and Toby took Abe's upper arm. The four of them stood by silently for a moment, other mourners staring at them as if they held some magical powers, as if they would do something to change the course of events. Lillian was such a doer, such a leader and organizer. Surely she would make some statement, commit some action that would lift the gloom. She would clap her hands and begin to dictate orders. *This half of the room into the kitchen. You people over there, prepare the table. We need this furniture moved.*

"Where's Sylvia?" Abe asked.

"She's upstairs. Doctor Wasserman got here earlier. He gave her something."

"She can't sleep forever," Lillian said.

"I know," Bill whispered. "Better talk to Hymie." He turned to indicate him.

"Oh, Abe," Lillian said, taking her husband's arm. He patted her hand and they started across the room.

"Hymie," he said, extending his hand. Hymie Goldstein looked up with what seemed to be incredible physical effort. He took Abe's hand and just held it. Lillian knelt down, squatted beside him, and placed her head against his shoulder. She sobbed gently, and tears began to come from Hymie Goldstein's eyes. His mouth quivered. Abe looked about nervously. They weren't helping. They were bringing everything to a horrible head.

"Lillian," he said. She lifted her head away and stood up, turning her back to them. Toby was at her side with a handkerchief.

"Looks like you were right, Abe," Hymie said. "You called it."

"I didn't call anything," Rothberg said softly. He hoped no one was listening.

"The kid became committed to the cause. I didn't stop him. I let it all go on and I never discouraged him. He appreciated that. But Sylvia's fears were right. She was right. What have I done?" he asked, his hands up.

"Easy, Hymie." Abe patted Hymie on the shoulder and the man's arms dropped to his lap. "He wasn't killed in a battle. He was mugged on a street. It could've happened to anyone."

"He was killed in battle," Hymie said, shaking his head. "The others keep dropping by. They know. Some of them are here now—his friends, members of the JDL. Look at their faces. They're plotting revenge, and I hope they get it."

"None of that's gonna do any good now."

"It'll do good; it'll do good. Those vermin have to be exterminated before they strike out again and again."

"I'm sorry," Abe said. "None of this makes any sense." He wanted to turn away and sit with Bill Marcus, but Hymie grabbed his jacket sleeve.

"Abe," he said becoming more animated. He leaned over, one hand on the arm of the easy chair. "I'm asking people who want to give something in Daniel's memory to give donations to Rabbi Kaufman."

"Who?"

"Kaufman. He'll be here soon. David's leader."

"Oh, Kaufman. If that's what you want, Hymie, that's what I'll do."

"It's what I want," he said. He clenched his teeth, and his eyes grew bigger. After a few moments, he sat back and looked dazed again. Toby and Lillian moved into the kitchen. Abe joined Bill Marcus by the picture window. He was talking to Doctor Wasserman. They paused as he joined them.

"Bad business," Abe said.

"Just horrible. We'll never be free of it. Never," Bill said.

"Hear anything about the killer?" Wasserman asked.

"No. Nothing."

"Sometimes I think we oughta go back to the old block police system, sorta make each neighborhood responsible for itself," Bill said.

"And make the city a thousand armed camps?" Wasserman asked.

"That's what it is anyway."

"Violence breeds violence. It's no solution," the doctor replied.

"So what is the solution?"

"I don't know. I do know that what you're suggesting isn't."

"The only solution for the Jews is a strong and powerful state of Israel," Marcus said. "That's the only reality our enemies will understand. They don't want to compromise and negotiate. We've got to be bigger and stronger and capable of delivering the greatest death-blow. That's the only solution. You're comin' up to the New Prospect for the holidays, aren't you, Doc?"

"We'll be up by the third night. I've got many things to do yet."

"Just as long as you're up to hear Chaim Eban."

"And contribute," Wasserman said, nodding his head.

"And contribute. Right, Abe?"

"And get in some golf if the weather permits," Rothberg said. It took the fire and enthusiasm out of Marcus's face. He smirked, but Wasserman smiled.

"Damn right. You're about my handicap, aren't you, Abe? Five, give or take a stroke?" Wasserman went on, still smiling.

"Sure, but on that course," Abe said, feeling a little more like talking, "everyone's handicap goes up fifty percent. Why I remember once . . ."

He stopped talking just as Rabbi Kaufman entered the house. Four members of the JDL stood beside him. Their presence brought an immediate silence. Two young men came out of the kitchen and joined them. All of them stood erect—their entire demeanor one of anger and aggression. It was as if a strong gust of air had come into the room. None of them wore expressions of sorrow or sympathy. Kaufman's face was tight, his lips pressed together, his eyes reduced to slits because of his nearly closed lids. He began across the room. A couple stood aside to make room for all of them. Everyone stepped back and turned.

Hymie Goldstein didn't realize they were there until they were right on top of him. He looked up slowly, and then the expression on his face changed radically. He seemed to have renewed energy. He lifted his hand and shook Kaufman's vigorously. His face registered the light of hope. Then he stood up, still holding the rabbi's hand. It was as if Kaufman could transmit strength.

They spoke softly. No one could hear the words, though nearly everyone strained to do so. Whatever he said to Hymie Goldstein encouraged him even more. He nearly smiled. Then he turned and shook hands with each and every one of the JDL members.

"I can understand how Hymie feels," Bill said. "I can't say I wouldn't be the same way if I were in his shoes,"

"It's not the solution," Wasserman repeated. Marcus turned and looked at him, this time with obvious disgust.

"I'll say this for you, Doc. Your kind must've been in the majority during World War Two. Otherwise why would six million of us have strolled into the gas chambers?"

"C'mon, that's not fair, Bill," Abe said.

"Exactly," Marcus replied.

11

Nessim looked out the study window and watched as a tray of coffee and small cakes was taken out to Clea and Yusuf. They sat in the warm sunlight of the spring afternoon and enjoyed the hospitality of their new sudden hosts, Paul and Beatrice Tandem. The house in Monroe was off on a side road, a thousand feet in. The long driveway and plush lawn with weeping willows and lines of hedges appeared as elegant and as peaceful as anyplace they had ever known. The house itself was a large stone and wood building consisting of twelve rooms. There were two floors and an adjoining two-car garage. Farther right from that was a shack for tools and garden equipment.

"Here we are now," Hamid said, entering the study with Paul Tandem. "All set to talk things over."

Nessim turned and took the easy chair near the window. Paul Tandem was a light-haired, blue-eyed, six-foot-tall, well-built man in his forties. He had a wide forehead, but his hair came down over it, hiding that characteristic. His face narrowed considerably below the cheeks, and consequently he had an unusually small mouth. He had a cocky demeanor.

Nessim immediately decided the man was cold and unfeeling, but there was something more. He had seen this kind of type A, hollowed-out individual who looked like the shell of a person before. Tandem had eyes of glass that went no deeper within him than was necessary. Nessim was sure he had fingers of ice, and when they shook hands, that was confirmed.

Paul Tandem was a man who walked and talked with Death, Nessim thought. Death was with him at the breakfast table in the morning. It sat beside him when he had his quiet moments in this study. Men like Paul Tandem made Nessim aware of his own mortality.

"I'm happy to meet you, Commander," Tandem said. He extended his hand, with its rather large palms but short stubby fingers. He grasped Nessim's hand and gave it a manly squeeze.

Nessim nodded.

Tandem went on, "Heard a great deal about you and your ability."

"Good," Nessim said. He looked to Hamid. He was impatient with small talk.

"We want to get right down to it," Hamid said. "We've deliberately left only a short time for preparations. El Yacoub will be here tonight."

"El Yacoub," Tandem repeated, smiling widely. He took pleasure in the sound of the name, but to Nessim he looked like he was lost in a daze.

"Sit," Hamid said.

Tandem moved quickly to the black leather couch. It was a

neatly kept study with paneled walls, a thick cream-colored nylon rug on the floor, and a desk with its supplies and contents carefully arranged. In fact, the room looked unused. Hamid began to unroll a thin piece of oak tag paper.

"Hotel floor plans?" Nessim said, looking over his shoulder.

"It's construction plans. El Yacoub will bring more detailed and more elaborate material to study. The Obermans—they own the hotel—have made arrangements for Eban to stay for dinner and overnight. He is to make his speech about 9 a.m. and then visit with some rich people in a cocktail party later that evening in the night-club."

"I see. This dining room holds all the guests?"

"They feed three thousand people," Tandem said. "At one time."

"The exact timing of Chaim Eban's schedule is not yet set, but he has to eat when everyone else eats. He has to show himself to the contributors as much as possible," Hamid said.

"What did the organization have in mind?" Nessim asked.

"Mr. Tandem here seems to think the structure is vulnerable. We do too."

"It damn well is," Tandem said. "I know something about construction. I was in that business for a while."

"I'm to collapse part of the building, is that it?" Nessim asked.

"Like Samson on the Philistines," Hamid said. "I suppose there are a number of possibilities," he added, looking at the diagram.

"This basement appears to run under the dining room, the night-club, and the lobby," Nessim said.

"The command would like you to use the Kennedy Airport method," Hamid said.

"Detonation through radio transmission?"

"Exactly. Tandem has suggestions about where to plant the plastique and detonator devices."

Tandem approached and pointed to a number of spots on the plans. "Steel girders," he said.

"El Yacoub's bringing much more detailed material," Hamid said again, "but we want to give you the main idea. Think it over."

"You'll get three thousand of 'em in the dining room," Tandem said.

"Is there any security in the basement?"

"Security? Hell no," Tandem said. "You're in the Catskills, not the Middle East. They don't patrol all over. Security is mostly a cosmetic thing."

"Cosmetic?"

"Yeah, for show, to make the guests feel secure and protected," Tandem said. "Not that they really feel threatened in any way," he added.

"The plastique?" Nessim said, turning to Hamid.

"The Claw will have it tonight when he arrives."

"You'll be able to enter this basement from a number of places," Tandem said. "But the best way is from the outside here"—he pointed to the diagram—"late at night."

"We have you in a room next to a fire escape," Hamid said. "It drops right near that entrance."

"It you went down through any of the lobby exits, you could be seen. That would attract some interest," Tandem said. "It's just something we can avoid," he added proudly.

Nessim looked at him. "Apparently you worked there?"

"I was head of their security for five years."

"Gave you a bad deal, did they?" Nessim asked, smiling.

"You might say that," he replied. "They killed my son."

Clea smiled tentatively and crossed her legs as Paul Tandem, Hamid, and Nessim came out to join her and Yusuf. Yusuf had been sulking the whole time. He knew that they had been discussing strategy, and he resented the fact that he was not permitted to be in on all of it. Nessim knew how he felt and tried to give him a reassuring look as they took seats.

Beatrice Tandem, a small woman with rather wide hips and a small bosom, stood up quickly. Her face was round, with puffy cheeks and a long thin mouth. Her nose seemed lost under the wide, smiling blue eyes. Nessim sensed something immediately childlike about her expressions. He had seen mothers like that in the Middle East. They became silly and giddy in the face of tragedy. It was the mysterious workings of the brain, setting up defenses against reality. He understood why she would be the way she was and did his best to make his awareness unnoticeable.

"More coffee?" she asked, clapping her hands together.

"Yes, yes," Paul said. "More coffee."

She scurried off, her long skirt flying out and snapping back with the exaggerated movement of her arms. There was a moment of silence.

"I meant to ask you, Hamid," Nessim began, breaking the short silence, "about that woman with El Yacoub."

"Brenda Casewell? Her husband was an American sailor. Remember that American ship the Israelis 'accidentally' attacked during the

'73 war? He was killed on it. We were going to use Brenda's apartment for a meeting place, but when El Yacoub discovered that empty one next door, he decided on that. He has an inbred, instinctive feel for caution. This way no one could tie Casewell in with us. She's rather a bitter woman and El Yacoub knew her grandfather."

"You see what I've been telling you," Nessim said turning to Yusuf. "We're careful from the top down. Caution is the sister of courage."

Yusuf nodded but looked away quickly.

"Isn't it peaceful here?" Hamid said. "Like an afternoon on Sheep's Head Hill by the Jordan, right, Nessim?"

"Yes," he said. He sat down. His eyes lifted slowly and confronted Clea. She looked frightened. He wanted to get her alone and hold her and tell her this was all nothing, nothing. He would do his work and they would still be together. It wasn't his time yet. The plan provided for his escape.

"While we're all here together like this," Hamid said, "I might as well describe how we're going to work your entrance to the hotel. The Claw was rather pleased to learn you and Clea were available."

"Clea?"

"Yes. The Jews are having this Passover holiday, you know. It's a big family gathering."

"What's the plan?"

"We have reservations for you and your wife in the name of Mr. and Mrs. Martin Jaffe."

"What about me?" Yusuf said suddenly.

"You're to stay here and wait until it's over."

"I want to go. I want to help."

"Well . . ."

"Tell them, Nessim. I can help. I'm ready."

"I'm afraid it's not possible," Hamid said.

Yusuf slammed the palms of his hands down on the arms of the wooden chair and stood up.

"Easy," Nessim said.

Yusuf looked at him and then walked off, toward the front of the house.

"He's too anxious," Hamid said. "El Yacoub was very upset by what happened in the city."

"Nevertheless, he is dedicated and wants to contribute. We should find a way to use him in this," Nessim said.

"You want him along?"

"I could use him. Planting the plastique. He could be of help since Clea is there, just to support the cover."

"Well, we will have to speak to El Yacoub, but frankly . . ."

"I'll speak to him," Nessim said quickly. "Leave it to me."

"Whatever you say. You know what has to be done once you're in the hotel."

"What exactly has to be done?" Clea asked. She looked from Hamid to Nessim and then to Paul Tandem.

"'We're . . .'" Tandem started.

"I'll talk to you about it later," Nessim said, cutting him off. He gave Tandem a strong look and Tandem smiled. Clea caught Nessim's visual warning.

"Do you come from the Middle East, Mr. Tandem?" she asked.

"No," Tandem said. "I come from upstate New York, Sullivan County."

"Sullivan County?"

"The county the New Prospect Hotel is in."

"Is it true that only Jewish people live up there?"

"Hell no," he said. "But the way they talk about it, you'd think so."

"It is true that they control all the money and the big businesses up there, is it not?" Hamid said.

"Not all of it. A lot of it. They're into everything. One gets in, he makes way for another and another. It's the way they work. Like termites."

"You must've had Jewish friends living up there," Clea said.

"Not many. My family always worked for 'em one way or another, but I never had any real friends," he said with a note of pride in his voice.

Nessim found him more and more distasteful. It was one thing to fight a war against the Jews for control of a homeland in the Middle East and to dislike them for their politics and military strategy, but to clump them with termites . . . Ironically, Nessim was not anti-Semitic. He considered it a personal weakness to generalize your hatred. It was the difference between a psychotic and a soldier. He could kill anyone if there was some strategic or political value in it, but wanton killing . . . It lowered and reduced the image he had of himself and his cause.

"We all have quite unusual backgrounds," Clea said in measured tones.

"And yet here we all are, together, fighting for the same cause," Hamid said.

"We've all been deprived of something by the Jews. You, your homeland; and me, my son," Tandem added, nodding.

"Your son?" Clea asked.

"Mr. Tandem's son worked at the New Prospect," Nessim said. He could see the utter confusion and discomfort Clea was experiencing.

"They promoted him into a waiter position," Tandem said with bitterness. "He was big for his age. He worked his ass off bringing them their second portions and their special juices." He added in a tone of mimicry, "This meat's too rare. This meat's too thick. This potato's too hard.".

"I still don't quite . . ."

"It happened over a Christmas New Year's holiday. He developed pneumonia. I never knew it. You see, the staff lived at the help's quarters. It's a separate building, away from the hotel proper. So the guests won't be disturbed by their presence after hours. But the head-waiter knew. Everyone in that damn dining room knew the boy was ill. He was walking around with a temperature of one hundred and three, his face flushed. He wasn't a particularly bright boy, you see," Tandem said, his voice cracking, his eyes watering. "But he gave the work all he had—to please them and make big tips. That's what it's all about up there, dontcha know, big tips. Those fat, rich bastards, filling up their stomachs, ordering him around while he suffered with pneumonia."

"I don't understand why he pushed himself so, if he was that sick," Clea said, as softly as she could. "I mean . . ." She looked to Nessim.

Tandem shook his head. "They made him work. They didn't care. He was so glad he was doing a waiter's job. They make big money up there for those holidays. You know what it means to a sixteen-year-old boy to make over a thousand dollars for ten days! He collapsed in the dining room and do you know what they did?" Clea didn't respond. She waited quietly. "They were so concerned about the guests getting upset they made him stand up and walk out on his own. It was almost two hours later before anyone bothered to call me. They left him in the back of the kitchen with a towel on his forehead. They said he wanted it that way. What did he know? When I got there, the kid was shivering like crazy. All the while, that damn meal was being served. No one paid much attention to him. They were all worried about their tips. Tips!"

"What happened then?"

"I got him to the hospital, but it was another hour before a doctor examined him. By the time he got treated, he was struggling to breathe. I knew the moment he died, saw him take his last breath. I swore then that they would all pay." Tandem had worked himself up. He was sitting forward, his fists clenched. "I never dreamed I'd get the opportunity. I'm grateful. Grateful."

"Did the hotel owners ever say anything, do anything . . ." Clea was sitting forward too.

"What could they say? It's a big hotel. Someone's in charge of the dining room, the kitchen, the staff. It's like an army. The generals don't know their troops. The managers came to the hospital, both of them, and they waited in the lobby with my wife. When I told them he had died, they could only say they were sorry. They were sorry," he repeated and smiled.

"Amazing lack of consideration," Hamid said.

Tandem nodded. "You see how my wife is. I am not blind, even though I pretend to be. She's been that way ever since."

"How did you come to know us?" Clea asked. She hoped Tandem would relax. He seemed ready to strangle someone to death at the slightest provocation.

Nessim was uncomfortable in the presence of his rage. He was too unpredictable. He decided then and there that Tandem would not have anything specific to do with the operation.

"Quite often, an officer in the Israeli army would stay at the New Prospect. It's quite the recreational center of the world for the Zionist movement, you know. I worked there as their chief of security."

"Oh," Clea said and looked at Nessim.

"I often got to talk to these soldiers. One time I met a Major Nussbaum, something of a secret service man for them, I think," he said, looking toward Hamid.

Hamid closed his eyes and nodded. "And quite efficient. One of their top people."

"He was a little high one night. We talked for hours in the lounge. This was before my boy died," Tandem said. "He described some Hezbollah strongholds and I remembered a name. The rest was easy. I made contact. I wanted to join up, fight with them, but they had other plans for me." He paused, then said, "I move around a bit these days. Then they set me up here."

"You don't own this house then?"

"No. It's sort of a checkpoint, a hideaway, a rest stop for members of the organization who move across the country. X-2 stayed here last month," he said proudly. "Of course you know he masterminded the massacre of the hundred Jewish tourists in Mexico City last year. We had a good talk."

"X-2?" Clea looked at Nessim.

"He's an American citizen with some political power," Hamid said. "His true identity must be kept as secret as possible."

"I see."

There was a long moment of silence. Beatrice Tandem's laughter turned their attention to the house again.

"You'll never believe this," she said, as she came outside, still laughing, "but I spilled a whole pot of coffee by mistake and had to brew a new one."

She started across the patio with a tray.

"Mr. Tandem forgot to mention one detail," Hamid said, turning back to Clea. "The dinner his son served while being sick was a dinner dedicated to the American Jewish Congress."

"Yes," Tandem said, a far-off look in his eyes, "and I've waited for years to serve them their proper dessert."

12

Barry worked the key in the lock as softly as he could, but when he had opened it and pushed the door, he ran into the chain lock.

"Damn it," he said and closed the door again, waiting to see if Shirley would just open it now. She didn't. He heard the television going and imagined her asleep on the couch as usual. There was nothing to do but press the bell button. The chimes played a rendition of "As Time Goes By," the theme song from *Casablanca*, Shirley's favorite movie. He had gotten it for her as an anniversary present. A little while later, the door was opened and she peered out at him.

"It's me, Shirl," he said. Sometimes she didn't wake up until she was off the couch for a few minutes.

"You? What time is it?" She wiped her eyes and massaged her cheeks vigorously.

"Two thirty, Shirl. Open the door, Shirl."

"Two thirty?" She closed the door, slid out the chain, and then opened the door. He stepped in. "Well?"

"Well what?"

"Did you get the Wallace Avenue killer?"

"Not yet," he said and went into the kitchen. She followed, dressed in her robe. "I've worked up an appetite sitting around on a stakeout," he added, opening the refrigerator. There was some cold chicken on a plate. He took it out and sat down, hovering over it like a cat with a mouse in its paws. She brushed her hair back and plopped into a seat.

"I let the kids stay up a half hour later because they wanted to see you," she said.

"Um."

He began to devour the chicken. She watched him eat, resting her face on the palm of her hand, propped up at the elbow.

"We've got a suspect," he said, nibbling at a leg bone as if it were corn on the cob, "but it looks like he's skipped out. Had the apartment staked out all day and most of the night."

"Sure he's skipped out. He killed someone. Who wouldn't skip out? You gotta be a detective to realize this?"

"I keep getting the feeling there's more to this one, but I can't get my fingers on anything substantial."

"Whaddaya mean by more?"

"I don't know," he said. "That's just it."

"Makes a lotta sense, Barry. A lotta sense."

"I hope that's not today's paper sticking out of the garbage," he said. She turned and looked.

"I think it is."

"That's not right. Really, so I get home late once in a while."

"Once in a while? Did you say once in a while?"

She got up and pulled the paper out of the garbage. She inspected it and decided it was clean.

"Thanks," he said, taking it.

"My mother's waiting for us to invite her over for the First Seder," she said as he unfolded the paper and spread it out before him.

He began reading. "You think she's sitting on the phone?"

"A good part of the day she is. My father probably wants her to call and invite us, but they invited us last year. I'm sure she's just waiting for me to call."

"That means your brother's waiting too."

"Don't I know it.'

"I'm not sure yet whether I'm taking the holidays," he said as he skimmed the paper's first page.

"Whaddaya talkin' about, Barry? How can you not take those days? You were almost a rabbi."

"Not really almost, close, but not almost," he said. "I'm right in the middle of this case." He lifted his chicken-greased fingers for emphasis.

"Murderers can wait for you to celebrate your holiday, Barry. My mother wouldn't understand."

"You called her," he said and pointed an accusing finger. "You've already called her and made the arrangements."

"I haven't. Honest. It's been bothering me day and night. I can't eat without thinking about it. Why do you think there's so much chicken left?"

"Just hold off."

"Until when, Barry?"

"Another day."

"It's not right. She invited us last year."

"So we'll fall behind one year. Man O Manoshevitz!" He turned the pages.

"We've got to give the kids some sort of religious environment. I mean, what do we give them? You're hardly home and when you are, you don't talk about religion much. I'm practically an atheist, except when it comes to the holidays. I mean . . ."

"Hold it," he said holding up his hand.

"What?"

"This item here. This piece on page five."

"What item?" She leaned over.

"'Catskill Hotel to Host Israeli Military Hero'; Chaim Eban is going to the New Prospect."

"So?"

"The New Prospect," he said, looking up. "The New Prospect."

"The New Prospect. So?"

"I don't know. That's the second time I've seen that hotel's name today."

"Wonderful. Fantastic. You know, I've never really appreciated the wealth of information you bring home, Barry."

"I wonder," he said. "I wonder . . ."

"Wonder what?"

"If it means anything."

"I'm really beginning to worry about you," she said. "Now, let's get back to our discussion concerning the First Seder. . . ."

"I was expecting you to call," Rabbi Kaufman said. Barry had called him first thing in the morning. He woke up thinking about the news article.

"I'd like to stop by and talk to you for a few minutes today."

"Stop by. You've had no luck?"

"I don't know what I've had," Barry said. "That's why I want to see you."

"Okay," Kaufman said. "Come. I'll be here all morning."

Barry met Baker outside their office at the precinct. Apparently no one had shown up at the Mandel apartment since they left.

"There's nothing on these people," Baker said. "It's as if they just appeared. No records going back anywhere. Apparently, we've come across some illegal aliens. I told Phil to turn it over to INS."

"That's what Rabbi Kaufman told me."

"So he oughta be working for the federal government."

"Remember that brochure we found in that empty apartment?" Barry said as they walked into the office.

"Brochure?"

"About the New Prospect Hotel. In the Catskills."

"Oh, yeah. What about it?"

"Guess who just happens to be going up to the New Prospect for the Jewish holidays."

"Rabbi Kaufman and his boys."

"No. Chaim Eban."

"Who?"

"An Israeli military hero."

"So?"

"You don't think there's any connection between all these leads and facts?"

"What leads and facts?"

"I was going to try it out on the chief, but I figured I'd see how you reacted first."

"You think these so-called conspirators are goin' to try to do somethin' against this military hero?"

"It occurred to me, yes."

"Talk about Jewish paranoia. Jesus."

"I'm going to tell the chief anyway," Barry said.

"He's a bit pissed off about this case," Baker said. "I had to tell him about the ice pick and how we got it."

"Well, maybe he'll realize this isn't just a routine matter," Barry said. Baker shook his head and smiled. A few minutes later, Barry was sitting in the captain's office, pulling on his shirt collar.

Captain Petersen—a stout man with thick, hairy forearms and a stomach that was as hard as the wall, despite its balloonlike appearance—paced back and forth. He had listened with his usual impatience, an impatience that always made Barry feel he had to rush his information before something else happened and took the chief's mind off what he was saying.

"So that's why I think I should follow these leads," Barry added.

"Leads, huh? So far you've told me one helluva dumb story, Wintraub." He spun around and slapped his left palm with the back of his right hand's fingers. "You got the address of the guy who works in this fish market. You went there because you were given the murder weapon by members of the JDL. Who they are, you won't say even though they were withholding evidence."

"I couldn't have gotten it otherwise."

"Did it ever occur to you that they might be settin' someone up?"

"We thought of that, but as Baker said, the Mandels are apparently a fictional family. Illegal aliens. INS is looking into it. There is some justification for our suspicions."

"Okay . . . So then you went to this apartment, found it had been left in a hurry, but happened on a newspaper with an ad circled. You went to the address in the ad, but no one lived there or had for two weeks. Why'd you go to that address anyhow?" Chief Petersen asked, arms out and palms raised. He wore a deceptive look of innocent curiosity.

"Thought they might be there or the people might know where they were. In any case, we'd learn more about them than we knew."

"Amazing. But when you got there, you found out no one was there."

"So the super said."

"So the super said. And then on the way out of the apartment, in which no one lived for weeks, you found this brochure from the New Prospect Hotel."

"And then when I saw the news article . . ."

"I know, I know. Look, Wintraub, suppose I pick up this phone now and call the Office of Security in the State Department and tell them one of my detectives thinks Chaim Eban might be in some danger when he goes up to the New Prospect. They're going to ask me why you think that, Wintraub," Petersen said, smiling and changing the tone of his voice. It was as if he was talking to a complete idiot. "You know, some hard evidence?"

"They won't laugh at you, Chief. The Israelis, especially, respect caution. They've come to understand it."

"Is that right? All right," he said. "I'll make the call, but frankly, I think we've got a simple one-on-one situation here. This looks like a revenge killing or a confrontation killing. Nothing more. Your mysteriously empty apartments, lost cats, and illegal aliens add nothing to that theory, Wintraub. These people split because the heat's on. Go out there and continue to try to trace them down. Just work on a murder, will ya, and not an international conspiracy."

"Right, Chief," Barry said, standing. Baker stood in the doorway, smirking as usual.

"Maybe you oughta go back to your JDL source. They're apparently doing a better police job than you are," Petersen said, sitting behind his desk.

"Yeah. Oh, listen, Chief," Barry said, turning back again. "I'll be taking those days for Passover after all."

"Baker, you team up with Thompson then."

"But I don't want to be taken off this case, Chief."

"Oh, of course not, Wintraub," Petersen said with excessive dramatic gesture, "we'll just hold a moratorium on crime until Passover ends."

"At least you can count on those thieves and murderers who are religious Jews," Barry said quickly.

Petersen's face froze. "Huh?"

"Don't forget that call, Chief," Barry said and marched out. Baker followed behind him, laughing.

"Hey, hold up. Where we goin' so fast?"

"Up to see Rabbi Kaufman. You heard the chief."

"You goin' to let me go in with you this time, Jew boy?"

"Yeah," Barry said. "See what you think."

Kaufman's wife greeted the detectives at the door. She was a thin woman with a quiet smile. She moved gracefully and spoke with her eyes. The look of peace in her face was the look of peace that comes after everything was over—the battles and the burials. Mentally, she had taken herself into all the avenues of the future, Barry thought. This was a woman who had come to grips with the possibilities her husband's work held early on. She was a woman of great strength or great emotional fatigue.

"This is Lieutenant Baker," Barry said as they stepped into the living room. Kaufman stood up and shook Baker's hand.

"You both looked worried."

"That's what comes of working with a man like Wintraub," Baker said. He smiled at Barry.

"Your illegal alien is gone," Barry said as he sat down. Baker took the easy chair to the right. Kaufman sat on the couch.

"To some other part of the city?"

"Maybe."

"Somewhere on East Ninety-Third, perhaps?" Kaufman said, smiling.

"How did you . . ." Barry looked at Baker. He shrugged. "You had us followed."

"A little insurance for our investment of trust. Don't be offended."

"Then you people have been staking out the Mandel apartment as well, I'd venture to guess."

"We have. Tell me about East Ninety-Third."

Barry related the story of the Lost and Found advertisement and the brochure they found in the empty apartment. Kaufman listened intently. His wife brought in some coffee and then left.

"What does all this mean to you?" Barry asked.

"I don't know. If I follow along with your suspicions, I run into contradictions."

"Why?"

"Well, Daniel Goldstein's murder is obviously an event on a much smaller scale politically than an attempt on the life of Chaim Eban. People sent to get Eban would have to be of high caliber and efficiency. Some of their best. Why would one or two of their best take the time and the risk to kill a member of the JDL and bring on a police investigation just when they're planning to do something as big as get Chaim Eban?"

"See?" Baker said. "I knew you were way off base with this."

"On the other hand," Kaufman said, "perhaps there are more terrorists involved here than we think. Maybe the Goldstein killing was meant to be some sort of diversion. How many people lived in the Mandel apartment, three?"

"You knew that before I did, I think," Barry said.

"Yes. All right," Kaufman said, leaning forward. "I'm beginning to worry about this situation a lot more. Let me be straightforward. As far as we know, the superintendent of the building on East Ninety-Third is no one. He was also telling the truth about the apartment."

"Wait a minute," Baker said. "You might have followed us to East Ninety-Third, but how did you know about the apartment?"

"We went back in the evening, suggesting I should say," Kaufman said, smiling, "that we were affiliated with the New York Police and asked some questions. Sort of a follow-up."

"That's impersonating a police officer," Baker said.

"Go on," Barry said with impatience.

"Well, now when I hear what you know, I wonder why they would go there too. What comes to mind is a meeting of some sort. Someone had to know that place was available. It was planned out in advance, right? We can assume that from the newspaper advertisement."

"And?"

"My first thought is someone in that building. It's a twelve-story building. You know how many tenants there are. It's going to take some time to look into that suspicion, time we might not now have, if your theory is correct. You called the Israeli ambassador, I assume?"

"My chief is calling the Office of Security. It's part of the State Department. They're responsible for the security of visiting dignitaries."

"But the Israelis will bring their own security. This Office of Security won't anticipate great dangers for Chaim Eban in a Catskill resort, especially one attended by thousands of Jews there to raise money for Israel."

"Perhaps they won't let him go up."

"On the basis of what you've got?" Kaufman said, eyebrows raised. "This is a very important rally. Israel is in desperate need for funds, especially now. Do you know what it costs a day to keep Israel protected? No, he'll go for sure."

"Well, we can't do anything else with the little information we've gotten so far."

"You don't even have real information. You've just got a theory," Baker said.

"Nevertheless," Kaufman replied, "it's good that you let everyone concerned know what you've come upon and what you think. There is, perhaps, one other party we should contact. I am friendly with the Obermans."

"Obermans?"

"The family that owns the New Prospect Hotel. I've stayed there on occasion. In my less militant days," Kaufman said, smiling. "If I call the son now, will you talk to him? He is a young man. David Oberman. He took over for his retired father."

"Well, I don't . . ."

"I'm sure he would appreciate hearing it from you directly. I have, as you well know by now, a certain reputation. He might not take me seriously."

"What could I say?"

"Just what you've told me and your superiors. The New Prospect has a security force of its own, and there is the welfare of the guests, too."

Barry looked to Baker. He smirked but didn't offer any resistance. "Might as well spread the paranoia," he said.

Kaufman turned quickly. "When you run into one of these people, Lieutenant Baker, you will grow paranoid instantly. They have a way of making you realize your own frailty."

"Okay," Baker said, putting up his hands. "I'll stay out of this."

Kaufman got up and went to the phone. David Oberman had to be paged and picked up the receiver down in the indoor pool. He was teaching Lisa Sue the backstroke.

"What is it?" he snapped at the concierge when he picked up. He always wanted to prevent the hotel business from coming between him and his kids. When he set off time for them, it was as important as anything else.

"There's a Rabbi Kaufman calling from New York, Mr. Oberman. He insists it's urgent."

"Kaufman?"

"Yes, sir."

"Okay," he said, "put him on." He waved at Tony Atwel, the lifeguard, indicating he should entertain Lisa Sue. The six-foot-four former Mr. America sprang up out of his seat and sliced through the water to come up right beside her.

"David. I'm glad I caught you. There's a New York City detective in my apartment right now and he has some information that should be of interest to you. When he is finished, I'll get back on for some small talk."

"Okay, Rabbi," David said and turned completely, putting his finger in his other ear to keep out all noise.

"Mr. Oberman, my name is Barry Wintraub. I'm a homicide detective," Barry began. "We had a murder here of a JDL member and during the course of my investigation . . ."

13

Nessim sat quietly on the bed and watched Clea brush her hair. She sat at a small vanity table and stroked her long strands with smooth even motions. They had both said little after they had retired to their room. Nessim knew she hesitated to ask specific questions, but she was anxious for him to tell her the significant details. Yusuf had shut himself in his room, still sulking.

"You mind being used in this plan?" Nessim began.

"No," she said.

She turned, her naked shoulders gleaming in the lamplight. She had a sculptured neckline. He loved to run his fingers down the side of it and trace the roundness of her shoulders and then move slowly, exploring her breasts.

"It will be a great event for the movement. Perhaps greater than anything we can do in the Middle East. It's why they sent me here. My opportunity."

"Will it be . . . Will we be in great danger?"

"No. I will set up an antipersonnel device that will take out Chaim Eban," he said. Instinctively, he knew he couldn't tell her that he would be creating an explosion that would destroy as many as three thousand people. "I have become expert in different kinds of detonation," he added.

"Don't try to explain any details to me," she said. "I'm hopelessly stupid when it comes to scientific data."

"Don't use the excuse you're a woman," he said. "One of our most effective front fighters is a woman."

"Will I have to do anything specific?"

"Just look beautiful and be Jewish."

"Jewish?"

"We are going as two Jews celebrating Passover up there."

"Oh. That won't really be so difficult. I've celebrated Jewish Passover with people in the Middle East," she said, turning back to the mirror. There was a knock on their door.

"Yes?"

"El Yacoub has arrived," Hamid said. "We'll be in the study."

"I'll be right there."

"We'll need a much better wardrobe if we are to go to a hotel," she said.

"I know. We'll be shopping tomorrow and we'll get what we need. It'll all be arranged."

"I can't help being very nervous about it. I wish I had your coolness."

"You will," he said. "You'll see. Don't worry." He walked behind her and touched her shoulders and stroked her hair. She leaned her head back against him and closed her eyes. He bent down and kissed her forehead. "I'll see you in a while."

El Yacoub, Hamid, and Tandem sat around a collection of drawings, photographs, and diagrams spread out on the desk in the study. Hamid made a place for Nessim as he approached.

"You are comfortable here?" El Yacoub asked.

"Very."

"Good. Let's get down to it."

"The materials?"

"It's all in the garage," Tandem said.

"It's the new plastique, the stuff that was used at the Belgium airport last month."

Nessim nodded, pleased. The source of and the acquisition of the plastique was one of the tightest-kept secrets of the organization, but Nessim knew that the improved material had come from Red China. It was somehow historically right that the Chinese would be in the forefront of explosives. They were said to have invented gunpowder.

"All right," Nessim said. "Show me what we have."

Tandem pulled out two large photographs and put them side by side. They were both blown-up views of the cement piers in which the steel girders that held up the ceiling structure of the dining room were set.

"About four by eight?"

"Yes," Tandem said. Nessim lifted the photographs and studied them.

"They'll go like pieces of cheesecake. How many?"

"We've got a V structure here," Tandem said. "There are five down this side and five down the other," he said pulling out the construction plans for the hotel. "And the one at the bottom. As you can see, there are five floors above the dining room."

"That's a lot of weight," Hamid said. Tandem smiled.

"A lot of weight? Think of it, besides the building materials, we are talking about plumbing—sewage pipes, fixtures, and don't forget the electrical wiring. There will be fires everywhere. Those who escape the crush might very well get burned to death."

"Many will fall through this floor, of course," Nessim said.

"The boiler should blow," Tandem said, pointing to its location on the floor plans. "That'll take the side of this section of the main building out."

"You realize," Nessim said, going over the diagrams, "that we will not just be dropping a ceiling and floor in a dining room. The way this hotel is built, the twenty stories of the adjoining part of this building will topple over too."

"They'll be buried in a mountain of rubble. It'll look like Berlin after the war," Tandem said.

"Incredible," Hamid said. "Just by taking out these supports."

"They're going out simultaneously," Nessim said. "It would be as if someone scooped your feet out from under you. All your weight comes down instantly. And if someone is leaning on you, as the main structure leans on these five stories of the hotel, he would fall along with you and over you."

"I want you to do one more thing," El Yacoub said. He lit a thin cigar and sat back. "These Israelis have a knack for getting themselves out of the most impossible situations. I don't want to take any chances of not killing Chaim Eban."

"Yes?"

"Plant some plastique under his table in the dining room, to go off with everything else."

"A backup."

"Yes. Will there be any problem?"

"No," Nessim said. He lowered the photographs. "There is one thing. I want my brother in on this. I'll need him and I can trust him."

"How do you mean? Helping to make up the packets and the detonators?"

"No. In the hotel. To plant the stuff."

"Impossible."

"Why?"

"We couldn't take the chance. What would be his cover? He'd have to go in himself, as a single."

"There are some singles during the holiday," Tandem said, "but most are families, couples, parents and children. That sort of thing. Of course, the rally will bring in all types."

"What about with Clea and me?"

"I don't like it," El Yacoub said. "He's impulsive. To have him there days before . . ." He shook his head. "I don't like it."

"I have an idea," Tandem said. "Why don't I bring Yusuf to the hotel the night you plant the stuff. I can sneak him in all right and . . ."

"I don't like that," Nessim said. He was hoping to keep Tandem out of the project once they left Monroe.

"It sounds like the best idea," El Yacoub said. "This way he needs no cover, presents no danger. He can go in and get out. He'll be there to help, if that's what you want—although, personally, I don't like having someone as inexperienced in on this."

"He'll be with me. I have taught him a great deal."

"I know and that's why I would agree to Tandem's suggestion."

Nessim saw that El Yacoub was determined about this.

"Okay," he said reluctantly, happy he could get something for his brother, "but it might be dangerous for Mr. Tandem to be seen around the hotel after all these years. It would attract some interest."

"Oh, I won't hafta go in with him. I'll take him to the garbage-truck entrance and explain how he should go about meeting you. It'll be easy."

"And, of course," El Yacoub said, "Tandem and Hamid will be waiting at a side entrance to take you and Clea out before the explosion." There was a look in the Claw's eyes. Nessim caught something of a message.

"It's our opinion," Hamid said quickly, taking the attention away from El Yacoub and Nessim, "that there will be such turmoil no one will know who got out and who got crushed or burned to death."

"It will be difficult in many cases. I'd better take these photographs and diagrams with me," Nessim said, gathering the material up. "I'll have to study every free moment."

"And if you have any questions about the hotel, just ask me," Tandem said.

"Thank you."

"It's me who should be thanking you," Tandem said. Nessim didn't look at him.

"Clea and I will have to gather up a wardrobe for the hotel," Nessim said.

"Yes," El Yacoub said. "Hamid will make all your financial arrangements. Tandem will take you two around to shops tomorrow at your convenience."

"Gladly," Tandem said. He was smiling wider now.

He's stupid, Nessim thought. *He's drunk on revenge. Such a man makes errors.*

"Okay," Nessim said. "Will you be here tomorrow?" he asked El Yacoub.

"No, but Hamid knows where to find me if you need me."

"Good night then," Nessim said. El Yacoub stood up and stuck out his hand. Nessim took it, but El Yacoub simply held on without shaking.

"You know what this project means to the cause. It will have worldwide repercussions. All of us will be watching and waiting."

"Yes," Nessim said. The old man's eyes were burning through him. His blood rushed to his face.

"Now and forever," El Yacoub whispered.

"Now and forever," Nessim said. Hot tears had come to the corners of his eyes.

He stopped at Yusuf's door on the way back to his room and knocked softly. A moment passed and Yusuf opened it. He was still dressed.

"I thought you might be sleeping."

"What for?" Yusuf said and backed away.

"You jump too quickly. You show your hand too fast. Haven't I taught you anything? Should I have left you in the Middle East?"

"Maybe. Apparently, I am of no use here. I don't know why they agreed to your taking me along."

"You will be of use," Nessim said.

Yusuf turned quickly and studied his brother's face. "I'm to be in on it?"

"Yes."

"Nessim, I . . ."

"But you won't be brought to the hotel until I need you. You'll help me plant the plastique."

Yusuf nodded quickly, great joy in his face. "Whatever you say."

"This will be the biggest action the organization has ever taken in the United States and we will be doing it," Nessim said, revealing deep emotion. Yusuf was touched. He grew very serious.

"I won't let you down, Nessim."

"You'll have to stay with this man Tandem for a few days. Don't spend too much time with him and tell him little. He's . . . He's not really one of us. The organization is using him. When this is finished, it is my guess that . . ."

"What?"

"He'll be taken out," Nessim said, remembering the look in the Claw's eyes.

"I understand."

"Get some sleep. I'll want you to help me tomorrow, making up the detonators and arranging the packets."

"Okay, Nessim."

"Good night."

"Good night," Yusuf said.

Nessim looked at his brother for a moment. He remembered the way their mother would curl his hair with her finger and pet his head when he was a baby. She had dreamed of him as a tall, beautiful Arab man. It saddened him to think of what he and his brother had become. He knew his mother would cry if she were alive. This sadness quickly turned to anger. Others were responsible for what they had become, not they. These others would suffer. In a few days, he would do a deed his mother would never have understood.

But she was dead.

And so was their father.

And, in a real sense, so were they.

He left quickly to return to Clea's arms, to feel her breath on his face. She was a beacon in the darkness, a respite on the journey to hell.

14

"You didn't call your mother, did you?" Barry practically screamed as he came charging through the door. Shirley put the milk back in the refrigerator slowly and closed the door. Then she turned and faced him. He stood there, panting. Apparently he had run up the stairs, impatient with the elevator.

"I did," she said.

"Oh no. You gotta call her back. You gotta call her back." He turned and raised his arms. "Shirl, you gotta."

"Why, Barry?"

"I was talking to David Oberman," Barry began, with exaggerated patience and slow tempo. "He's the owner of the New Prospect Hotel in the Catskills."

"The New Prospect again?"

"Listen, will ya. I told him about this case."

"Which case? The Wallace Avenue killer case?"

"Will you stop calling it that. It's a lot more than that. I just know it."

"So what else is it?"

"Listen for Christ sakes. I followed some leads that took me to the New Prospect."

"You went to the Catskills today?"

"Jesus, Shirl."

"Okay, talk."

"There's a possibility that something might be happening up there. Remember that article I read in the paper you almost threw out?"

"So I threw it out. Look, if I left all the papers around that you didn't read . . ."

"Forget that. I don't care. Throw everything out. Just listen. That gave me the clue, see. I talked to this David Oberman and he was quite concerned with the possibilities."

"What possibilities?"

"I don't want to get into every detail, Shirl. Anyway, to make a long story short, he asked me what I was doing for the Passover holidays. He knew I was Jewish, see."

"You told him you almost became a rabbi?"

"No, Shirl. I didn't discuss my life story. So then he says would I consider spending the holidays up there, as his guest."

"Just you?"

"No, all of us."

"As his guest?"

"That's right. Although he has security, he'd still like me around since I've been working on this case." Barry held up his hand to stop her from speaking. "For now, just call it a case. No special names."

"The New Prospect? For the holidays?"

"That's right. Free. You know what that's worth?"

"That is something. I'll have to get a new outfit. At least one new outfit."

"Get two."

"Two? You mean it?"

"I mean it," Barry said, sitting down. "So you see, that's why you've got to call your mother back."

"No, I don't."

"But you said you called her and asked her to Passover."

"I did, but she turned me down."

"She turned you down?"

"My brother asked them first."

"Morris? But he's a bachelor. He always tags along. He . . ."

"Apparently he's got a girlfriend now and he wants to show her off to Mom and Dad. She's going to cook. I'm expecting him to call and ask us any moment. I've been sitting by the phone."

"At forty, a dedicated bachelor, your brother's thinking of getting married?"

"Don't you think it's time, Barry?"

"It's time; it's time. What are you going to tell him when he calls?"

"The truth. We're going to the Catskills for the holidays. You know what my mother's going to think?"

"No, what?"

"That your job's finally paying off."

To an outsider, check-in at the New Prospect for Passover would seem like massive confusion. People, eager to begin their festivities and take advantage of their first day at the hotel, arrived early and in large numbers at once. Cars were lined up in rows outside the front entrance, and bellhops were working as fast as they could to unload the luggage and put it on the carts. Guests were shouting orders and greeting one another. The parking lot attendants waited on the sidelines. The moment a car was unloaded and the guests ushered into the hotel, they slid in behind the steering wheel and spun away to park the car in the large lots built away from the hotel proper. For all the service personnel, speed meant money. As soon as they finished with one guest, they could go on to another. All this added to the air of excitement, creating a hectic rhythm. People spoke quickly and moved in jerky motions.

The guests followed their luggage into the lobby, almost as if they were tied to the handles of suitcases by invisible cords. Children were everywhere, clinging to their parents or holding on to the luggage carts. The main desk was overwhelmed. Mrs. Aldelman and her assistants moved continuously around the little area, pulling out confirmations and assigning room keys. Miraculously, they kept out of one another's paths. Guests, impatient before they even began their wait, whined and barked out their names, trying to catch someone's attention. There was an endless "Just a minute, sir. I'll be right with you, sir. He's first, sir. We'll be right with you."

Lillian Rothberg, dressed in a baggy pants suit with a half-moon collar, stood by the entrance of the dining room that was just off the lobby and greeted people she knew personally. A large photograph of Chaim Eban was encased in a glass frame by the door. She stood near it as if his image could give her some extra official sanction. She was all smiles. Her fingers moved in and out of hands. She kissed cheeks, laughed, and moved from couple to couple as if she floated on some invisible cushion of air. Her hair, plastered into place by the hotel beautician, bounced in one piece as she walked from side to side. Some of her friends sounded envious when they approached her.

"Have you met him?"

"Did you see him?"

"Is he here?"

"No, darling," she said. "I've only talked to his attaché at the Israeli embassy. He'll be flying in from Washington, you know. Landing by helicopter out here in two days."

"I can't wait to meet him."

"I can't wait to hear him speak."

As soon as the Marcuses arrived, Toby joined Lillian as an official greeter. The two of them stood by like mothers at a wedding. Lillian had ordered a few thousand buttons that read WE ARE ALL ZIONISTS AT HEART. They were placed in open boxes on the reservations desk. Children grabbed them in handfuls and put five or six on themselves.

With the weather good, the atmosphere hectic but exciting, and the prospect of a week to ten days of vacation ahead of them, the crowd got into a festive mood rather quickly. Some guests, calmer and more resigned to the wait and the procedures of hotel bureaucracy, gathered in small groups and talked. Most were dressed for a stay at the hotel and already wore brightly colored shirts, slack outfits, and casual pants. Children were draped in showcase attire, but quickly forgot they were to behave like mannequins. Childless couples and singles were less frantic. They had no one to settle in but themselves. Many took to the direction of the lounge and left the bellhops with sizable tips in advance, telling them to take care of their things and deliver their room keys to them in the bar.

The music had already started. A small combo, consisting of a piano player, a saxophone player, a drummer, and a trumpet player, wailed rhythm and blues in the dimly, but colorfully lit lounge—an enormously long bar consisting of an elegant marble top and cushioned chairs with backs, a rich red shag rug, and glittering mirrors and chandeliers. A dozen bartenders worked frantically, but quietly, up and down the bar. On entering the lounge, a guest immediately got the feeling he had moved into the late, late hours of night, when indeed it was early afternoon. Laughter traveled in waves. There was a New Year's Eve atmosphere.

Toby Marcus looked longingly at the entrance to the lounge. She wanted to bathe herself in the erotic shadows and sexy lighting that made eyes speak, lips look wet and inviting, naked shoulders and necks stimulating. Bill was already helplessly lost with a group of loud, cigar-smoking buddies, arguing issues and theories. They would organize their poker game as soon as possible and spend the remainder of the afternoon in the midst of smoke and talk. Her daughter, Dorothy, found a few of her friends and drifted off to the teen rooms. Bill joined Toby as soon as he had gotten their keys, but he was anxious to get back to his friends as soon as he could.

"You wanna go up to the room and freshen up?"

"I'll stay with Lil for a while."

"Okay. I'll settle us in and see you later," he said.

She nodded and deliberately stretched out her hand to greet someone.

"I simply must get myself a drink," she said as soon as Lillian turned her way. "My nerves are screaming."

"All right, but we've got to get together before dinner tonight and meet with the Obermans. I want to do this thing right. We want Chaim Eban's schedule worked out to the minute."

"Certainly," Toby said. "I'll call your room," she added, then she kissed Lillian on the cheek and backed herself toward the lounge.

When she passed through the entrance, she breathed relief. The cool air and the subdued lighting triggered a quicker heartbeat. She searched quickly for Bruno. Sometimes he was in the lounge, mixing with guests. But she didn't see him. She smoothed down her dress, patted her stomach gently, and walked toward an empty stool. After she sat down, ordered her drink, and brought it to her lips, she turned around, crossing her legs so that the bottom of her dress moved up around her knees, and waited for someone to approach her and make her feel eighteen again.

15

Lieutenant Barry Wintraub stopped at the security booth at the front of the hotel driveway and rolled down his window. Shirley was sitting in the back with Jason because Keith just could not ride in the car for a period longer than twenty minutes without fighting with his brother. Barry and Shirley conceded that fact and agreed that she would sit in the back and one of the kids would sit in the front. Naturally the boys fought over who would sit there, so Barry timed it, sharing the front seat between them. Once they were separated and unable to make each other unhappy, they hated the car ride more.

"Yes, sir," the security policeman said. He had his clipboard in hand. All the names of the guests with reservations were there. "First letter of your last name, please."

"W. I'm Lieutenant Wintraub. Mr. Oberman told me . . ."

"Oh, yes, sir. We've been expecting you. One moment, please," he said, turning. "Hey, Mike, Lieutenant Wintraub's here."

"Be right there."

"Everybody knows Daddy," Keith said with great satisfaction.

"Just other cops," Jason said.

"Not just other cops. Everybody."

"Just other cops."

"Shut up you two, will ya," Barry said. "I'm sorry. My kids. You were saying?"

"Yeah. My partner here will drive you in. Mr. Oberman wants you taken to a special entrance so you don't have to get caught up in the check-in rush. It's pretty hairy right now."

"Special entrance?" Shirley said. "Not a back entrance?"

"No, ma'am. A side entrance that leads right into Mr. Oberman's office."

"That's great," Barry said, trying to ease Shirley's concern right away. "Great."

The other security guard came around, and Barry pushed over to let him take the wheel. Right off, Keith opened his mouth.

"Where's your gun?"

"I don't have one, son. We all don't really need a gun for this job."

"My father has one. What kinda cop doesn't have a gun, Dad?"

"A cop in the Catskills," Barry said. The security policeman laughed. They started down the driveway. The kids pressed their faces against the windows and gaped.

"A lotta people up?" Shirley asked.

"Oh, yes, ma'am. We're overbooked."

"Overbooked? You mean there'll be people without rooms?"

"No, ma'am. Everyone's got a room, but some people are to be housed in the old house."

"Old house?"

"Yes, ma'am. Your family will be going there. After I take your husband in to Mr. Oberman's office, I'll get you and the kids settled."

"Old house?" Shirley said. "No wonder it's free."

After they came to the main building, Barry and the security guard got out and walked through the side entrance to follow a short corridor up to the back door of David Oberman's office. The security guard knocked and then opened it. David stood up behind his desk as they entered.

"This is Lieutenant Wintraub, Mr. Oberman."

"Good," David said, extending his hand. Barry walked over to shake it.

"I'll settle in his family in the meantime," the security guard said. David nodded.

"Sit down, Lieutenant. It's personally a great relief to see you here. I'm glad you could arrange it."

"Well, I had the days . . ." Barry looked around as he sat down. The office was big and lush. Thick peach-colored carpet covered the floor. There were bookcases to the right of Oberman's desk and paintings on the far wall and left wall. He noted the portrait of a rugged-looking elderly man directly in front of the desk. The desk itself was a hardwood, probably oak, he thought. It was covered with papers and office supplies.

He was surprised at how young looking David Oberman was. In Barry's mind, anyone who ran a hotel as big and as famous as the New Prospect would have to be well along in his years. David looked to be in his mid-thirties, and his well-tanned skin and baby blue eyes, combined with thick wavy hair, gave him a rich, George Hamilton Jr.

look—although he had a much larger frame and a sturdier-looking set of shoulders.

"Now then," David began. "Have you learned anything new since we spoke?"

"No, not really. We know these suspects are illegal aliens, apparently from the Middle East. They've left the city, as far as we can tell."

"And you think they've come here?"

"Possibly."

"To kill Chaim Eban?"

"That's my theory, although I hafta tell you, no one but Rabbi Kaufman sees it as clearly as I do. My partner thinks I'm paranoid and the chief in my precinct thinks I'm blowin' up the whole thing."

"Let's hope you are," David said. "But just in case, it's good to have you around. Do you think you might recognize these people if you saw them?"

"I have a general description of one. Other than that, I'm just going to hafta start doing a little police work around here."

"I'll get the word out to my people to cooperate with you in every way, but I'd appreciate us keeping the details totally to ourselves. We don't want to unduly frighten hundreds of people."

"I understand."

"My chief of security is not really a policeman in the sense that he's had any police training. We keep outsiders off the grounds and try to give the guests a feeling of protection. That's all. His name is Tom Boggs."

"Tom Boggs?"

"That's right," David said, smiling. "The football player. He used to come up here frequently. When he found himself struggling with the team, we offered him the position. We can have a meeting later tonight. Now, from what I understand of the preliminary arrangements, one agent from the Office of Security in the State Department is accompanying Chaim Eban. It's token, but everyone would expect him to be relatively safe up here, I suppose."

"I know. That's more reason why they would do it here, though."

"You've got a point," David said.

"I'd like to begin by checking out all parties of three: two men and a woman."

"Two men and a woman? Well, I don't expect we have many of those. This is a big place, but I don't think it's the week for that sort of stuff," David said, smiling. "Let me introduce you to Mrs. Aldelman. She's in charge of reservations and runs the front desk. Sort of my right hand around here."

"Fine."

David buzzed the front.

"Can Mrs. Aldelman step in here a moment?"

"She'll be right in, Mr. Oberman," a thin, female voice said.

"Good." David turned back to Barry. "Your family will be on the second floor of the old house. Actually, that place is more homelike, warmer. It's where I was brought up."

"Oh."

"Yeah. My father lives on the first floor. Retired, but he still sticks his nose into things from time to time," David added. "You're in room 214. It has a nice view."

"Fine. That will make my wife happy," Barry said. He turned as Mrs. Aldelman came into the office. Then he stood up.

"Mrs. Aldelman. I want you to meet Lieutenant Barry Wintraub of the New York Police. He's here doing some unofficial police business at my request."

"Pleased to meet you," Gladys said. Her glasses were down on the bridge of her nose, and there was a smear of ink across her chin. Barry noted that all her fingers were stained at the tips.

"I'd appreciate it if you'd cooperate with him and give him whatever information he needs."

"Right now?" she said, grimacing.

"No. He'll settle in and see you after things quiet down."

"Fine," she said. She smiled quickly at Barry and turned completely to David. "We're having a small problem with the Marxes. Mrs. Marx claims she specifically booked a second-floor room and we have her in a fifth-floor room."

"So what's the problem?"

"I've booked all the second- and third-floor suites. She's going to be calling you soon."

"Okay, I'll deal with it," he said and smiled at Barry.

"I guess you have your work cut out for you," Barry said. "I'll leave you now and see you later."

"Fine," David said. Barry started for the back door. "Oh, and Lieutenant, . . ."

"Yes?"

"You've got your work cut out for you, too."

Barry nodded. Mrs. Aldelman peered at him over her glasses. Then he left.

16

Nessim stood looking out the window of their room. From where they were located, it was possible to see down to the garbage truck entrance of the hotel where Hamid would be waiting to take them away after the walls came tumbling down. Including staff and guests, the New Prospect had a running population of nearly thirty-three hundred people. It required the services of a full-time sanitation crew and had about as much garbage in tonnage as a small village or town. The hotel had its own trucks that carried the refuse to the county dump.

The New Prospect was fenced in on all sides, but a highway ran alongside it on the east end. It was from this highway that people came up from New York. Across the highway, the hotel had its parking lots and a part of its golf courses. A constant line of cars was driven into the parking lot on check-in and check-out days. The regular traffic along the highway was continually interrupted. One of the New Prospect's security men tried directing traffic around the guests' cars. Nessim watched with some interest. Then he turned and looked at the closed suitcase near the bed. It carried fire and death.

Clea was in the bathroom, showering for dinner. It amused him to see how much she had been taken by the hotel. He himself had been surprised by its luxuriousness: thick, rich-looking carpeting along the lobby and up the stairways; expensive-looking chandeliers and fixtures; and large, sumptuous rooms. It was like a palace all right. They had penetrated someone's kingdom.

What amazed him was how easy it was to enter the hotel carrying enough plastique to blow it up. The Middle East was a maze of security—searches, X-ray machines at airports, personnel hired simply to watch and look and study. That was a world of continuous pessimism. Everyone expected there'd be attempts to deal individuals death. But that was not true here.

The Jewish people at the New Prospect were as vulnerable as could be. It would be easy. What were they—arrogant or stupid? The world was being ripped apart by factions struggling until the bitter end and they frolicked about as if all was hunky-dory. The vessels and the tools of war would come out of the things these people said and did here, and yet they felt completely safe, apart from it all. Nessim thought, *Do they think we are stupid perhaps?* If so, they would change their minds in a few days.

He walked to the bathroom doorway and turned the knob slowly. Then he pushed the door open and confronted Clea, nude, drying herself. She turned and looked at him.

"Don't dry yourself," he said. "I want you wet."

"But we'll spoil the sheets."

"I don't care." He smiled and she tossed her hair back. Then he retreated to the bed and stripped. She came out, beads of water on her arms and shoulders and breasts. He pulled back the covers and patted the bed beside him. She came to it and he kissed her wet skin, ran his lips over her nipples, sucking up the drops of water around them.

"Oh, Nessim."

"It's like a honeymoon," he said and laughed. But there was more to it. The thoughts of death and violence always brought him to a pitch of intense excitement. There was something sexual in delivering death. He couldn't explain it, but it excited him in an erotic way. He was going to manipulate people, turn them, spend them, and drive them into pain and agony. He always enjoyed this sense of power. It was often the same with his sex.

Clea moaned beneath him. She closed her eyes and opened her body to his touch. He felt between her legs, slid his fingers gently into her, massaging, touching, bringing her up to a pitch of intensity that had her moving her own body to the rhythms of his stroke.

He made love as hard and as determinedly as he had ever made love. Once, in the middle of it, she opened her eyes and stared up at him to see if he was really enjoying it. He seemed wild and violent. The look on his face must've frightened her some. She closed her eyes and turned her head. When it was finished, he turned over on his stomach and lay there, breathing hard. After a while, he felt her hand on his back.

"Nessim, are you all right?"

"Sure. Why?"

"You weren't making love to me."

He turned and looked at her, propping himself on an elbow. She looked worried.

"What? What do you mean?"

"You were doing something else, not making love."

"You're crazy. What else?"

"I don't know."

"Don't talk silly," he said, but he was embarrassed that she had seen through him so well. "C'mon," he added, sitting up. "Let's get dressed and walk around this place. We've got to be guests. I'm curious anyway."

"Okay."

"Remember now. If people ask, we're from Israel. Jerusalem. We can talk about the new city."

"What do you do again?"

"Irrigation engineer."

"I'll try to let you answer all the questions," she said.

After they were dressed, they went to the lobby, walking through it down to the stores, looking at everything just the way any tourist would. They saw the indoor skating rink, went to the big glass floor that overlooked the indoor pool below, and then strolled through the game room. Clea played some computer tennis against Nessim and beat him once out of three times. They laughed, studied the pictures of famous entertainers and politicians set along the hallways, and made their way to the lounge. Music drew them inside.

"Dinner's not until seven," he said. "Let's take a table over at the far end and have a drink."

"Fine."

They maneuvered their way through the crowd, into the darkness of the lounge. The band was much louder as they went deeper and deeper inside, but when they got to the far end, they found they could talk at a relatively normal volume. A waitress in a short skirt and bright red tank top came to them.

"Whiskey sour," he said. He turned to Clea. She nodded. "Make it two."

"On the rocks?"

"Yes."

"Is Chaim Eban here yet?" Clea asked when the waitress left them.

"No. Two days more."

"How . . . Where will you get him?"

"In the dining room," he said.

She didn't reply. She looked out at the crowd of laughing, loud people. He studied her face. There was such quiet beauty in it. Here they were, he thought, in the dark shadows, together, talking about killing. The people around them drank, listened to the loud music, pressed their bodies against each other, wore beautiful bright clothes, sang a song of life. They would all be dead in less than seventy-two hours. Those women with the low-cut dresses, those men with the rich suits—all alive and excited in their prime. They had come to this hotel for pleasure and they would find pain.

As he studied them though, he thought he detected some rather remarkable differences between these people and the people he made war against in the Middle East. These people looked softer, paler. It made him conscious of his own dark color and Clea's too. Very few of them had the hardness about their eyes. A very funny thought came to him—these were domesticated Jews, provided for and spoiled. There was almost something degenerate about them. It occurred to him that he was in no way afraid of them. They would be no challenge. They didn't even know he was in their midst. It nearly made him laugh aloud.

The drinks were served. He took out a cigarette and offered her one. The light danced against her eyes. She blew the smoke up into pink clouds.

"Still nervous?"

"Not so much yet. Maybe later," she said cautiously.

"Don't think about it. Think only about enjoying yourself. You're a guest of the New Prospect," he added, smiling. Then he turned and lifted his glass. When he brought it to his lips and looked out at the crowd again, he thought he saw a familiar face. A woman caught his attention at the bar. A few people covered her from his view. He struggled to get another glimpse.

"What is it?"

"I thought . . . someone. Can't be," he said, sitting back again.

"Yusuf looked so unhappy this morning."

"He always looks unhappy. Believe me, he's not so unhappy."

"I don't think he liked being left with Mr. and Mrs. Tandem. She makes him nervous."

"Hamid's there too. He can keep to himself. Listen," Nessim said. "Late tonight I'll be leaving the room. Don't be concerned."

"I expected it," she said.

"Well, I . . ." People at the bar shifted their positions and the woman who had caught his attention before was now in view, but she had her back to him.

"What is it?"

The woman at the bar paid her bill and then turned to leave. He saw her face clearly and was sure. It was Brenda Casewell, the woman who had been with El Yacoub at the East Ninety-Third Street apartment. Why was she here?

"Nessim?"

"Nothing," he said and took another drink of his whiskey sour to mask the anger in his face.

The last thing he wanted Clea to think was that something was not right.

17

After his family had checked in and was settled, Lieutenant Barry Wintraub took them for a tour of the hotel. He got as far as the lower lobby of the main building. There the hotel had a clown performing. About two hundred children were seated on the rug watching him go through his antics, which included some magic tricks. Shirley and Barry left the kids and continued on their own to look at the indoor pool. They stopped at the nightclub and watched the stagehands preparing for the evening's entertainment. Then they moved on down to the stores and over the enclosed walkway that connected two different sections of the building to return to the kids.

All the while Barry considered the lethal possibilities. Given the assumption that some terrorist organization was planning to attack Chaim Eban, where would they do it? Where would they have their best chance? Was escape part of the plan or was this going to be another suicide bomber? Rabbi Kaufman had mentioned the fact that he thought the Arab organization had sent some of its top people to do this deed. If that were the case, they would probably not want to lose them.

Of course, Chaim Eban could be shot at from almost a hundred places while he moved through the building. Later on, when he met with the Israeli security and the man from the State Department, Barry would discuss placing people at advantageous positions in the lobbies and halls to prevent such an occurrence. He wondered what precautions, if any, were to be taken with Chaim Eban's quarters.

"You know, Barry," Shirley said, "I am good company, but I'm getting tired of talking to myself."

"Huh?"

"I asked you three questions in a row and you walked on as though I wasn't even here."

"Oh. Sorry, I was thinking."

"Figured that. Didn't think you were hypnotized, although a while back there you were glued to the movements of a certain young lady's rump."

"Rump?"

"Don't try to tell me you missed that, too. If she had those pants on any tighter, she'd have to have skin grafting."

"Really?" he said, turning around.

"Forget it. Did you see about the babysitting service? I'd like to get away from our offspring tonight."

"Right. I'll see to it now. You wanna stay here with the kids or join me at the front desk?"

"I'll watch the clown. Being with you sorta trained me for it."

"Very funny," he said and kissed her on the cheek. As he walked back, he studied people. It was going to be nearly impossible to spot anyone he could consider suspicious. What made him think he could? He conjured up a picture using the description Gitleman, the fish market owner, had given him of the young man. Then he thought about the blouse he had picked up in the Mandel apartment. He pictured a certain form and shape on the basis of it, but how does one go about imagining the female terrorist? He wondered. He should have spent more time talking to Carl Bradsand at the FBI office. When he got to the main desk, he found a young receptionist, all smiles. She wore a nametag that said, "Happy Holiday, I'm Mona Langer."

"Hi, Mona. I'm interested in getting some babysitting service tonight."

"Fine. Time?"

"Pardon me?"

"Time that you want the service?"

"Oh. Er . . . The show starts when?"

"First show will start at ten."

"Good. 9:45."

"Name and room number?"

"Barry Wintraub. I'm in the old building. 214."

"Fine," she said. "They'll be a girl there about 9:45."

"Is Mrs. Aldelman around?"

"I believe she's in with Mr. Oberman. Let me check."

She disappeared into the back office. Barry turned around and for a split second, his eyes met Nessim's. He and Clea were just going into the lounge. Barry thought the girl was rather attractive, but other than that, he saw nothing unusual about them. Mrs. Aldelman stepped out of the inner office.

"Oh. Yes, Lieutenant?"

"I was wondering . . . I know you've been working hard, but I'd like to do some researching as soon as possible now. I'm going to take my family back to our room, and then I'd like to come back and look at your check-ins."

"Certainly. I might be able to give you a girl for an hour too, if you'd like." Mrs. Aldelman seemed much more relaxed and pleasant, Barry thought.

"Wonderful."

"I'll be in the back when you're ready," she said.

He thanked her and went back to join Shirley and the kids. When they got to their room, the phone was ringing. It was David Oberman.

"I had occasion to speak to the Israeli ambassador a little while ago," he said. "I described some of our situation up here and he told me that he would be sending someone up tomorrow. His name's Trustman and he's with Israeli security."

"That's good," Barry said. "Pretty soon you'll have more cops and the like up here than guests. I hope it's not a waste of energy."

"It doesn't hurt to take these precautions. I'd rather not have any kind of incident in the hotel. From a purely selfish point of view, it would do a great deal of damage to what's left of the hotel industry up here. We're relatively free of that sort of business. People take vacations to escape the real world."

"I understand."

"And we do owe a special responsibility to Chaim Eban."

"I'm going over to do some research at the reservations desk right now," Barry said.

After he hung up, he helped Shirley coax the boys into the shower to clean them up for dinner. "Where are you running off to?" she asked as he scooped up his jacket and headed for the door.

"I've got a half an hour or so and figured I'd get some investigating done."

"Just be sure you don't investigate any of those tight pants women."

"Right, Shirl," he said and hurried out.

When he stepped onto the front porch of the old main house, Barry stopped to take in the view of the modern structure just across from it. Rooms were lit up as high as the twentieth floor. He had the feeling that he was back in the city, but the open space around the hotel building gave him the sense of freedom and abandon that so attracted the tired city dweller. He was, after all, in the country. The night sky, filled with stars now because of the early twilight, was open and somehow more alive. He was filled with a new sense of energy and importance.

The lieutenant watched staff members outside the hotel move about the front entrance and the driveway like soldier ants around the dirt hill. The hotel crawled with life and activity. There were the sounds of car doors slamming, voices shouting orders, and car horns beeping. He saw a group of about six chambermaids laughing and talking as they made their way out of the hotel and down to the help's parking lot.

When he returned to the hotel lobby, Barry found it filling up quickly as more and more guests, dressed and perfumed, had come down to wait for the signal for dinner. They were as immaculate as storefront mannequins. Children looked trapped and imprisoned by their fresh clothing. All their movements were restrained by the watchful eyes of parents and grandparents. The adults milled about, sat on the lounge chairs, and carried on quiet discussions. Way off in a far right corner, a small group had gathered in front of a large color television set placed on a shelf. Barry went right to the office.

A heavy young woman sat before a board made up of what seemed to him to be a thousand tiny lightbulbs. Some were red and some were blue. She wore earphones and her hands, despite their swollen nature and thick fingers, moved with remarkable accuracy as she pulled plugs and jabbed others. The wires attached to them made an incredible maze across the board, yet she somehow found the ones she wanted when she wanted them. In the few moments that he watched her, he got the impression that she was part of the whole mechanism. She never turned from the board and her hands moved at the beck and command of the lights and the buzzing from within the abdomen of the switchboard.

Mrs. Aldelman beckoned to him and took him to a desk in the far corner. Another young girl sat nearby, looking very serious and officious. She wore a tan blouse and dark skirt. He thought she was cute and was grateful that she didn't wear tight pants.

"This is Jenny Thomas," Mrs. Alderman said. "She can help you for about a half hour."

"That's about all I have right now anyway," he said, smiling.

Jenny watched Mrs. Aldelman, intent on her command.

"Just tell her what to look for. There," she said, indicating a small stack of papers, "are all our check-ins to date."

"Thank you."

"You're welcome," Mrs. Aldelman said and put her glasses firmly back on her face.

Turning to Jenny, Barry said, "Pull out any party of three consisting of two men and a woman."

"Two men and a woman? In one suite?"

"No. Doesn't hafta be. Just as long as they checked in together, in a single party so to speak."

"Okay," she sang, "but I don't think there'll be many of those."

"Might make it easy to find then," Barry said. He sat down beside her and started going through the lists.

The names, rooms, and the home addresses were all down in columns across the pages. He was beginning to think that all his work might be futile because there was a strong possibility that the three broke up their group and checked in under separate names. There were so many possibilities.

"I've got one here," Jenny said.

"The Feinsteins?" He looked at the list. "Do you know them by any chance?"

"Yes. Two men in their late sixties or even early seventies. One's the wife's brother. They're always together."

"Forget that, but keep looking for that sort of thing."

"Sure," Jenny said, a half smile on her face now. "If I find what you want, will you tell me what it's for?" she whispered, an eye on Mrs. Aldelman across the room.

"Maybe," he teased. He looked back at his sheets.

He saw it nearly fifteen minutes later. It hit him like a slap across the face. The numbers had been in his mind all the time, buried with all the other details and facts he had accumulated during the past few days, so it wasn't unusual for him to be jolted by them. What bothered him was the fact that he never considered the possibility of it being there. He had overlooked that detail. *How stupid*, he thought. *It better be the end of that kind of stupidity.* He lifted the sheet off the table.

The fact that it was there before him, typed clearly in black and white, made him aware of the fact that he had one big advantage going for him in this affair. They, whoever they were and wherever they were, did not know that he was here, that he had come specifically because he believed something was planned to occur. He was hunting for a relatively unknown prey, that was true, but the prey did not know the hunter was among them.

"You can stop looking," he said. "I've got what I want."

"Oh?" Jenny looked over, but she could never discover what it was that excited Barry.

There, next to the name Brenda Casewell, was the address from East Ninety-Third Street.

"I want to make a phone call," Nessim said to Clea as they got up from their table in the lounge. "I saw some pay phones in the lower lobby. Let's go there."

"Where's your cell phone?"

"I can't make a call in here, and I don't want to go out on the hotel grounds to do it. It might attract attention. Just come along," he said a bit sternly.

Clea followed him out. She had been with him long enough to sense when something was troubling him. It was nearly impossible to see it in his face or hear it in his tone of voice, but there were always vibrations in the air, a kind of current that had developed between them. Most of the time it was smooth and calm. She bathed in the warmth of it, enjoyed the touch of his invisible fingers. But now she sensed static. It had come so suddenly, seemingly without any warning and it worried her. She reached for his hand. He gripped it unusually tightly.

She did not question him further. It was not the way with Nessim. He would only move into his shell, throw up thicker walls and protection. It was best to simply wait. When he was ready, if he was ready, he would talk. As hard as it was for her to get used to the idea, they were in a battlefield of sorts. That was the only real preliminary preparation Nessim had made with her.

"You must think of us as being involved in a war. Think of it all the time, if you can, and you'll never be careless. In a setting such as the one we are about to enter, there will be a great tendency to question our entire purpose. Everything will be so peaceful and benign. It will be difficult to think of these people as the enemy or as plotting and working against us, but that is what they're doing. That is the main purpose and thrust of their whole activity. The man they will be honoring has the capability to engineer many strategies of death and defeat for our people. There is no way to measure the immense good we will be doing by destroying him and that potential."

She listened to him quietly, thinking to herself that she had somehow become his private student. He was tutoring her in the ways of terrorist war, but even more so in the ways of reality. As she listened, she thought she was getting an even better insight into who he really was. Nessim was the most complicated man she had ever met. He was capable of great passion and softness, yet he was as deadly and as ruthless as anyone could imagine a man could be. He had never broken out into hateful tirades against the Jews. He had never demonstrated viciousness before her. He was as quiet with his violence as he was with his love, but he was also capable of great passion and physical lovemaking, so she assumed from that that he was capable of great hate.

They walked silently and quickly through the lobby, down the carpeted stairway with the beautiful thick banisters. The thickness of the carpet muted their steps. She was touched by the elegance of the hotel, which had the capability of making everyone who was a guest in it feel like a king or a queen. That was its magic and its power. Nessim stopped by one of the phones and took out all his pocket change, setting it on the little shelf before him. The phones were not enclosed. He was bothered by that, but he would have to make do. Clea waited quietly by his side.

He lifted the receiver and followed the directions printed on the phone. When the operator came on, he filled the phone with the required change and waited, pressing his body up against it and hunching his shoulders over it in a sort of protective gesture. He was happy that Hamid answered.

"All is well," Nessim said quickly, "but there is one thing. The woman from the Ninety-Third Street apartment is here."

There was a silence on the other end. Nessim listened intently, skilled in detecting meaning from the rhythms and nuances in the voices of people.

"She hasn't made contact with you, has she?" Hamid asked.

"No, but why wasn't I told about this and why is she here?"

"She's insurance," Hamid said. "It's the Claw's way. Chaim Eban must not leave the New Prospect alive. If something should go wrong, if your work doesn't succeed, she is prepared to do the job."

"But why wasn't I told?"

"It's the Claw's way," Hamid said again. "He believes each person is part of a strategy and must know only what he or she has to know to do the job. This way there can be no betrayals or mistakes that would harm another part."

Nessim was silent.

"You can't find fault with this," Hamid added. He sensed how Nessim felt.

"Another man might be more upset."

"Only a man with more ego than we need."

Nessim felt the verbal blow. Hamid was right about that, but he wasn't thinking so much about his own damaged pride as he was about possible damage to his strategies.

"How is Yusuf?"

"Impatient, but don't worry."

"Okay," Nessim said. He hung up.

Clea looked at him closely for some indication or hint as to the true result of his phone call.

"How was Yusuf?"

"He's all right."

"Something has angered you?"

"In a small way. It's not important now." He looked at his watch. "The dining room doors will be opened now. Let's go up."

She wanted to say something more, be more affectionate, ease or comfort him in a way, but two laughing couples came down the corridor. Nessim moved away from the phone quickly.

It was a nervous and overly cautious gesture that frightened her. They walked toward the stairway again. But it was only a few moments later that he relaxed. She felt the muscles in his hand ease and his grip become more loving.

When they entered the dining room and stopped to give their name to the maître d', Nessim was all smiles and warmth again. Her heartbeat slowed to its normal rhythm. She looked about at the immense room and became interested in the upcoming experience. Their mission was forgotten for the moment.

18

"What are the possibilities that this is just a coincidence?" David asked. He leaned back in his chair. Dressed in a blue suit and white tie, he was all set to play host to three thousand people for the First Seder of Passover. Barry sat at the edge of his seat.

"Oh, that's always a possibility. Not sayin' it isn't, but don't forget, this address at East Ninety-Third Street was the lead that started me on this in the first place."

"Um . . ." David nodded slowly. "Well, I'm going to want Tom Boggs in on this right now." He leaned over and pressed the intercom. "Have Boggs come right to my office," he said and looked at his watch. "It's six forty-five. I've got to get to the dining room. We'll be opening the doors in fifteen minutes."

"My wife must be going crazy."

"I'll have one of the bellhops go get her and the kids and escort them over. You'll be sitting at table five. It's situated immediately adjacent to mine, where Chaim Eban will be eating in two nights."

"Good."

"Tom will know how to handle things in the hotel itself. He is fully aware of our policies and how we like things done on the hotel grounds."

"Right."

"He should be here at any moment. I'm sorry I can't stay to introduce him. But he knows about you now, so . . ."

"Don't worry."

"Talk to you later," David said. He stopped as he came around the desk. "Do what you have to do, but remember to keep everything as subtle as you can."

"Understood."

Barry stood up as David left. He walked around and studied some of the plaques and awards the Obermans had received over the years. A few minutes later, Tom Boggs walked in. At six feet two inches and weighing nearly two forty, Boggs was a powerfully built man. He had thin blond hair and blue-green eyes. The only thing that marred his good looks was a small scar under his chin where he had been gouged by a shoe spike during a game. Barry didn't recall his facial features, but he did remember seeing him play years ago.

"Tom Boggs," the man said, extending his hand.

"Barry Wintraub."

"We've got something going here, is that it?" Boggs asked, moving around the desk. He took David's chair quickly.

"Mr. Oberman's told you why I am here?" Barry said. Boggs nodded. He sat back in the chair. Barry went on, "I've gotten a good lead and I want to check it out immediately."

"How?"

"I want to get into a room and search it."

Boggs nodded, but didn't say anything.

"Figured this would be the best time. Everyone's down for dinner, the suspect included."

"Male or female?"

"Female. Brenda Casewell's the name. She's in room 416."

Boggs looked at his watch.

"Okay," he said quickly. "Let's go right to it."

Barry liked his firmness and was relieved that Boggs offered no cautious, hesitant lines. *His sports training's responsible*, Barry thought. *It's made him a man of action. On the hotel grounds, he is pretty much in control of things the way he might be on a football field.*

"Good," Barry said. "For a moment I was afraid you'd be worrying about search warrants and that whole bag."

"We're a sneaky group of bastards when we have to be," Boggs said with a grin.

They walked out of the office and went right to an elevator. It opened to let a group of guests out. They stepped back to let them pass.

"How many security men in plainclothes like yourself?"

"Four. We have six uniformed men on a rotation around the building and the grounds. We're not prepared for any kind of an attack though," he said as they entered the elevator. "Just how sure are you guys about this terrorist possibility?"

"Not sure at all. Just working on some leads."

"Don't mind tellin' ya, it's the most exciting thing's happened up here since we had a streaker go through the lobby during one of the Senior Citizen weekends."

"What happened?"

"Nothin'. Most of the old people didn't see him or hear him or care, for that matter."

"No other security problems?"

"Some gate crashers occasionally. A few robberies here and there. Once in a while we have a fight or two over at the staff's quarters, but other than that, this is a soft job. Until you came along, that is."

"Maybe it'll stay soft. Although I know you're not really a softy," Barry said. Boggs smiled.

They stepped out on the fourth floor. A couple, waiting for the elevator, stepped in after them.

"Down this way," Boggs said. Barry followed close behind. They stopped at 416 and Boggs knocked softly. There was nothing happening inside, so he knocked louder. Still nothing. He took out a ring of keys and fit one into the lock. Barry looked behind him, but there was nobody in the corridor. Boggs opened the door and they stepped inside.

"Know what you're looking for?"

"No," Barry said, going right over to the dresser. He pulled out the top drawer and ran his hands under the clothing. He did the same with all the drawers. Then he spotted the suitcases on the floor in the closet.

"What's this woman look like?" Boggs asked.

"Don't know. Just discovered her name next to an address in the check-in sheet, that's all," Barry said. He snapped open the second suitcase. There was some more clothing in it. He lifted out a blouse and held it in the air before him, recalling the blouse in the Mandel apartment. This one was nowhere near the same size.

The Casewell woman, whoever she was, was bigger in the shoulders and probably bigger breasted too. He imagined her to be a chunkier woman. There wasn't that same strange, enticing odor either. This was a different woman. He was sure of it. Perhaps David Oberman was right. It was all a fantastic coincidence.

"Whaddaya lookin' for? A blouse for your wife?"

"Just tryin' to picture the woman," Barry said. "Clothes make the woman," he added, smiling. Then he folded the blouse and put it back.

"She didn't bring as much as most women do," Boggs said. "That closet's only half full. Shit, that's about a weekend's worth."

"Yeah." Barry contemplated the clothes in the closet for a few moments. Then he ran his hand through it, pulling the dresses apart, one by one. He stopped when he got to a raincoat. It felt much heavier on one side. "Wait a minute," he said and put his hand in the pocket. When he pulled his hand out, it held a .45-caliber automatic.

"Holy shit," Boggs said.

"Yeah," Barry said. "Holy shit."

Toby Marcus was in a bitchy mood. Bruno hadn't come looking for her in the lounge as she had hoped he would. She wanted him to find her surrounded by men. Consequently, she drank two or three too many and had a gruesome headache behind her right eye. She forgot she had to sit with the Obermans and wouldn't be anywhere near Bruno in the dining room. And Dorothy came up from the teen room, or wherever she was, much too late to shower and change for dinner. She had to go like she was.

She yelled at the kid and that probably didn't do the headache much good. Bill didn't give a damn. He had taken a nap right after playing cards and woke up just in time to shower and shave himself. *He is always in his own world anyway,* she thought. *Half the time he doesn't know we exist.*

Then Lillian Rothberg called because they were supposed to meet with David Oberman before dinner. Naturally Toby wasn't in the suite when Dynamite Lil had first called, and she was quite perturbed about that.

"He was going to meet with us before dinner. I had the time set aside, Toby. You know he is a busy man."

"I don't know how I forgot. You said you told me right before I went into the lounge?"

"That's right, dear. He'll meet with us right after dinner, though."

"Why can't we just discuss it all at the table? We'll be together and . . ."

"That's no place for that sort of thing, Toby. It's the First Seder. His family will be there . . . the kids, you know. It won't take us long, darling."

"Right," Toby said. She wasn't going to argue with Dynamite Lil, not with the headache she had. She took some aspirin, showered and dressed, and fixed her hair for dinner. Even though Bruno would only see her from a distance, she wanted to be sure she looked damn good.

They joined the crowd waiting outside the dining room doors. When the maître d' opened the room, the crowd headed for it as though some kind of vacuum power was sucking them all in. Those unsure of their tables checked at the front desk. The maître d' and his assistants greeted as many people as they could personally.

The New Prospect dining room was a handsome room for one so

large. Although it ran in a rectangle with a small L lip on the entrance side, parts of it were designed with different decor. The room could be partitioned into five different rooms, if need be. Sliding electric doors were housed in the walls and would move out and across to cut up the sections. Because of that, the parts were paneled in different colors and textures. With the large curtains that draped down from the ceiling and the heavy floor beams that ran across the top, it somehow all blended in well to give an interesting and tasteful effect. There was a continuous circulation of fresh air, and rows of big, crystal chandeliers ran the length and breadth of the room.

All the tables were round, and although each had a hard plastic top, all were composed of heavy wood with large heavy legs. Most sat twelve people. Though they were spaced well apart, they were more or less sectioned as well so that each busboy and waiter could find his or her station. Small compact cabinets were located every five or six tables and it was from these that the busboys brought silverware, extra dishes, napkins, and other table properties. A coffee heater and glass coffeepots were placed atop each busboy's cabinet.

As the crowd entered the dining room, the busboys and waiters stood by their stations, watching and waiting expectantly. The group of people who eventually settled around their tables represented potential tips of varying sizes for the holiday. The seasoned dining room staff knew how to interpret and analyze the guests. They knew what a table of young people meant and what a table composed mainly of elderly guests purported. They knew what a table of children meant too. Most of the younger kids would be served in the children's dining room, but the teenagers and preteens would sit with their parents.

The acoustics in the dining room were remarkable for an area of its size. Voices carried well from one end to the other. Of course, when needed like it was needed tonight, a public address system was employed. As the dining room filled up, the murmur and hum of voices grew louder and louder. The clinking of dishes could be heard as busboys rearranged settings to fit requests. The room developed a symphony composed of music from tinkling glass and silverware.

A long, rectangular table was set up front in the dining room. It was reserved for the rabbi and the cantor, their wives and children, and a choir hired to sing along with the cantor. The Seder would begin with the rabbi leading the traditional Passover services. It was customary, on Passover, for the youngest son of a family to answer what was known as the Four Questions. Serving as the symbolic youngest son for everyone in the dining room, Bobby Oberman sat at the rectangular table next to the rabbi. He had done this before, so he was not unduly nervous. Bobby was a very independent boy anyway, developing his self-image under the wing of his grandfather and being a product of his tutelage.

When it was apparent that just about all the guests were seated in the dining room, David went to the microphone by the Seder Table, as it was now called, and introduced the rabbi, the cantor, the choir, and his son. Throughout the room, yarmulkes were placed on heads as the services began. When it came time for Bobby to answer the Four Questions, he stood up and, in a clear, firm voice, spoke into the microphone.

"Wherein is this night different from all other nights?" the rabbi asked.

"For on all other nights we may eat either leavened bread or unleavened, but on this night only unleavened.

"On all other nights we may eat other kinds of herbs, but on this night only bitter herbs . . ."

Bobby's voice echoed throughout the room. Elderly people nodded and smiled. Some moved gently back and forth in their seats, moving to the rhythm of the rabbi's and Bobby's voices. The dining room had become a prayer hall. The atmosphere was somber. The voice of the cantor carried into every corner and appeared to touch everyone with its melody. Some were actually moved to tears by the words and music. Perhaps they thought of loved ones who were no longer with them.

The services proved to be as emotionally beautiful as ever. When Bobby was finished, he ran back to David's table and his father and mother hugged him. His grandfather gave him a glass of wine and sat back with pride, smiling.

"And to think," Gloria whispered to Solomon, "we had to talk you into coming for this."

"I was coming. I was coming. I just enjoy knowing you want me to come," he said in a voice of uncharacteristic softness. She squeezed her father-in-law's hand.

Halfway across the dining room, Clea and Nessim sat quietly and watched the services. With a yarmulke on his head, he was indistinguishable from any other young Jewish male in the place. They sat at a table with five other couples, three of whom had come up to the hotel together and were closely knit. Their conversations centered around themselves, and after the preliminary introductions and some small talk, they paid little attention to Nessim, Clea, and the other couple, a man and a woman in their early forties, both with rather sad faces. They sat staring at everything most of the time, speaking short sentences and whispering when they spoke to each other.

Nessim thought they appeared rather timid and withdrawn, and they were a remarkable contrast to the boisterous and gay group of three couples with them. The woman's name was Amy and the man's name was Seymour. They introduced themselves as Amy and Seymour Kleinman, the woman's name first. Clea thought that meant the man had taken the woman's name in marriage. Nessim only smiled when she asked him, but it made her reluctant to initiate any conversation for fear of a real faux pas.

Nessim was grateful for the uninteresting people at their table. He was worried that Clea would grow attached to people, even in the short span of two days, and would think of them when the building was brought down. As it was, he had uneasy feelings about the way she was going to react to the carnage. The room, now a mass of humanity, crawled, hummed, and beat with a rhythm of life that reminded him of a crowded street in Jerusalem, especially during tourist season.

He couldn't help but look up at the massive ceiling above them, studying its construction. In his mind's eye, he could see where certain chunks and sections of it would fall. He envisioned the people at the various tables surprised by the collapse of wood, pipe, metal, and cement. He saw where the heavy beams would snap and visualized just how they would slam down on a table of animated elderly people, talking now with their hands, almost all at once in their enthusiasm. He studied a table consisting of two families, set directly under one of the rather big chandeliers. It would fall like a sharp metal bomb, its pieces splattering and sending projectiles of glass and metal into the faces of the people around the table.

Tables close to the walls would be sandwiched by the crumbling plaster and wood. The floor and the sides of the room would close in on them like giant mouths, swallowing them into a stomach of fire and smoke. He saw three immense paintings across the far walls and imagined how they would come slicing down in the guise of guillotines, decapitating and cutting through the bodies of the people in their paths.

As Nessim perused this potential scene of death and disaster, he thought up freak lethal scenes. Silverware jumping and spinning from the vibrations and explosions flew through the air and into people. Heavy tables turning over over would crush and break bones. Some of these tables might actually be lifted into the air and sent smashing into a group at another table, squashing them as a flyswatter squashes a fly. The room was as deadly as any gas chamber. A common water glass would become as lethal as stilettos on springs.

There would be more screams, more hysterical shouting, more cries for help than in the worst Middle Eastern battle scene. For these people, it would be as though the world had come to an end.

The hotel was as good as placed atop a volcano. The survivors would never forget the chaos, the human pain and agony, the horrible scenes of death, the maiming, the streams and pools of human blood.

It would take days to organize and free the bodies mangled and twisted around parts of the building. All the while, the newspapers and television networks would bring the scenes to the world. The availability of the media and the improvement of communications would make the aftermath of this act as terrifying and as significant as ten times the death and destruction of a World War II battle. Most likely he, Clea, and Yusuf would be spirited out of the United States and taken back to the Middle East. He would be known forever as the man who completed the Seder Project.

19

"As you see," Shirley announced when Barry walked up to their table, "I do have a husband."

Barry smiled at the people around the table—another couple with three teenage children, a girl and twin boys, and the wife's parents. The grandparents looked up at Barry as though he was some kind of domesticated monster. The children seemed dazed or bored into a stupor. Their parents smiled back stupidly.

"Sorry I'm late," he said, sitting down.

"You missed the ceremonies," Shirley said. "They were just beautiful, just beautiful."

He shook his head but didn't offer any explanations. It was apparent from the silence around the table that everyone was expecting something.

"This is Mr. and Mrs. Rosenblatt," Shirley said, introducing the old couple first. Barry nodded and smiled in their direction. The old man gave him a quick smile, but the old lady just nodded back, her face still screwed up in a reproachful gaze. "And their daughter, Lucille, with her husband, Morris, and their children Betty, Michael, and Martin. That's Michael," Shirley said pointing to the boy on the left.

"No, I'm Martin," he replied.

"I'm always mixing them up myself," Morris said and stood up to lean across the table and shake hands with Barry. Barry stood up too. Lucille smiled and mouthed a hello.

"Evening," Barry said. "Well, what's the menu?" He picked up the long card beside his setting.

"No hamburgers, Dad," Jason said with a mournful expression.

"This isn't McDonald's," Shirley chastised. "For once, you'll eat well."

"He doesn't eat well at home?" the old lady said quickly. Her question carried the subtle tone of criticism.

"You know children. I make them the best meals, but they pick and pick."

"You said it," Lucille said, trying to rescue Shirley from her mother. "But wait until they get to be Michael's and Martin's age. These two don't stop. The refrigerator is a swinging door in our house."

The twins smiled together, but their sister still looked bored. Keith began tapping his fork on the still full soup bowl.

"Stop it. Aren't you going to eat any of that?" Shirley asked Keith as she eyed old lady Rosenblatt.

"It's ugh. It tastes like . . ."

"Never mind," she said quickly. "So," Shirley said to Barry in a soft voice when the Rosenblatts started a conversation of their own with their daughter and son-in-law, "where the hell were you?"

"Got involved. I'll tell you later. It's good that I'm here," he added in as important and as impressive a voice as he could muster. She was affected.

"Really?"

"Matter of fact, Shirl, I'm thinking of asking you to help on this."

"Me?"

"We'll talk later," he said. He caught sight of Tom Boggs walking through the dining room and heading for David Oberman's table nearby.

"Dad," Jason said, tugging on Barry's jacket. "Dad."

"What?"

"Who washes all these dishes, huh? Who?"

"They've got help for that, Jason. Don't worry about it."

"They've got a dishwasher machine," Keith said smugly. "Whaddaya think, stupid."

"Your wife's been telling us you're a policeman," Morris said suddenly in an attempt to break out a general conversation. "Detective?"

"That's right."

The teenage girl became a little more animated, but Mrs. Rosenblatt still looked quite disapproving. Barry didn't offer any additional information about himself and his work and the conversation just seemed to linger there, suspended in the air as Morris and Lucille sat staring at him with stupid smiles on their faces.

"Must be interesting," the woman finally said. "Are you like Sam Spade or something . . ."

"More like the rabbi who slept late," Shirley said and laughed at her own joke.

"Pardon?" Morris still smiled. His face looked stuck in that expression.

"Barry was going to be a rabbi."

"Really?" Mrs. Rosenblatt said. She took another look at him. "He doesn't even look Jewish."

"I'm afraid," David Oberman said, leaning over toward Lillian Rothberg, "that I'm not going to be able to walk around and greet people with you."

"Oh?"

"Something's come up. Gloria will though."

"Fine," Lillian said, eyeing Gloria Oberman. She really didn't want to greet people with Gloria Oberman at her side. None of the men would pay attention to her. They'd be hypnotized by the former model. But, it was better than nothing, she thought. At least she'd make some new contacts.

"Whenever you're ready," Gloria said. "I don't drink coffee."

"Really?" Toby Marcus asked, picking up Gloria's remark quickly. She had always worshipped Gloria's looks. The woman was a goddess to her. There must be some secrets, something magical that she did to keep so beautiful. "Is that for . . . health and beauty reasons?"

"Well, too much coffee does affect blood pressure," Abe Rothberg said.

"It's mostly because I never liked the taste," Gloria said, smiling. She said it so matter of fact and naturally that Toby felt deflated.

"Oh," she said. "I thought . . ." She looked off, across the dining room. Bruno was standing away from his tables now, the meal completed. He looked as handsome as ever, but he wasn't looking her way.

"If you'll all excuse me then," David said as he stood up.

"I would never let anything ruin my meal," Solomon Oberman said. "Especially a Seder meal."

"So you admit things were easier then, huh?" David quipped and smiled.

"Easier?" His father just laughed at that. David patted him on the shoulder.

"I'll talk to you later, Dad," he said and went out. Gloria and Lillian excused themselves as well and started their rounds in the dining room.

Barry saw David Oberman get up. He caught his nod and quickly gulped down his coffee.

"Well," he said, "you'll have to excuse me." Then added, "I have to make an important phone call."

"Huh?" Shirley said. Barry gave her as chastising a look as he could.

"Is it . . . about a case?" Lucille asked, leaning toward him.

"I'm not supposed to talk about it," he said, winking.

"I understand," she said, but she couldn't hide her look of disappointment.

He got up and put one hand on each of his boys' shoulders. They both looked up expectantly.

"Behave yourselves," he said. "If I'm not back in a while, you can meet me in the lobby," he told Shirley. She grimaced.

After he left, Mrs. Rosenblatt leaned over to whisper in her ear.

"I think you'd be better off if he was a rabbi, no?"

"Ugh," Jason said overhearing her comment. "Then we'd hafta eat kosher pizza and I hate it."

The twins laughed and their sister smiled for the first time.

*   *   *

"Don't say anything until we get into my office," David said as Barry joined him. They walked out of the dining room together and met Tom Boggs in the office.

"I've spoken to the maître d'," he said. "She's at table 34. We'll follow a bellhop to the table so we can see her."

"What's he going to give her?"

"It'll be a mistaken message, but we'll be able to find out who she is."

"Come back to the office when you're finished," David said.

As soon as they stepped back into the lobby, Boggs signaled to the bellhop and he started for the dining room.

"If my wife sees me going in again, she's going to think I'm crazy," Barry said.

They watched the bellhop enter and then followed him. When he got to table 34, he stopped and asked for Brenda Casewell. Barry watched closely as a woman in her late thirties, early forties, with short hair looked up to respond. Both he and Boggs studied her face as she read the message and then handed it back to the bellhop, smiling. Then they quickly left the dining room.

"Whaddaya think?" Boggs said as they walked to David's office. "Ever see her before?"

Barry just shook his head. David was waiting at his desk. They sat down and once again described how they found the gun. David took on a posture and expression of Kennedy-like seriousness. It reminded Barry of some pictures he had seen of the young president alone in the White House, seated at his desk, contemplating some national problem.

"We're not supposed to be searching rooms without a search warrant," David said, more like a thought spoken aloud than a revelation of new facts. "This could really be sticky."

"Of course," Boggs said, "she could have a permit for that gun and it could all be on the up and up." He waited for some support, but Barry just smirked. "Maybe she's afraid she'll be mugged in her room. Some of these New Yorkers live in constant terror."

"But if we ask her about it, she'll know we were in her room, and if she is innocent, I could get myself into some kind of a legal hassle," David concluded. He turned to Barry. "What are your thoughts?"

"I don't think she's innocent, but I'd like to play it cool for the next twenty-four hours at least and see if she contacts anyone else in the hotel. She checked in by herself, but others could have checked in separately. She's never been here before, according to your records."

"We'd have to shadow her constantly," Boggs said. "I'll put Hardik and Cooper on it, split shift. And we'll keep track of all her phone calls. We'll start immediately."

"And after this day or so?" David asked. "What then?"

"I have an idea," Barry said. "It's a little outlandish, perhaps, but..."

"Go on."

"We're interested in neutralizing this woman and the potential evil she could do. Let's get her into a compromising situation. Have her arrested for something else ... like stealing. An accusation will be made, the room searched, the gun will be found ..."

"Stealing? But how ..."

"Just leave that part to me," Barry said. "We'll wait until the morning of Chaim Eban's arrival. That way, whoever's behind this won't have much time to reorganize plans."

David stared at him and thought.

"Can you do this without a major scene in the hotel?"

"No problem," Barry said. "I did something similar last month, using a policewoman as the supposed victim."

"All right," David said. "Tom, get right on it."

Barry and Tom Boggs stood up.

"We'll fill in the man from Israeli security as soon as he arrives tomorrow," Barry said. Since the discovery of the gun he felt he had to take more of a leadership role. He could see that David Oberman appreciated it.

"When I first spoke to you, I thought, well, things like this are happening now. I'll take precautions, but honestly, I never deeply believed . . ."

"I know," Barry said. "No one ever seems to believe it will happen to them. It's like there's something working inside us, a defense mechanism, linebackers," he said, looking at Boggs, "keeping us from facing ugly truths."

"You've got a great responsibility, Tom," David said, turning to Boggs. He nodded.

"I know. Nothing like this ever touched me. Only thing I can compare it to is the Super Bowl game I was in."

Barry laughed. There was a moment of comic relief. Then the three men looked at each other. It was as if they all felt a fourth presence, one that would leave darkness and death.

20

The excitement of opening night in the New Prospect's nightclub was electric. The anticipation was visible in everyone's conversation. After dinner, most of the guests relaxed in the lounges. Some visited the stores. Others took walks through the hotel and around the grounds. Many went back to their rooms to change again for the show. Reputed to be one of the world's largest nightclubs, the Astro Room, as it was now called, had a dome ceiling filled with hundreds of colorful small lights that gave it the appearance of a Technicolor night sky. It was dazzling.

Small tables were set on tiers around the lower floor. There was a large clear area in front of the gigantic stage. This was used for ballroom dancing, usually during the intermission between the first and second shows.

Keeping more or less within the theme of the holiday, David had booked Darnel and Dede, a pair of Israeli singers who were exploding onto the scene and gaining fame and fortune on their

American tour. Their single records, which preceded their arrival, sold in the millions. Darnel was a tall, handsomely built Sabre whose dark hair floated over his forehead in a gentle wave. Thousands of women had fallen in love with his picture on the front of *Time* magazine. And Dede, a Middle Eastern version of Cher, only with smaller facial features and a slightly fuller figure, had already made her Israeli army pants and jacket into a popular new fashion item. Some of the guests in the audience wore modified versions of her outfit.

Besides singing their hit records and talking in conversational style about Israel, their act consisted of taking popular American songs and singing them in Hebrew. They had arranged a number of songs so they could harmonize, one singing in English, the other singing in Hebrew. Crowds loved it, especially in the Catskills. Because of their growing fame and fortune, the duo had to expand their act to include their own accompanying band.

Nessim sat back and blew smoke from his cigarette with cool indifference. The longer they were at the hotel, the more powerful and godlike he felt. From their table on a raised tier, he could look down at the buoyant crowd. He fantasized deific actions. Perhaps he would arrange it so that particular woman or that particular man would not be killed. He could perform miracles. Any moment these people might turn in his direction and go down on their knees to beg for mercy.

"Nessim? Nessim?" Clea said.

"I'm sorry."

"You looked . . . so deep in thought. It was frightening. You didn't hear a word I said."

"I was in deep thought, like you said."

"The longer we're here, the stranger you become," Clea said.

He touched her hand. "Don't worry. What were you saying?"

"Those two down there, by the stage. The ones just sitting down now. They're the owners of the hotel?"

"Yes."

"And they will be with Chaim Eban when you . . . when it happens?"

"Yes."

"It gives me the chills."

"Think about your mother and father and it won't," he said harshly. He crushed his cigarette viciously in the ashtray. She looked away. In a moment he regretted his anger. "Actually, I'm glad we made this show. I've heard these people sing, have I not?"

"On the radio. They've got a good sound, but whenever I hear them, I think about going back to the Middle East."

"Maybe we will. After . . . after this is all over."

"Really?"

He smiled at her obvious happiness. "I think so. We will have done our work here."

The thought comforted her somewhat and she turned to watch the show. Nessim caught sight of Brenda Casewell at a floor table to the right of the stage. He watched her more than he watched the performers, waiting to see if she would look up at him. Her presence was still very annoying to him.

Boggs's man Hardik sat just one table behind her, but there wasn't any way Nessim could tell he was watching her. She had come in by herself and now sat with two other women. Apparently, from what Hardik could see, she did not know them before she had joined them at the table.

Of course, Nessim thought, *there is always the possibility they did that as a precautionary measure. These people are clever.* He recalled headlines and television shows.

Barry had made up his mind he would give Shirley a good evening. After all, he thought, things might become hairy during the next few days and he wouldn't be able to spend much time with her. When the babysitter arrived, they left quickly to go to the nightclub for the show. Shirley wore her new outfit, and he had complimented her twice on how nice she looked. All his antics before and after dinner seemed forgotten. She hadn't even asked him what he meant by his using her in the case. She was too excited about going to the night-club.

"I called my mother," she said, "at my brother's house."

"So?"

"You know my mother."

"Whaddaya mean? She was mad?"

"Not exactly."

"She didn't enjoy dinner there?"

"Not exactly."

"What then?"

"You know."

"If I know, why am I trying so hard to find out?"

"She asked me if we enjoyed the First Seder and I said we did. I guess I said it too enthusiastically."

"Why?"

"She wanted to know how I could enjoy a Passover eating with a bunch of strangers."

"What about the meal your brother's girlfriend cooked?"

"All she would say is nice, and you know what nice means."

"No, I don't. What does nice mean?"

"It means she wasn't crazy about it."

"That's what nice means?" He thought for a moment. "So that's what she meant when she said I provided you with a 'nice' home."

"Well, sometimes 'nice' means other things to my mother. You can't go by one 'nice.'"

They joined a couple from Philadelphia who had a two-drink start on them. Offering up only first names, Larry and Ellen, they avoided substantial conversation and only joked and laughed. He was a rather loud, chubby man with dark hair who shouted back at the comedian. She laughed at almost everything her husband said or did; Barry and Shirley got more entertainment out of them than they did the show.

Barry spotted Hardik a number of tables down to his right and followed the line of vision until he located Brenda Casewell. They had decided that, for the time being, Barry would stay away from the other plainclothes security men, avoiding any possibility whatsoever of anyone's suspicions and fears being aroused. He forced himself to listen to the comedian, for his mind was reluctant to do so. He had the increasing tendency to look around the room analytically, searching for a clue, a lead, an inclination. Ever since he had discovered the gun in Brenda Casewell's room, he had the growing feeling that something way beyond his wildest imagination was going on here. Something . . . terrifically . . . terrible.

THE TERRORIST'S HOLIDAY

*   *   *

At eleven o'clock, Toby Marcus excused herself from her table, whispering into Bill's ear that she thought she was about to get her period. Besides being a way for her to get away from the table, it was an ingenious way of avoiding him sexually and saving herself completely for Bruno. She told Bill to stay there while she went up to their room to check things out. He nodded quickly, lost in conversation with another couple. She made her way up the aisle and rushed out to the lobby. Frantically, she looked around, her heart beating madly. Then she saw him. He was standing by the main desk talking to one of the receptionists. He saw her too.

She headed for the elevator, not looking back at him. When she stepped in, she saw him turn away from the main desk, that powerful shoulder of his moving slowly around. The door closed, but not before she caught sight of his face and clicked his smile into her mind. It carried her up the elevator shaft with as much lift as the elevator.

Bruno and she had developed a kind of visual language between them. It was a system of communications necessary to people screwing around on the sly. A look, a glance, a smile, a movement of the head—any and all of it were just as effective as complete sentences, even paragraphs. They could tell each other in a moment if or when getting together was possible. She was somewhat proud of this body talk that had grown between. It added a nice touch of excitement to the whole affair.

Getting out of the elevator quickly, she fumbled through her pocketbook for the room key. She left the door slightly opened and moved through the suite, closing and locking the door to Dorothy's room out of some moral instinct rather than out of any practical necessity. Then she got out of her dress, unfastened her bra, and quickly slipped off her panties. She'd be naked by the time he came through that door.

When the first show ended, people in the audience began to pay more attention to one another. Some took advantage of the hotel orchestra and went up to the dance floor. Others, feeling high and quite jovial, went right onto the stage to dance and clown around. The rest of the guests milled about their tables, ordered drinks, or left the dining room to stroll through the lobby.

Nessim saw no point in staying around and inviting the interest of hotel guests. He decided they should return to their room. "I want to sleep for a while," he said. He could sense the tension growing in Clea.

She nodded and remained silent until they paid their check and left the nightclub. Actually, Nessim wanted to study the photos and diagrams some more before he descended into the basement. It would be best if he knew exactly what he was looking for and where it would be. Because he would plant the explosives and detonators tomorrow night, it meant that the materials would be there for an entire day, and the possibility of someone discovering them would be that much greater. Obviously, he had to do the work at night when he would be assured of greater privacy. What he would do tonight was mark out the spots where the explosives would be placed on the cement footings. He'd want them as hidden as was possible.

According to what Tandem had told him, the area had little

human traffic, but there was some. Chambermaids went through the hotel that way, large carts filled with sheets and pillowcases were pushed into the big laundry rooms on the other side of the building, and service personnel occasionally went into storage rooms to gather supplies. He also had to look out for custodians who maintained the great boilers that sent heat up through twenty floors of the main building.

Of course, few, if any, of these people would be down there in the late hours. Once the packets were well placed and the receivers were set, he could detonate the explosives whenever he wished. What Nessim had created was not really as innovative as it seemed. However, the command was very pleased with the potential of his work.

Plastic explosives have to be detonated by an electrical impulse. In this case, it need be no greater than that of a penlight battery. The battery was activated by a simple switch that moved on the command of an FM frequency. The detonators had tiny receivers in them, built to respond to only one frequency, a frequency beyond the range of ordinary radio FM transmission. When the detonators' receivers received the frequency message, they would close the switch, activating the penlight batteries, thereby sending enough electrical impulse to detonate the plastique. The explosion could be commanded and controlled from a safe distance, limited only by the power of the FM transmitter. The whole process was similar to the radio processes used by space experts to order and manipulate machinery on the moon and on Mars.

Since the methodology of this sabotage was somewhat involved and unique, Nessim had agreed to utilize a more conventional system for the backup explosion at Chaim Eban's table. The Claw's great reliance on caution required it. If something happened to the transmission, or for some unknown reason, the detonators did not function properly, or only a few did, Nessim would have a different system for the plastique under the table. After all, all the packets would have to explode simultaneously in the basement for the plan to work. The building would have to be unsupported on all sides at the same instant.

He would use a watch to trigger the detonator under Chaim Eban's table. This meant that he had to plant that bomb during the course of the day of Eban's arrival. There were times when the dining room was completely empty—a good one being right after the staff had set the tables for dinner and left. He would do it then. It was the most dangerous part of his work, as far as he was concerned, for if he were caught doing that, he couldn't detonate the major explosions later.

All these thoughts played on his mind now and he wanted to devote all his attention to them. Suddenly, the noise and the excitement of the hotel had become annoying. He had to get away, go up to the room, and relax a little before his first exploratory trip to the basement.

Clea felt the tension building and walked quietly beside him. She began to feel a greater and greater separation building between them. Nessim was leaving her spiritually, becoming this second individual she had really never grown to know. In time, he would become the complete stranger and she would be alone. During those hours by herself, she would wonder about many things and she was afraid now of what the conclusions might be.

She wanted to love him.

She wanted to think only of her parents.

She wanted to believe in their cause.

She wanted to be happy for their success.

But how she had enjoyed the singing of the two Israeli perform-ers in the nightclub. . . .

21

After it had come to life with such a dynamic force, the hotel was reluctant to go to sleep. The lounge bar closed at three, but the band played on for another hour. Their music, although quiet and subdued, catering now to the slow-moving couples who embraced to dance, traveled out the door and made its way across the lobby and into the immediate darkness around the hotel. The hotel staff wound down slowly. Many of the dining room personnel and bellhops stayed up late to play cards, drink, and talk over the day's labor. Naked lightbulbs dangling in the help's quarters remained lit, and the low murmur of voices continued in nocturnal rhythms punctuated by an occasional loud laugh or heavy curse.

The security staff had shrunk down to three men—a uniformed guard at the main gate, a guard at the front entrance, and a guard at the entrance used by the hotel staff to get to the help's quarters across the road. Cooper had relieved Hardik and stayed silently and very uncomfortably in the shadows of the fourth floor, watching the door to Brenda Casewell's room.

Very little traffic passed now on the highway that ran alongside the hotel grounds. Almost all the lights of the rooms were out, but the floodlights splashed on the sides of the building and kept it from fading completely into the shadows. And of course, the pole lights along the driveways of the hotel remained lit. The main lobby had its big chandeliers dimmed considerably, but the room remained lit all night. A night clerk sat behind the big desk reading a newspaper. He looked up whenever a couple would finally retreat out of the lounge. The emptiness of the room made them conscious of their own voices and they would invariably whisper as they walked to the elevators.

The women looked spent—their hairdos loosened, strands fallen from their molded places. Makeup faded and smeared, eyelids drooped. The vision of the men beside them was clouded by the alcohol they had consumed. Some had cigarettes dangling from their mouths. It was as if they no longer had the strength to hold them securely. Trails of smoke made them cough and squint their nearly closed eyes even more.

Although the window displays remained lit up, the stores were all shut and dark. The corridor leading past them remained highly lit up. Late snackers were coming and going from the hotel luncheonette that stayed open until four thirty in the morning. Their specialty for the wee hours were bagels and cream cheese. The sound of tinkling coffee cups and silverware traveled up the corridor. In fact, the lateness of the hour, the silence in most parts of the hotel, and the emptiness of the large areas all seemed to amplify the noise.

Across the hotel grounds, the old main house was nearly in complete darkness. Two lights remained—the entrance light so the latecomers wouldn't trip going up the wooden steps to the front door, and a small lamplight in the living room used by Solomon Oberman. He sat by a window, staring out at the hotel. He had always had great difficulty falling asleep. He was so active and energetic during the day that his nerves cooled down slowly, moving on a kind of echo and rebounding through his body. After his wife's death, his insomnia had grown worse. He didn't tell his son about it though. He was never one to share his problems with others. He had withstood so much in his life, battled alone so many times, that he didn't know how to share hardship with someone else, even his own son. Besides, he knew David and Gloria would only want him to see a doctor and a doctor would fill him with some sleeping pills that would leave him groggy and dull the next day.

Solomon had always had a deadly fear of pills anyway, believing in the natural ability of the body to combat its illnesses and problems instead. If his body wished to remain awake long into the night, he'd let it and certainly wouldn't battle with it. After the late news and some light reading, he'd often come to the window and watch the hotel to see the comings and goings of the late staffers. He liked to count the number of windows still lit in the main building and keep a record, matching the hour with the number of windows. Some guests kept their lights burning all night. He imagined them to be older guests deathly afraid of the darkness, especially in a strange place.

Usually, he would tire by two thirty or three and sink into sleep. He seemed to only need a few hours of night sleep and took an afternoon nap to make up for it. Tonight, because of the beginning of the holidays perhaps, because of all the excitement associated with it, because he remembered sharing so many First Seders with his wife, he sat up even later. It was already three fifteen and he felt no need to turn away from the window.

At three thirty, he decided he'd have to try to go to sleep and forget—pushing his redundant thoughts back into their chambers in his mind. He was about to turn away from the window and do just that when something caught his attention. It was incredible, especially considering the hour of the night. He wouldn't have been able to see it so well either, if it weren't for the floodlights over the sides of the building. They were especially designed to illuminate the fire escape, and there, coming down it slowly, was a figure, a man. He reached the end and stopped at the side of the building.

Solomon opened his window completely to get a totally unobstructed view of the incident. The man just stood there for a few moments. Then he approached the basement door. He jerked it open, stood silently looking in, and then disappeared into the building to descend the steps. It was a most peculiar scene, and Solomon could make no sense out of it whatsoever. He knew it would bother him to just forget it so he went to his phone and called the main desk. He recognized Charlie Gordon's voice.

"Charlie, this is Mr. Oberman."

"Yes, sir," Charlie said with apparently little surprise. "I always can recognize your voice, Mr. Oberman. What's the problem?"

"You know any reason why someone should be coming down the fire escapes tonight?"

"Fire escapes? No, sir. Not unless there's a fire. How many people are climbing around on them?"

"I just saw one man."

"No, sir, Mr. Oberman. There's no reason for that. You sure that's what you saw?"

"Of course I'm sure," Solomon said harshly. "I know when I see someone walking down a fire escape."

"Uh-huh. Well . . . maybe I'd better leave a note for your son to read tomorrow, huh?"

"I saw this person go into the basement," Solomon said with tenacious determination. He knew from the sound in Gordon's voice that the desk clerk wanted to humor him and hang up as soon as he could.

"Basement?"

"That's right. Through the outside entrance. You tell one of the security men. Who's on duty in the lobby?"

"Larry Hardik."

"I don't remember him, but you tell him to go down there and look around right now."

"Yes, sir."

"No reason for a guest to go sneaking around the hotel this late. I don't like it. You make sure you tell him that I don't like it."

"I'll tell him. Yes, sir."

"Yeah." Solomon hesitated, but he didn't hang up.

"Okay?"

"Listen, you call me back as soon as he comes up from the basement check," Solomon said.

"Right, Mr. Oberman. Will do."

Solomon hung up and went back to the window to watch the outside basement entrance and wait for the return call.

Nessim had left Clea behind reluctantly. Her body was so warm, and she looked so childlike asleep there. Strands of hair lay gently over her cheeks, and her lips were parted slightly. He watched her breathe and moved the hair off her cheeks by running the tips of his fingers down the sides of her face. Then he slipped out of the bed and moved quietly to put on his clothes again. When he stepped into his shoes, she turned over. He waited.

"Nessim?"

"Yes. I'm going out."

"You'll be careful."

"Yes."

"Will you be long?"

"Not very long. Go back to sleep."

She didn't reply, but he knew she was watching him. He moved to the door, opened it slowly, lifted his hand to indicate he was going, and disappeared outside. The click of the door left her in total silence.

Nessim moved on cat's paws. He opened the side window slowly, taking great pains to avoid any squeaking. Then he stepped out on the fire-escape landing and closed the window almost all the way. He turned and looked out at the hotel grounds. He was surprised by the brightness of the floodlights against the walls of the building. It made him cramp up and cling to whatever shadows he could find. A car went down the driveway away from the hotel. He watched it go to the front entrance and saw the figure of the security guard move in the little booth. The car hesitated and then pulled away. The sound of its engine and tires was heard in reverberations.

There were no other signs of life outside—no human voices, no people walking on the grounds. He started down the fire escape slowly and carefully. It would be terrible to have an accident, slip now and twist an ankle or break a leg. They had placed him perfectly. It was a short distance down this fire escape, and the location of the room on the second floor made it especially easy to get to it. The good planning encouraged him. He would have great success.

When he stepped to the ground, he waited just to be sure no one had seen him. He listened once again for the sounds of life. Now the music from the lounge could be heard. It was soft enough and distant enough. He looked about, spotted the door to the basement, and approached it. When he tried the handle, it didn't move and he feared the door was locked. He didn't panic. Instead he turned harder and jerked it. Sure enough, it was just a stubborn doorjamb.

After he opened the door, he stepped back and waited again, listening this time for voices from within. It wouldn't do to walk down those steps and come upon some hotel staff people at this hour. There'd be great difficulty explaining his presence. A small-watt bulb threw a dim light over the small stairway. He walked inside and closed the door softly behind him. All was perfect so far. This would be the easy entrance and exit tomorrow night.

He descended the stairway slowly, using his memory of the maps and pictures of the hotel he had studied to visualize what he would find. He stood quietly at the bottom of the steps and listened. He could hear the hum of the transformers and the sound of the water heaters in the basement. To his immediate left, perhaps twenty yards away, was the elevator that went up to the lobby and above. It was open and waiting like a sleeping beast of burden to be nudged and directed into use.

There wasn't an unpleasant odor in the basement, but there was the smell of storage, dampness, and closed-in areas. The plaster walls were unpainted, naked and rough to the touch. A series of dim neon lights ran down the corridor ceiling, spaced out for the most efficient use. Directly across from him was an open area cluttered with old furniture, chairs with broken arms, couches with damaged legs and cushions.

Nessim turned slowly and looked to the right. There were still no signs of people, no sounds of voices or footsteps. The basement appeared sufficiently deserted. It was a good time to prowl. He knew from the floor plan that there were a series of rooms along the way. Some housed electrical equipment and some served as storage areas. The linen area was all the way down the corridor, well past what would be the location for the explosives. As he moved down the corridor, he kept track of what was above him on the main floor of the hotel. He wanted a vertical knowledge of where he was at all times. Plumbing was helpful in outlining and delineating locations. He knew just about where he was under the lobby. When he came to the first steel girder on his left, a surge of excitement moved throughout his body.

Three of the columns were immediately visible. They stood in the cement footings exactly as pictured in the photographs. He looked up slowly, following their ascent into the ceiling of the basement where they disappeared into the body of the building. He approached the one on his left slowly, running his hands over the cold metal, eyeing it like one would contemplate an adversary. Then he moved farther into the belly of the building, locating each girder. Two had to be reached on hands and knees. He thought Yusuf would be better at getting to those, and since they were already quite hidden, placement of the packets wouldn't be as crucial.

He went back toward the front and studied the girders, imagining how they would kick out when the explosives blew away their footings. Perhaps, for a few seconds, the skeleton structures of the upstairs floors would crack with surprise. The sound of the explosions would stop conversations dead. Everyone would hear the tons of materials collapsing above. That realization alone might kill some of the older people, some of those who had spent a good part of their lives supporting and working for Israel.

He chastised himself for dreaming too much. He was down here now to do work. Specifically, he wanted to mark out the exact locations for the plastique; place each packet with its detonator in such a way as to avoid discovery by a passing staff member or custodian. He took out a black Magic Marker and began drawing small squares on the cement footings.

Nessim had marked off the first one only when he heard the footsteps in the corridor. Someone was approaching from the right, walking slowly, cautiously. He held his breath and waited. The footsteps got louder. He backed against the wall and inched his way farther into the shadows. Suddenly, a security guard appeared in the hallway. He stopped about ten yards in front of Nessim and put his hands on his hips as he stared ahead. Then he turned slowly.

It seemed to Nessim that the man was looking right at him. Nessim worked his hands down to his pockets and quickly searched for the knife he had placed in his pants. The guard looked away, shrugged to himself, and then started back up the hall the way he had come. Apparently he hadn't seen him; however, Nessim waited until the man's footsteps could no longer be heard. Then he slipped out of the shadows and listened for a while longer. There were no voices.

What brought a security man down here? Nessim retraced his steps mentally, trying to figure if he had done something to attract any attention. Maybe someone heard the basement door open or close. Maybe the guard was just looking for a friend. Whatever, it made Nessim work with a quicker sense of urgency now. The appearance of a security man also made him think about Yusuf being brought in to help him tomorrow night.

It was, of course, possible for him to do all the work by himself. It was true it would take longer, and the longer he stayed down here planting explosives, the greater the chance of being discovered. However, he wanted Yusuf with him for other reasons besides the efficiency they could accomplish together. Yusuf needed guidance and needed to be part of what he was doing. Yusuf had no one but him. His brother had no other life interest. They were both married to the cause. It struck him as both ironic and perhaps tragic that all he could give Yusuf was the opportunity to vent his hatred and vengeance.

When Nessim was finished, he retreated the way he had come, pausing on the steps to the outside door to look back and contemplate the scene that would occur tomorrow night. At this time the next day, he and Yusuf would be planting the plastique. Then, the following evening, when Chaim Eban sat down to dinner with just about three thousand people, Nessim would stand outside the building in the darkness and trigger the transmitter.

Despite the unexpected appearance of a security man, Nessim felt confident. The planning and all the groundwork had been completed.

All that remained was for him to put the processes into effect, and that was, after all, what he had become an expert at doing. He felt good about it all and turned to go out and back up the fire escape to his room, where he was sure Clea lay awake, waiting and worrying. He'd hold her in his arms, kiss and stroke her hair. They would fall asleep embracing.

"Nothing," Larry Hardik said, coming back into the lobby. He held his arms out. "There's no one down there. Who the hell would be down there this time of the night anyway?"

"Beats me. Just tryin' to humor the old man."

"Yeah, well, why didn't they tell me that would be a part of this job? I mighta asked for a little more pay."

"Sure, sure. Whaddaya complainin' about. I gotta call him back, don't I? Maybe I should make up somethin.'" Gordon thought for a moment. "He's a pretty stubborn old man. When he says he saw somethin', he says he saw somethin.' We ain't gonna convince him he didn't."

"What's to make up? At three thirty in the mornin' somebody's crawlin' around fire escapes and goin' into the basement?"

"I know. I'll tell him it was some teenage kid foolin' around with his friends. He'll believe that. He always complains about what the kids do around the hotel."

"Do what you want," Hardik said. "Just leave me out of it."

"Yeah. You're a big help." Gordon picked up the phone and rang Solomon Oberman's apartment. It took the old man quite a while to answer the phone, and Gordon began thinking he might have gone to sleep.

"Did I wake you, Mr. Oberman?"

"Hell no. I told you to call me, didn't I?"

"Yes, you did."

"Well, what was it?"

"Er . . . Seems like we had a bunch of teenagers foolin' around. You know, one took a dare from his buddies. Somethin' like that."

"Teenager? This late at night?"

"Yeah, well, you know how some of these modern parents are, Mr. Oberman," Gordon said and winked at Hardik.

"Teenager, huh. Hope you scared the shit out of him."

"We sure did. He won't be doin' that anymore. No sir. Lucky you saw it."

Solomon Oberman sensed something insincere in the desk clerk's voice, but couldn't fathom why the man would lie to him. That just didn't make sense now.

"Yeah. All right. Good," he said and hung up.

Gordon wiped his face and hung up too.

"He believe ya?" Hardik asked.

"Yeah."

"You gonna tell David about it?"

"You kiddin'? Forget it," Gordon said. "He'd only be embarrassed about his father sittin' up all night starin' out his window."

"I suppose you're right," Hardik said.

"How many lottery tickets you get today?"

"Twenty. You?"

"Twenty. Maybe we'll both be lucky. We're due for some luck around here."

"You can say that again."

Gordon repeated it and Hardik laughed.

The laughter seemed to linger as if the building had picked it up and echoed it in jest.

22

Tom Boggs, David Oberman, and Karl Trustman, the man from Israeli security, stopped talking as Barry came into the office. It was the day of Second Seder, and Barry had joined the others for a briefing.

They all turned his way. Boggs was leaning against the wall with his arms folded against his body. David sat behind his desk, and Trustman, who sat on the couch, stood up to greet Barry. Trustman was a five-foot-eleven man, powerfully built with a bull neck that seemed to emanate directly out of his deltoid muscles. He looked like a power weightlifter. Barry noted the thickness of his wrists when he stuck out his hand to shake.

They eyed each other during the introductions. Karl Trustman had a narrow face with a wide forehead and bushy eyebrows. His deep-set eyes and small mouth held together with tight, thin lips gave him the look of a man in deep thought. His gaze was steady and firm. There was an aura of cool, collected calmness about him. He had control of every part of his body, directing it with total energy toward the object of his concentration. His grip was strong. He had the demeanor of a man resigned to the belief that life was a series of continuous struggles, but he wasn't overwhelmed or fatigued by it. He was prepared for it.

"As I understand it, Lieutenant, we could be in great debt to your insight and perception."

"Thank you. How far along are you all in the briefing?"

"We've told him all about Brenda Casewell," David said.

"Uh-huh." Barry sat down. "I called my partner in New York last night and he's checking her out, but of course, we don't have the time to wait around."

"I agree," Trustman said quickly. "You're going to arrange for her to be taken out of the hotel before Eban's arrival?"

"Yes."

"Good. Other than that, there hasn't been any indication of any danger to Chaim Eban, correct?" He asked his question quickly and directly, as if he were driving toward a set conclusion.

"I don't believe she's the only one here to do him in," Barry said.

"But there isn't any other evidence, hard evidence, to discuss, is there?" Trustman said. He seemed impatient.

"Well, she's not the woman who lived in the apartment we investigated in New York. She's associated with those people, but . . ."

"You haven't located any of them here nor have you been able to run down any hard leads confirming their presence, is that correct?"

Barry began to feel like someone under interrogation. He looked at Boggs and David Oberman, but they were stone-faced, staring and listening.

"No, not what you would call hard evidence."

"Good. Then I won't recommend Chaim not appear tomorrow."

"Oh, I see." *So the primary concern,* Barry thought, *remains Eban's ability to raise the money.*

"Perhaps you don't," Trustman said, perceiving some unhappiness in Barry's expression. "I'm not trying to create a rosy picture here and deliberately avoid the possibility of evil or ugly actions occurring, but we Israelis are used to the fact that danger lurks around us continually. Since the Arab fanatics have turned to terrorism as their main form of offensive war, every Israeli man, woman, and child is constantly on a battlefield, no matter where he or she is. Eban knows this better than any of us. He lives with it daily."

"I understand," Barry said. He recalled Rabbi Kaufman's intensity and recognized the similarity.

"Of course, I would appreciate your permitting me to work with you for the next day and a half."

"Certainly," Barry said. "I'll go back over the check-in lists to see if I can come up with any more leads. In the meantime, I assume that Casewell has made no significant contacts. Is that correct, Tom?"

"Right. What's more, no one's approached her."

"Maybe when we put the pressure on her tomorrow, she'll make an effort to contact someone," Barry said.

"Well then, there's not much more we can do, is there?" David said. He seemed relieved.

"One thing," Trustman said. "Have an alternate suite for Chaim Eban. Keep him booked into whatever you had, but at the last moment, make the change."

"That's not a bad idea," Barry said. "Thinking of some kind of sabotage, perhaps?"

"It's a precaution," Trustman replied, but he didn't make it sound like anything special.

"All right. I'll do that," David said. "In fact, at the last moment, we'll book him into the old main house. On the top floor."

"Good. Well then," Trustman said, turning to Barry, "what are your immediate plans?"

"I'll go back and join my wife in the dining room for lunch and afterward I'll spend time in the office."

"Mr. Trustman will be at your table tonight and tomorrow night," David said. "We want to keep him near Chaim at all times."

"Fine."

"And I'm in room 515 if you need me and I'm not around."

The buzzer rang and David picked up his receiver.

"Hold on," he said turning to Barry. "It's for you. New York."

"Thanks." He got up and took the phone. "Hello. Yes, this is Wintraub. Hello, Baker, you black . . . What's that? Go on."

Barry listened for a while. "What about the Casewell woman? Uh-huh. Thanks. We'll be in touch."

"Got something?" David asked immediately.

"An Arab boy was murdered last night, killed in a manner similar to the way the JDL boy was killed, only whoever did it wasn't as neat. The boy was beaten badly too. He was confirmed as an illegal alien. INS has picked up the entire family."

"Think there's some connection with all this?" Trustman asked, his eyes narrowing. Barry had the feeling he knew the answer but was simply after confirmation.

"No question. My first guess is that the boy was somehow involved in the JDL boy's death, and it was a revenge murder. The police are thinking about the possibility of a kind of underground war erupting in New York because of all this."

"What about the Casewell woman?" Boggs asked.

"No permit for a pistol registered in New York. Landlord told my partner she works for a travel agency, but he's not sure which one. He really didn't seem to know much about her."

"She must be the one," Boggs said. They all looked at him.

"I find it hard to believe they would place such an important mission in the hands of one woman," Barry said. "Don't you?" he asked Trustman. He didn't agree or disagree. His neutral expression was cold, unnerving.

"If we panic and call off this rally, they would be victorious without firing a shot," he said.

"We've got a lotta people to think about here," Barry said.

"Hold on," David said, lifting his hand. "Let's not go haywire. I'm with Mr. Trustman on this. We'll keep security tight and continue the investigation, but let's not frighten a few thousand people on the basis of what we have."

The three of them turned to Barry. He was the only one working with a relatively objective viewpoint. The others had interests that complicated matters. The Passover holiday was, after all, one of the best vacation moneymakers for the hotels, and the amount of money that could be raised for Israel was very significant. He had no choice but to simply nod back in understanding.

When the phone rang in the Wintraub's room, Shirley screamed from the bathroom, "That's my mother!" But when he lifted the receiver and said hello, he heard Rabbi Kaufman's voice.

"Anything yet?" he asked.

"I'm working on one suspect, a female who just happens to be from the East Ninety-Third Street apartment house and carries a pistol."

"Dangerous, but there are others perhaps more dangerous there too."

"And how do you know this?"

"Sources are not important. Information is important. Two men and a woman. One man in his early thirties, the other in his early twenties. The woman is around twenty-four. The older man is called Nessim, the younger, Yusuf. He's your Joseph Mandel. The woman's name is Clea."

"Joseph Mandel's apartment was in her name," Barry said. "Mrs. Clea Mandel. You believe they're all here?"

"Perhaps."

"There's a man from Israeli security here. His name is Karl Trustman. Do you know him?"

"My relations with Israeli security are a bit strained these days. We don't see eye to eye on crucial points."

"One more question, Rabbi. There was a murder last night, an Arab, illegal alien. Young boy. Apparently he was beaten, perhaps to make him talk."

"I read about it," Kaufman said in a neutral voice.

"I hope that's your full involvement, otherwise . . ."

"One case at a time, Mr. Detective. These people you're tracking . . . they are capable of great acts. Let your imagination run wild. Nothing is beyond them. Shalom," he said. Before Barry could reply, Kaufman hung up. Barry sat there with the receiver still in his hand.

"I guess that wasn't my mother," Shirley said.

"Huh? Oh, no, no."

"What's the matter?"

"For the first time, I just had a feeling of impending doom. Maybe it was wrong to bring you and the kids up here with me."

"And leave us on Passover?"

"You could have gone to your mother's."

"Thanks a lot. We'll take our chances with Chaim Eban," she said. He looked at her and laughed.

The festivities of the Second Seder were just as beautiful and as well coordinated as those of the First. Everyone in the hotel dining room seemed to be in an even more festive mood. There was much more noise, more music, and much more laughter. The dining room staff was also caught up in the jovial atmosphere, and the usual tension created by the pressure of service was absent.

Toby Marcus was radiant. Her sexual encounter with Bruno brought new color into her cheeks. She was filled with a revitalized energy and dominated conversations at her table. Her husband enjoyed her and found himself stimulated by her vibrancy. She paid more attention to him too. She seemed to have greater interest in him since her involvement with Bruno. Her affair improved all of her relationships.

Because of the anticipated arrival of Chaim Eban, Lillian Rothberg stepped up her activities. The itinerary was well planned out and the protocol established. She took an even firmer control of the family's affairs, planning out what each family member would wear the day of Eban's arrival and what each would do. She visited with more guests, stimulated more interest, and made more contacts.

Abe Rothberg grew tired just watching her. The more active she was, the more withdrawn he became. He longed to retreat to the sanctuary of card games and steam baths. All the noise and excitement was just confusing to him. A lot of people were running around looking important. It was hard to believe anything really significant was to occur.

Across the room, Nessim sat even quieter than he had during the First Seder, but like that first meal, no one at the table seemed to notice nor care. Clea watched him carefully, waiting for the slightest signal of his intentions. He was beginning to show some signs of nervousness, but only someone who had lived with him awhile would notice. His gestures were quicker. His sentences shorter and abruptly to the point. He looked at everything with a cat's curiosity. His silences made her somewhat uncomfortable, and he seemed to withdraw deeper and deeper into himself. He didn't touch her hand or give her his comforting smile. He was impatient with the smallest thing, and for the first time since she had known him, he muttered oaths of hatred and vengeance under his breath. It was as if he was psyching himself up for the job he had to do.

When Karl Trustman came to Barry's table, he introduced him as an advance man from Chaim Eban's staff. The Rosenblatts and their children were thrilled by his presence and asked him question after question concerning Israel and the wars with the Arabs. Barry was grateful for that. He was no longer the object of their intense attention. He relaxed and really enjoyed the Seder meal.

But the final words of advice Rabbi Kaufman had given him were continually cropping up in his thoughts now. "Let your imagination run wild. Nothing is beyond them." What did that mean? What were the possibilities here? They could make various kinds of attempts on Eban's life—try to shoot him in the lobby, in the dining room, perhaps while he made his speech. They might attack him in his suite or sabotage the rooms. Perhaps they would try to get him immediately, as soon as the helicopter landed.

All this was sort of conventional. Something more lingered between the words Kaufman had uttered. Of course, the rabbi didn't know himself, but he probably hoped to stimulate Barry's imagination. *What makes him think I'm more capable of concocting gross acts?* he wondered. *The only advantage is that I'm here. I'm here,* he thought and looked around.

Eban would be eating in this room tomorrow night, sitting only a short distance away. Perhaps they would try to poison him. He'd have to check into that and be sure no one could tamper with the food, but he was sure Israeli security had thought of that as well. Thinking these thoughts was stabbing in the dark, all right. Later, after dinner, he would get together with Karl Trustman, tell him what Rabbi Kaufman had said, and discuss the possibilities. He was sure Trustman could come up with more imaginative lethal acts.

And there were still the check-in sheets to reexamine, although his faith in that process was dwindling.

The sounds of the cantor's voice drew him into a more soothing frame of mind.

Much later that night, Nessim opened the suitcase and neatly arranged the plastique explosives and the detonators. He taped each packet securely and once again checked the detonators. All the switches were in working order, all the batteries were fully charged. When he was satisfied, he took out a cloth sack and placed each packet within it. The sack had a strap that went over his shoulder. He tested its weight and was sure that it would provide no problem to him as he climbed down the fire escape. Then he looked at his watch. It was nearly time.

Clea had gotten up too. She was unable to just lie there and watch him prepare. She lit a cigarette and sat in the corner of the room, observing him quietly. He didn't seem to notice her. All his concentration and attention was on his work. He was a technician of the highest order now, completely involved in his mechanisms and systems.

They had never really discussed the method of his sabotage. She had deliberately avoided it. Fearful of the full significance of what he was about to do, she chose to remain naive and stupid about it up to this point. She permitted herself to understand that Chaim Eban was to be destroyed. He was, after all, a military man whose work meant death to people of her father's blood and heritage.

Although Nessim had rarely fanned the flames of her hate and revenge, he often made pointed remarks designed to keep her on one track—*The Jews in Israel were responsible for the death of your father and mother, and the Jews in America support the people of Israel.* She understood in a vague way that Chaim Eban was to be blown up in the dining room. She knew that it would mean the death of people around him. What she didn't comprehend at this moment was the number of surrounding people who would be killed, nor did she understand that the true intent of Nessim's mission was to eliminate as many of these people as possible. For El Yacoub and the Hezbollah, that was of equal, if not greater, importance.

Nessim had kept that from her, always stressing the significance of killing Chaim Eban. He didn't emphasize the need to kill anyone else. Her understanding of explosives was even less than that of the average layperson. Most of all, she had no idea about the lethal potential and the power of plastique. The packets Nessim had in his cloth bag were relatively small. It was impossible for her to conceive of their intensity.

Without questioning him about it, she imagined that he had concocted a plan whereby he would plant these explosives somehow directly under the feet and the table of the Chaim Eban party in the dining room. This was the reason he was going down into the basement. Now, as she watched him work, the questions began to develop in her mind, only she was hesitant about asking them.

"When you're finished with this tonight, will we be leaving?"

"No," he said. He didn't look up.

"Do you have to do something more to make it work?"

"Yes. I must do something in the dining room tomorrow."

"Will we go after that?" Her voice betrayed her eagerness to leave the place of death.

"We will leave the building just before dinner, but we won't leave the grounds until . . ." He stopped and looked up at her. "Until it's finished. Then Hamid will be waiting for us at the help's entrance."

"Is Yusuf in the hotel now?"

"He should be working his way to our rendezvous in the basement, yes."

"Maybe I should go down into the basement with you," she said. He smiled at her. "What for?"

"To . . . help. I could watch out or something."

"No, you'd just be an added worry on my mind. Stay here and wait."

He looked at his watch again and then lifted the cloth bag to his shoulder. She stood up. He was silent, staring and thinking. She approached and touched his arm.

"Be careful."

"I will."

He kissed her and went to the door. First he looked down the corridor; then he stepped out and went right to the window. He opened it and crawled quietly onto the landing. She watched through the open doorway. He looked back, closed the window almost completely, and began his descent down the fire escape.

Yusuf weaved his way through the shadows of the corridor. Tandem had gotten him into the building through the garbage truck entrance succesfully. They had waited until the custodial men disappeared into a back room, and then Tandem directed him through a doorway that led to the basement. He had given him explicit directions about how to travel through it and drew a fairly good map from memory.

Their car was parked a considerable distance down the highway, away from the hotel. Although it was a main road, there were no lights. Except for the beams of an occasional car, there was complete darkness. It was a moonless night with some overcast as well. Hamid waited within the car, a dark shadow seated in the back.

As soon as Tandem and Yusuf had left the automobile, Hamid had taken out his pistol and screwed on the silencer. He knew what had to be done. The Claw's orders had been definite. The moment Tandem got back into the car, he would shoot him quickly in the back of the head. His value to them would be completed after he had helped Yusuf to get to Nessim. They knew Tandem lived for a single act of great revenge and would probably lose interest in them and their cause when it was all over anyway. What's more, he knew too much. After Hamid killed him, he would put his body into the car trunk and they would dump it out somewhere off the country road later.

But Tandem had plans of his own. As he watched Yusuf disappear anxiously through the entranceway, he waited for a sufficient time and then followed him in. He remained way back, listening to be sure Yusuf was far ahead of him. When Tandem came to a stairway leading up to the main floor, he stopped, looked down the corridor, and then went up.

Yusuf reached the rendezvous point successfully and crouched in the darkness to wait for his brother. His heart beat madly. He saw the steel girders before him. He had, of course, seen them in the photographs, but being here now, able to reach out and touch them, was a totally overwhelming experience for him. All his dreams, his visions of grand destruction and death were about to be realized. He longed for the sound of Nessim's footsteps in the corridor.

23

Solomon Oberman couldn't believe his eyes. When his son had failed to mention anything about the incident he had reported to the main desk the night before, he thought something was peculiar. Although David was very busy, he wouldn't have forgotten something like that. He finally asked him if Charlie Gordon had left any messages for him and David said, "Nothing unusual. Why?" He described it to him, and David said he would ask Gordon about it.

Then Solomon thought, *Well, maybe it was just a bunch of teenagers fooling around and it wasn't that important.* What he didn't believe, however, was that the security man and Gordon had taken sufficient action to be sure it wouldn't happen again. To them it was probably just a harmless prank. Solomon still had the belief that you had to ride herd over the staff and let them know you were always around. He never liked the idea that David lived in a house away from the hotel, even though the house was on the hotel property. It was the difference between David's "modern" approach to the business and Solomon's traditional way. The old concept of a resort was that it served as home and a place of business at the same time. The guests got that feeling; the staff had that feeling; and it helped build the warm image of the hotel.

In any case, his suspicions about the effectiveness of Gordon and the security man were confirmed. He had deliberately sat by the window as late as he had the night before, and sure enough, there was the same dark figure making his way down the fire escape. He watched him for a moment and cursed. Then he went to the telephone.

He hated to do it, but there was no alternative. Because he was actively away from the hotel now, the staff just didn't pay enough attention to him anymore. He had lost touch, and they had forgotten his authority. Perhaps that annoyed him more than anything else. It certainly hurt his pride, and he was very angry about it. But most important, something crazy was going on at the hotel, and it couldn't be permitted to continue. After all, they had insurance obligations and who the hell knew what these kooky kids were capable of doing. Maybe they were terrorizing guests in their rooms. Maybe they were stealing. It had to be stopped, even if it meant his getting dressed and going over there himself.

He dialed his son's number. It rang twice. He knew the phone was right beside David, near the bed. He was only sorry it would wake Gloria, but he imagined they had received emergency calls late at night before.

"Hello." David's voice cracked with sleep.

"David, listen to me," he began.

"Dad? Are you all right?"

"I'm all right," he said quickly, impatient with his son's concern, but understanding it. "When I'm ready to die, I'll let you know in advance."

"What's the matter?"

"You remember that story I told you at Seder tonight?"

"Story? . . . It's Dad," Solomon heard David say and imagined Gloria waking up. "What story?"

"About those kids crawlin' on the fire escape. The ones Gordon and your new man, Hardik, found after I called them."

"Oh yeah. What about it? Jesus, it's three thirty in the morning, Dad."

"They're out there again," Solomon said, ignoring his son's comment on the time. "Some fear your new security man put into them."

"On the fire escape again? You saw them? You're sure?"

"Of course I'm sure. I saw them just now. Down the fire escape, comin' down from I don't know which floor, for God sakes, and going into the basement again. Maybe they're botherin' people in their rooms, peepin' in or somethin'. Maybe they're stealin', David. This is not a funny business."

"No one's complained about it, Dad. As far as I know, that is."

"You better call the main desk and tell them, David. We can't have them out there on the fire escape and who the hell knows what they're doin' when they get into the basement."

"Right, Dad."

"I'm sorry I had to call you, but . . ."

"It's all right. What were you doing up so late anyway?"

"I . . . I couldn't sleep so I sat up for a while reading," he said.

"Last night too?"

"It's the lousy hotel food," he replied, trying to cloak his problem in a joke. David was silent for a moment. "I'm all right," Solomon repeated.

"Okay, Dad. Don't worry, I'll call the main desk and make sure they take action. Don't worry."

"Apologize to Gloria for me, but tell her that's what comes of marrying a hotelman."

"She knows," David said. Solomon could hear the smile in his son's voice.

After he hung up, he went back to the window. What the hell were things coming to anyway? If parents couldn't control their children, then the children oughta be placed in homes where people could take care of them, he thought. Especially teenagers. You'd think they'd have a little more respect on Passover, he concluded and shook his head in disgust.

When Yusuf saw Nessim coming down the corridor, he nearly shouted for joy. It took all his self-control to simply stand and move out into his brother's view. Nessim moved quickly to his side and they embraced.

"No problem getting in?"

"No. Tandem gave me perfect directions, and it was easy getting past the custodial people."

"And Tandem—you left him outside?"

"At the garbage truck entrance. I'm to meet them at the car. It's down the road, well hidden. Hamid is waiting with it."

"Good." Nessim was visibly relieved.

"How has it been going here? You're a Passover Jew?"

"No problem. I've studied this area. We must work fast," he said, pulling Yusuf out of the corridor. "Watch now as I plant the first packet. Then you will plant the packets on the farthest two girders. You'll have to crawl to the cement footings there. The basement slants, and the walls are closer. Their placement has been marked off for you."

Yusuf just nodded. Nessim went to the first cement footing and began his work. After the detonator was attached, the plastique was molded and stretched so that it embraced the footing like the long legs of a giant daddy longlegs spider. Nessim worked his lethal sculpture carefully but quickly. Yusuf had seen and done it before under his brother's tutelage, but the significance and the importance of this job required that he get renewed instructions.

"Be extra careful with this switch. If these ends should touch, even for a split second, you'll ignite the explosive and blow yourself all over this basement."

"I understand."

"All right," Nessim said as he completed the implanting of the first packet. "Then go ahead. Take the two deepest girders." He handed him the two packets, and Yusuf, holding them gingerly, went off, deeper into the belly of the building.

Nessim watched him for a moment and then started on the second girder's footing. He had just completed it when he heard the sound of footsteps in the corridor. This time he recognized that two people were approaching. He moved quickly back to find Yusuf and warn him.

"What is it?"

"Some people are coming. Stop work and wait."

The two of them came back toward the corridor and leaned into the shadows so they could watch relatively unseen. But this time, whoever it was had brought a flashlight. The beam moved over the wall as if it had a consciousness of its own. It moved in and out of dark shadows, behind crates and under platforms.

"Maybe they know we're here," Yusuf whispered. He took his long switchblade out of his pocket.

"*Shh.*" Nessim squeezed his arm hard.

Two security guards appeared. They stepped right by the first girder. Although they were both unarmed, Nessim took the .25-caliber automatic out of his belt. Yusuf shifted his weight in anticipation. They could hear the guards talking.

"Well, just like it was last night. What'd I tell ya, Marty. The old man's drinkin' or something."

"Maybe, or maybe there are some kids fuckin' around," Marty said. They were both standing only a few inches away from the first packet of plastique, now firmly placed on the cement footing. The first guard leaned against the girder and took a cigarette out of his top shirt pocket.

"We'll stay down here a while so it'll look like we're really bustin' our balls searchin' the place, but hell, I ain't gonna go crawlin' around all over this filthy basement lookin' for some kids, are you?"

"Hell no."

"What the hell would they be comin' down here this time a night for anyway?"

"I once caught two teenagers screwing down here."

"No shit."

"Yeah. Found 'em in the paper room, doin' it on a coupla cartons of toilet tissue. I heard this moaning and groanin', see, and peered in. There's a coupla asses, moving and grindin' away.

I flipped on the light and the girl, she screamed. The poor son of a bitch had his dingle danglin' in the air."

"Whatcha do?"

"I put the light out again and walked away."

"Big-hearted bastard."

They both laughed. Then Marty lifted the flashlight again and directed it in front of them. He brought the beam around in a slow circle. Nessim and Yusuf anticipated it and when it reached them, they knelt even farther down.

"If they see the plastique," Nessim whispered, "I will have to shoot. Move out quickly. I'll go up and get Clea and join you at the garbage truck entrance."

The beam of light was just above their heads. It lingered there a moment and then moved on to the right. Nessim rose slowly and watched as the guard leaning against the girder suddenly took his cigarette and poked it out by pressing it against the cement footing, only inches above the line of plastique.

"Let's get the fuck outta here now," the guard said.

Marty grunted and they started back down the hall. Nessim and Yusuf remained in the shadows a while longer. Then they stepped out slowly and walked farther into the corridor to check after the guards.

"We'd better hurry now, huh?" Yusuf said.

"No. They've checked out the area. They shouldn't be back. Perhaps someone saw you enter the basement or saw me on the fire escape. In any case, do it carefully. I want this right."

"I will," Yusuf said and went back to his girders.

Nessim stayed out in the corridor listening awhile longer before going back to his cement footings. When he had completed his work, he stuffed the cloth bag behind some pipes and joined Yusuf near the first girder again.

"I wish I could stay with you," Yusuf said. "I wish I could be at your side when you detonate all this."

"You'll be close enough to see and hear it all."

"Maybe you'll need help tomorrow, when you plant the backup."

"No. In any case, stay close to Hamid. I'm still worried about this man Tandem."

"He's been no problem," Yusuf said. Nessim simply stared at him. "All right," Yusuf said. "Let me do something," he added, suddenly smiling. "Give me that marker."

"Why?"

"Just give it to me. Only a moment more. Please."

Nessim handed him the pen and watched as his brother knelt down at the cement footing and began to draw. He created the picture of a small hawk with a sword through it.

"Our symbol," he said. Nessim laughed. Then they embraced again. "Thank you, my brother," Yusuf said, "for making me part of the Seder Project."

"Pray for the day when there are no more Seder Projects," Nessim replied, but Yusuf did not seem to hear or understand him. "Take care going back out. You must not be seen now."

"I won't be. Kiss Clea for me."

"I will."

"See you tomorrow night," Yusuf said. His face was lit with anticipation.

Nessim squeezed his arm and then indicated he should go. He

stood there watching Yusuf move quickly through the corridor and away, clinging to the shadows like a creature of darkness and death. When he was out of sight, Nessim turned to look at the girders and their loaded cement footings once more. Then he made his way to the basement door. The great death was waiting. It was like a sleeping beast that need only be nudged.

24

Nessim opened the door to his room slowly and walked in to face a smiling Paul Tandem, seated on the chair by the dresser. He stood staring in disbelief and then closed the door quietly behind him. Clea, a look of confusion on her face, stood in her bathrobe on the other side of the room. She seemed to have put the most distance possible between herself and Tandem.

"What the hell are you doing here? Are you crazy? How will Yusuf get out safely?"

"Relax," Tandem said, folding his arms across his body and leaning back in the chair, forcing it to tip against the wall. "He knows his way in and out now. It's easy. Don't need me to babysit him."

"Why did you come into the hotel? If they saw you, there'd be questions, wouldn't there?"

"No one's seein' me unless I want them to. I know this place better than the Obermans know it. Is everything set?"

"I don't understand . . . Why . . ." He looked at Clea.

"He came to the door. I thought he had been with you in the basement," she said.

"Is it all set?" Tandem asked again, a more demanding tone of voice directed at Nessim.

"It's all set."

"Good. Now listen to me," he said, sitting up straight again. "There's going to be a slight change in plans."

"What change? Who ordered it?"

"I'm to trigger the detonators and I ordered it," he said, bringing his hands up from his sides. When he did so, he held a snub-nosed .38-caliber revolver in his right hand.

"You can't do this now," Nessim said, eyeing the gun. It wasn't pointed directly at him.

"Oh, but I can and I will. You see, I set out to help you people somehow, someway, to strike out at them Jew bastards, but I never dreamed you'd have something as beautiful as this going, and I never dreamed it would all come roostin' home in the damn New Prospect. No sir. I haven't been able to think of anything else since I learned of this plan. It's beautiful and it's my time, my time," he said, tapping his chest with his thumb. "And I want to own it all."

"But you'll have your revenge if you'll just . . ."

"I want the moment, the pleasure of the damn moment. You don't need it. You just need the job done. What's the difference to you? Give me the transmitter," he said, lifting the pistol higher so it now pointed directly at Nessim.

"What if something should go wrong with the system? Don't you see I need to be on top of it all the way? That's why I'm still here."

"Bullshit. You're here to plant that secondary explosion under

Chaim Eban's table tomorrow. You could've left the hotel tonight and blown these people to hell whenever you felt like it."

"You're wrong," Nessim said. He looked at Clea. She was staring at him now, a look of pain on her face.

"I'm not wrong. What was it we said back in Monroe—it'll be like Samson bringing down the stadium on the Philistines." He looked at Clea and smiled. "Three thousand of 'em, crushed in a mass of timber, cement, and steel. Boy, you people are somethin' else."

"Is this true, Nessim?"

"I won't give you the transmitter," Nessim said. He considered the situation. If he went for his own pistol and shot, the sounds would bring people and the whole project would be ruined. He couldn't do it.

"Oh, I think you will," Tandem said. He changed the direction of the pistol so it faced Clea instead of Nessim. "There's going to be two shots here, and don't think I won't find that transmitter anyway."

"Listen to me."

"Bullshit. You listen to me. I get the transmitter. I'm going down to that basement and wait it out. I have places to hide down there, understand. At dinnertime, I'll trigger the explosion from just outside the building, same as you would do. If you want, you can join me and watch me do it. That make you feel better?"

"Why can't you join me?"

Tandem smiled slowly.

"You guys didn't think of that before, did you? You used me, got all the information, pictures, and diagrams. I steered you in and out, made it all possible for ya, but no one said, 'You go along, Tandem. You earned it. You be there.' No sir."

"We thought you'd be seen. It would raise questions. You yourself said . . ."

"Maybe, or maybe you were all just finished using me. I want to be the one holding that transmitter," he said, pointing his thumb at himself. "I'll press the button that brings down this hotel. No one else. I earned it, damn it," he said, his face straining. Clea shook her head and backed against the wall. "Now give me that fuckin' device. NOW!" he shouted.

Nessim looked at him for a few moments and then moved slowly to the suitcase. He opened it and took out a small leather pouch. The transmitter was actually a modified FM wireless microphone. It was no bigger than the palm of his hand. As he took it out of the pouch, he considered leaving the battery out of it so Tandem couldn't trigger the detonators on his own, but then he realized he'd eventually check for that and what if he didn't get the battery to him—the explosives wouldn't be set off and all the work would be wasted. No, he had to give him the loaded device. He stared at it for a moment and then turned to give it to Tandem.

"Easy," Tandem said. "Put it on the bed there."

Nessim placed it on the blanket. Tandem looked at it for a moment and then looked at Nessim.

"Is the battery in there too?"

"No."

"Put it beside it. Go on," he demanded. Nessim reached into the pouch and took out the small round, flat-surfaced battery and placed it beside the transmitter.

"You must be sure that the transmitter is not on when you put the battery inside it; otherwise, the mere contact of the points will send out the signal."

"I know, I know," Tandem said. He was hypnotized by the device.

Nessim considered jumping him. Tandem seemed to sense it. He raised his pistol again.

"Step back now. Back."

Nessim obeyed. Tandem reached out and took the transmitter into his left hand. Then he scooped up the battery and put it into his shirt pocket.

"Where will you wait?"

"I told you. In the basement."

"They've been inspecting it—security guards."

"Have they?"

"Someone might have seen me or Yusuf enter the basement."

"Don't worry, they'll never find me."

"How will I find you?"

"I'll be right outside the basement entranceway at 7:20 p.m., but I won't wait for you. Be there on time or you won't get to see me trigger it," he said, smiling, and looked at the transmitter again. "It's like having a small atom bomb in your hands."

"You can't detonate until 7:20 because I'll have the secondary explosion set for that time and I don't want it to go off before or after," Nessim said. "We'd better synchronize our watches."

"Yeah, sure," Tandem said, but he looked uninterested. Nessim worried about that. He walked over to his suitcase again and took out a small watch without a wristband.

"This is the one I will be using on the packet I place in the dining room," Nessim said approaching. "Put out your watch."

Tandem did so, but he held the pistol straight up, pointed at Nessim's head.

"Careful, buddy. I know you people are trained to cut throats quickly."

Reluctantly, Nessim synchronized the two watches, winding both to be sure they would not run out. Then he stepped back, looking at Clea. She was frozen in her position and wore an expression of horror and fear. At that moment, Nessim hated Tandem more than anyone else in the entire hotel, in fact, in the whole occupied territory which included Israel proper.

"Great," Tandem said. "Everything's cool now." He stood up. "Don't do anything stupid. Move back to that bed and sit down. Do it," he commanded. Slowly, Nessim backed up to the bed and sat. "It's all going to work out the way you planned it anyway, so don't go callin' in the dogs. Hear?" He walked to the door. "See ya at 7:20," he added, smiling as he backed out of the room. When the door was closed, Clea began to sob.

"Bastard," Nessim said. "I knew he was dangerous. I knew he couldn't be trusted. He's a man crazed with revenge."

"How are you any better?" she said, looking up through tear-filled eyes. "You're planning on killing all those people, Nessim. All those people!"

"You knew it."

"Maybe deep in my mind I feared it, but I prayed it wasn't true. You told me you were here to kill one man. Of course some would die with him, but all of them? My God, Nessim, there are so many children."

"There are so many children in Jordan and Palestine and Syria. What about our children?"

She shook her head and walked away. He got up and followed her, angry now that she was so outraged.

"You live in a dream. What did you think my work was—a game of checkers? You always knew what I had to do in this country and how I had to do it. Why this sudden remorse?"

She didn't respond. Instead she went into the bathroom and ran the water to splash her face. He followed, worked up now by what had happened with Tandem and by how she was acting toward him and the mission. He had never felt so frustrated.

"I don't know," she said, shaking her head. "I don't know. Suddenly, looking at that man's face when he spoke about the death of three thousand people—his sense of pleasure." She turned to him. "You're united, both out to do the same thing."

"But for different reasons." He nearly shouted.

"Will that really matter after it's done?"

"Of course. It's a blow for the cause, for our people, for my father," he said, pounding his fist into his hand. "For your father," he added softly.

"My father would never want this," she replied.

He stared at her. He realized now he had been wrong to hide the details, the intentions, the full significance of the mission from her. Instinctively, he had played it down, knowing all along how she would react. And he was afraid of her reaction, afraid of what it would awaken in him.

It was a mistake to have met her, a mistake to have fallen in love, to have taken her with him to America. Sardin was right. She would make him hesitate, reconsider. She was soft and human and kindled compassion within him. It was the one thing a terrorist could not tolerate, the one thing a terrorist must smother inside of himself—compassion. A front fighter for the cause must only think of the cause. They were the enemy—all of them, the entire hotel's population. To think of them as just ordinary people would be tragic and self-defeating, and that's just what she was causing him to do. He hated and loved her for it.

"You don't understand," he finally said and turned away. She stepped out of the bathroom and touched his shoulder. He looked at her, but only for a moment. There was too much soft beauty confronting him.

"Oh, Nessim, what have you become?" she asked.

"I was always what I am now, ever since the first day you met me. You were either deliberately blind to it or . . ."

"Or you hid it well from me. And if you did, you knew yourself you were something you hated. Because if I hated it, you hated it."

"Leave me be," he said, pushing her away.

"You're right. I knew, but I refused to know. I suspected, but forced myself to believe other things—thinking of you as just a different kind of soldier doing your duty as you were commanded to do it. I'm partly to blame, but looking at that man . . ."

"I'm not like him," he insisted. They stared at each other for a moment.

"I pray to God you're not," she said.

He turned away from her and began to undress again. He wanted to get back into bed and think. Everything was going crazy around him. Tandem's betrayal, Clea's shock and outrage, his own new doubts—all of it happened too quickly. He had to digest it. Then he thought of Yusuf's pleasure and eagerness, how that always annoyed him, terrified him. He saw part of himself in his brother and he hated it.

After a while, Clea turned the lights out and lay down beside him. He felt her hand search for his and find it. They lay there in the darkness, silent.

A new thought made its way into his visions of tomorrow. Tandem now had the massive lethal capability in his possession. What was to stop him from triggering it at any time, during breakfast or lunch? What guarantee was there that he would sit it out in that basement and wait for dinner? How important was the death of Chaim Eban to Tandem anyway? He wasn't in this for the political reasons. He was only out for some crazy vengeance. He could grow impatient, eager. Perhaps he would put the battery in prematurely and accidentally set off the plastique. Anything was possible.

And then, Clea and he would be in that dining room, potential victims of his own creative death. What irony! When he closed his eyes, he saw the ceiling and fixtures coming down on them. He saw Clea's broken body bleeding beside him. Earlier, when he had envisioned it all in the dining room, he hadn't even looked up over his own table. What was above it? Was there a chandelier there? A heavy beam? Was the boiler directly below them? He couldn't remember.

All this happened because the command made use of a man like Tandem. That had bothered him from the start. Where was their sense of principle, their ideals? They corrupt and destroy themselves by choosing madmen for allies. His father once told him that men on a battlefield were indistinguishable from men in asylums. They babble, they talk to themselves, they defecate in their pants, they see visions. Perhaps Clea was right, but even if she was, it was too late.

I have to get that transmitter back, he thought. *I have to.* And then he thought, *But even if I do and we're not in there at the time, the explosion is going to kill us because it will kill what we had between us.* Her fingers tightened on his hand. *But that's our sacrifice for the cause,* he concluded.

He tried desperately to remember his father in death, but he could only think of him in life. He had Yusuf on his shoulders and was bouncing him as they walked. Yusuf screamed with delight and his father laughed. Yusuf's small hands had clumps of his father's hair between the fingers as he grasped it for security. The memory made Nessim smile and then it tore at his heart. He wanted to cry, he wanted to be afraid, he wanted to be sorry, but most of all, he longed for the protection of his anger and his dedication. Where was it when he needed it the most?

Clea's fingers loosened their grip, but he clung to them. He clung to them desperately, like a man clinging to life. He finally found sleep, and when he awoke in the morning, her fingers were still entwined in his.

25

Yusuf hesitated when the entranceway through the garage came into view. He heard voices and stopped. As he waited, he began to think. They had experienced a close call back there. Those two security men had been inches away from discovering the plastique. What if they had? The project would have been aborted and all the planning lost. Perhaps they would have had to shoot their way out of the hotel and either Nessim or he or both of them might have been killed. It was too close, and considering how near they were to the time of the explosions, what a shame it would have been. He looked back down the dark basement corridor. What if the guards or someone went back to that spot before Nessim triggered the plastique?

The material remained exposed. Granted, it wasn't easy to see it, but someone might. They should have planned for that. There should have been some consideration of the possibility.

True, the Claw had asked Nessim to plant a backup device, but that was only designed to kill Chaim Eban and a few people at his table. The main thrust of the project could be lost.

Yusuf knew what he had to do, despite the fact that Nessim wouldn't approve and no one had suggested it. He had to go back there and guard the explosives, linger in the darkness, well hidden, and wait. It was a considerable time, but he could do it. Afterward, they'd all be grateful to him, and it would have been his way of really making up for his mistakes in the city. They would especially be grateful if someone did discover the plastique and he stopped him before he could report it.

Hamid would wonder why he didn't return. At first, they would be worried that he had been caught leaving the basement, but after a while, they would realize that wasn't the case and they would know he was still in the hotel. They'd realize what he was doing. They might send Tandem back for him. That was always a possibility; but if he came back, Yusuf would explain it to him.

He turned away from the entrance to the garage and scurried back up the basement corridor. When he got to the girders again, he stopped and considered the possible hiding places from where he could observe. He decided to go in a ways and sit behind one of the girders. It was very late now, so he could get a few hours of sleep. In the morning, he'd watch and he'd wait.

When neither Yusuf nor Tandem returned, Hamid could only think of one reason—they had been discovered. It meant, of course, that Nessim wouldn't plant the explosives. The entire project was ruined. He shook with disappointment and got into the front of the car to drive away. He'd have to report this failure to the Claw. He wondered what sort of danger Nessim would be in now and if they would be able to get him out of the hotel safely.

It was probably all Tandem's fault. Somehow he had messed things up, Hamid was sure of it. He drove back toward the hotel slowly, expecting all sorts of police cars parked in front of the garage entrance, their roof lights turning. But it was deadly silent and deserted there. The pale, sickly glow of lights coming from the garage lit an empty area. There wasn't a man in sight. He hesitated, wondering. Perhaps they were discovered inside. But Tandem wasn't to go inside. It was very confusing. All he could do was report to the Claw and wait until morning. Then he would risk a call to Nessim.

Paul Tandem clutched the transmitter closely to his body and came down a side stairwell as slowly and as cautiously as he could. There'd be no mistakes now. He had planned it all this way. As soon as he had understood their strategy and realized the potential in it, he plotted his betrayal. Of course, it really wasn't a betrayal. He was just changing the order of things. What difference did it make how it was done as long as it was done? They'd hate him for it, and they might even want to kill him for it, but he'd be ready for them later on. Right now he couldn't think of that. He had what he wanted.

Holding the transmitter and having the small battery in his pocket wasn't enough, though. He had to see the plastique planted and confirm in his mind that it was all there, ready to blow the building and kill the people. He'd inspect Nessim's work and then he'd go into hiding. There was a rather large shelf near the ceiling in one of the storage rooms. He'd make a spot for himself up there and sleep and wait. When he was ready, he'd come down to do the job.

*   *   *

Yusuf heard footsteps and pressed his body hard against the wall behind him, staying safely in the protection of the darkness. While he did so, he took out his knife and released the blade. The cool metal reassured him. He waited. Lucky he had made this decision, he thought. Lucky he was here. A figure appeared on the right, moving slowly, suspiciously. Was it Nessim returning to check something? This man approached in an unusual manner. He wasn't a custodian or a security guard. Who was it?

He leaned out of the shadows to get a clearer view. When the figure moved into the light, he saw that it was Paul Tandem. Back for him already? And coming from the opposite direction? It didn't make sense. He didn't want to call out for fear that someone else somewhere in the basement would hear him. So he moved silently down the side of the wall toward Tandem.

Tandem stopped at the first girder and knelt down to study the plastique packet and the detonator. He smiled appreciatively and touched the plastique. Then he looked up the girder and nodded to himself. Yes, it was all going to go. Everything was ready. He looked down at the transmitter and then put it safely into his top pocket, next to the battery. Just then, he heard someone in the shadows. Feet scraped against the concrete floor. He peered into the darkness and saw Yusuf beckoning.

"What the hell are you doing here yet?" he asked.

Yusuf raised his finger to his lips. "*Shh.*" He continued to beckon for Tandem to approach.

Could Nessim have called out for help? Did he somehow make

contact with Hamid already and did Hamid send Yusuf back? How could they do it? Yet he had to be careful. A man with Nessim's capabilities might have done anything by now. They were pretty damn sneaky people. They might have had some code all along and never told him. Maybe they had anticipated his action and were set for it.

Tandem fingered his pistol. No, he wouldn't shoot the bastard. That would bring people down the corridor. The sound would reverberate against these walls and bounce up and down the basement. Yusuf continued to beckon. Why didn't he just come out? He wanted him to go into the darkness too. He was acting strange. Tandem smiled to himself. *All right, buddy*, he thought, *we'll play it your way*.

He moved toward him slowly. Yusuf remained crouched against the wall. When Tandem got closer, he saw the knife in Yusuf's hands. Yusuf held it to his side. He wasn't thinking about it, but to Tandem it appeared as though Yusuf was trying to be sneaky, keeping it down against his thigh.

"Where are you comin' from?" Yusuf asked. "Did Hamid send you?"

"Hamid?" Tandem stood a foot back.

"Yes. I'm staying here," Yusuf said with determination. "To make sure nothing goes wrong with the plan."

"Nothing, huh?"

"Nothing," Yusuf said, his face screwed in confidence, his mind made up. Tandem saw it as a challenge. He did not understand Yusuf's fanaticism. He eyed the knife and moved slightly to his left. Yusuf remained crouched; set to spring, Tandem thought. He imagined this was his intention.

"You go back," Yusuf said and gestured with his knife.

"I'll go back, sure," Tandem said, and then he lashed out with a quick kick of his right foot. The boot caught Yusuf just under the chin, snapping his head back with such force that a thin line of blood ripped across his lower neck where the skin tore. His head smashed against the cement wall just behind him and he sat down hard. He still clutched his knife.

Tandem didn't hesitate. He drove another kick into Yusuf's ribs, feeling the bones give way. Yusuf groaned in surprise and pain and tried desperately to turn out of the path of the foot that was coming down toward his Adam's apple. He put his left arm up and caught the heel against his elbow. The contact stunned his arm, sending a vibration through his body, but he was able to swing his right hand around fast enough to drive the knife into the top of Tandem's boot. It caught his foot just above the ankle. The leather of the boot prevented the blade from going in too deeply, but the pain sent Tandem back.

Yusuf struggled to get to his feet before Tandem charged in again. He didn't understand the reason for the attack or the viciousness of it, but he understood that he was suddenly battling for his life. A series of sharp, needlelike pains ripped down the side of his body where Tandem had kicked him, but he got to his feet anyway.

He crouched in readiness, knife out. Tandem began circling to his left and then to his right. Yusuf's head was spinning. He fought the dizziness frantically, sensing that his mind was trying to turn off, black out, and retreat from the ugliness of the pain and the threat of death, but he refused to lose consciousness.

"What's wrong . . . with you? Why are you . . . doing this?"

"You ain't gonna stop me, you little bastard," Tandem said. "It's mine, mine." He touched his shirt pocket, but Yusuf did not understand.

Suddenly Tandem launched at Yusuf, coming at him the way a ballplayer slides into base. It was the beginning of a scissors-grip takedown. His legs caught Yusuf's left ankle between them and Tandem turned his body, holding the ankle. The effect was immediate and hard to resist. Yusuf had no alternative but to go with the pressure. He went over, slapping down hard on his right side. It drove excruciating pain into his body. The knife slipped out of his hand and rolled a few feet away. He reached for it in a futile act of desperation.

Tandem was on him immediately. Yusuf felt the weight of Tandem's body forcing him against the floor of the basement. It was useless to fight it. Despite his great reluctance to do so, he knew now that he had to scream for help. He kept thinking it would mean the end of the project, but he had no alternative. It was, after all, a matter of life or death—and disappointingly, he chose life. He wasn't the front fighter he dreamed of being. In his attempt to let out that howl, that scream for help, he instantly came to despise himself. His animal drive for life forced him to do it, but his thirst for meaning condemned him for it.

Just as Yusuf began to scream, Tandem caught him around the throat with his forearm. It had the effect of smothering the attempt. Now, with the man's body pressing him down and the pain chasing him all over his body, Yusuf made his final effort. Tandem's grip was viselike and the bone of his forearm like steel. Yusuf tried turning his neck to deflect the pressure onto a less vulnerable portion, but it was impossible.

The pressure soon began to cut off his air. He pulled at the arm with all his might, but it did not budge. It did not give a fraction of an inch. He began to choke and cough in little spurts. He thought he tasted his own blood popping out along the inside of his throat. His tongue got caught between his teeth and he bit into it spasmodically.

When he knew he was going to die and there was no longer any use to struggle, he released his fingers from Tandem's arm. As the darkness began closing in, he wondered only one thing—why? He wanted to simply ask it—to have that one last favor. But it was not to be. His lips mouthed the word unseen and then his body went totally limp.

Tandem squeezed on for a few moments after Yusuf died. He knew he had killed him, but the muscles of his body had been launched into a frenzied pace and it was impossible to just call them to an immediate halt. His whole body, tensed and set, with all his strength driving toward the great hold on Yusuf's neck, cooled slowly. He took his arm away and let Yusuf fall to the floor. Then he stood up and leaned against the wall. The muscles in his arm and shoulder twitched. It was only then that he began to feel the pain in his foot where Yusuf had managed to stab him. The great effort to kill had made him forget it.

He slipped his boot off and touched the spot. It was damp with his blood. He hopped into the light and looked at it. There was a small gash. The blood was deceptive. It wasn't half as bad as it looked. He went back to Yusuf's body and ripped a piece of material out of his shirt, using it to tie the wound on his foot. Then he put the boot back on, experiencing some annoying pain as he did so. He cursed and sat back against the wall, staring at Yusuf's body.

What he would do now, he thought, was drag the body all the

way back against the far girders and stuff it in behind one. No one would discover it before the great explosions and then it would join in with a few thousand others. He laughed at the irony in that.

Then he tapped his shirt pocket to make sure that the transmitter was still there. It wasn't.

A surge of great fear shot through him. He panicked, stood up quickly, and began a wild search for the small device. Had they crushed it in the battle? Had it slid away, under something, never to be found? He got down on his hands and knees and began crawling in small circles around and around Yusuf's body. He tried to keep his cool. *I'll do this scientifically*, he thought, *until I find it. I'll make larger and larger circles gradually. I'll look forever.*

But he didn't look long before he found it. When he did so, he sat up and inspected it carefully. It looked all right. *If there was only a way to test it and be sure*, he thought. He remembered that the battery had been in his pocket too. He felt for that. It was there. All was okay again. He breathed a sigh of relief and turned back to the problem of Yusuf's body.

He was tired, nearly exhausted because of the great physical and emotional drain, but he had to get that body out of there now. He started dragging it by the feet. It was so heavy it took all his remaining strength to move it. When he finally got Yusuf's body hidden behind the deepest girder, he collapsed beside it and tried to catch his breath. He was there for the longest time, and nearly fell asleep. When he looked at his watch, he was shocked to discover that more than an hour and a half had gone by since he first confronted Yusuf. It was just about sunrise.

He got up and made his way slowly back to the main corridor. From there he moved to the storage room. By the time he crawled up on the high shelf and made a place for himself, he was shaking with fatigue. He closed his eyes, holding the palm of his hand up against the transmitter in his pocket. It was all still his. They had tried, but they hadn't taken it away. Now they would have to live with him in control. The thought comforted him and he was able to fall asleep with a smile on his face.

26

Although it was early morning, Nessim had been lying there with his eyes open for quite a while, so when the phone rang, it did not wake him. Clea stirred and wiped her eyes. He lifted the receiver and said hello. It was Hamid. Nessim sat up quickly and swung his feet out over the bed.

"Neither Tandem nor Yusuf came out of the hotel last night. Mr. Y. is very upset. Can you explain?"

"Only about Tandem. He . . . has the transmitter."

"How?"

"I met him in my room afterward. There was no other way." His tone of voice told all.

"So that was why he was so anxious to bring Yusuf into the building."

"Yes."

"And now, where is he?"

"Somewhere below."

"Yusuf?"

"Probably remained. Stubborn."

"All was set then?"

"Yes."

"Do you think Tandem will follow our schedule?"

"No way of knowing. Says he will."

"About number 2. Do it as soon as you can now. The sooner the better, Mr. Y. says."

"I know. Sometime before lunch, perhaps. Then I will search for Yusuf."

"Is that wise?"

"I must do it."

"Very well. I shall go on as planned and be where I am supposed to be."

"Understood," Nessim said. He heard Hamid hang up.

At first the thought of Yusuf being in the basement angered him, but then he realized he might very well have met up with Tandem, and Tandem was a crazed lunatic. If his brother discovered that Tandem had betrayed them, he would surely try to take him and get the transmitter back.

"What's happening now?" Clea asked.

"Yusuf didn't leave the hotel last night as he was supposed to."

"What did he do?" She sat up, pushing her hair back.

"He must've stayed in the basement. I told him to go, but he was anxious to be right with me when I . . . detonated the explosives. He wants to be part of all of it."

"Then he'll be down there all day, waiting somewhere in the basement." She shook her head and lay back.

"I'll go down and look for him later."

"What about Tandem?"

"I don't know."

"Will you try to stop him?"

"Stop him? I'll try to get back control of things, that's what I'll do," he said.

She turned over on her side, giving him her back. He took his pistol off the night table and inspected it.

"I won't go down to breakfast," she said. "Or lunch. I won't leave this room."

He considered it. He was wondering how to keep the two of them out of the dining room anyway. Thoughts of an anxious Tandem holding that transmitter worried him. Of course, he'd have to think of a way to get her out of the building itself during the meal hours. The whole structure should topple, and they were located above the dining room.

"Okay," he said quickly. She turned around and looked at him.

"You don't care?"

"If it's what you want. We can eat in the luncheonette. Maybe go for a walk."

She studied him for a moment. He was too easy about it, putting up no resistance. After all, she had been brought along to maintain a semblance of normalcy, harmlessness—just another Jewish couple on Passover. Why didn't he complain?

"What if you don't get back control of things?" she asked. He didn't reply. "Tandem will do what he wants when he wants, is that it?"

"I don't know."

"Then if we were in the dining room, we might be . . . He could explode it at any time—during breakfast or lunch, couldn't he? Couldn't he?"

"Yes," he said. He slammed his fist against the mattress.

"Then I will go down."

"What?" He turned quickly. "What if I don't find him?"

"Then disconnect your bombs," she said, her face solid with determination, "and make it impossible for him to do anything."

He considered. There was a much greater risk of being seen down in the basement during the day and he hadn't planted the backup bomb in the dining room yet. If someone saw him near the girders . . . Yet, it was the solution for the present. *Actually*, he thought, *all I'd have to do is block the contact, so even if the switches were closed, there'd be no electrical impulse.*

"You know," he said, smiling at her. "You've got an idea."

"Then you'll do it?"

"I'll do it right now," he said and reached for his shirt and pants.

Two chambermaids, both at least in their late fifties, spoke in low voices as they approached Nessim in the basement. He tried looking as casual as he could. No one would know he didn't belong down here if he kept his cool, he thought. *I can always say I have some business with the stagecraft people or the laundry.* The chambermaids did stare at him as they passed in the corridor, but they didn't stop to talk. He didn't look back, imagining they might be doing the same thing and it would look too suspicious. A custodian came down the corridor, walking very quickly. Nessim continued at his same pace; the man, muttering to himself, didn't even look at Nessim as they passed each other.

There was no one else in the basement corridor for the moment. He stopped and looked around. The doorway to one of the storage rooms was wide open. Where would either of them hide? He wondered. It would have to be in one of these rooms. He approached the doorway slowly, listening attentively for voices or sounds. There were none, and when he looked inside, he saw that it was simply a room for cleaning equipment—powders, brooms, mops. It smelled of ammonia. He walked on.

He approached the girder area slowly, thinking as he did so that if someone came down the corridor now, he'd just walk past and return afterward. He couldn't risk being seen going into the belly of the building. That would look too suspicious, especially to a custodial person. He heard women talking some distance behind him, but when he turned, they weren't yet in sight. Without any further hesitation, he scurried in between the first girder and the wall to disappear within the protection of the now very familiar shadows.

He waited as the women, more chambermaids, passed the area, and then he began work on the first detonator. If Tandem triggered them, they would close, permitting a point to touch the positive side of each penlight battery, thus completing the circuit. He placed a small piece of cardboard against the little batteries securely. There'd be no contact and therefore no detonation until he removed each. He would also be able to tell whether or not Tandem had indeed triggered the transmitter prematurely—for if he did, the switches would have been thrown.

He moved quickly, covering each detonator as he came to it. He reached the last two and, cursing to himself, crawled in to get at the one on the left first. That done, he came out of the area and crossed the belly of the building to take care of the one final detonator remaining on the right.

Seeing Yusuf's hand immediately upon approaching the girder, he jerked back with surprise. When he touched it, he felt the cold skin, and the shock of recognition became a surge of terrible fear. He tugged at the arm and his brother's body slid out toward him, the eyes still opened, the face stuck in an expression of intense pain.

"Yusuf," he said. He brought his fingers to his brother's face. During the last few years, Nessim had grown accustomed to the feel of death. It had become an all too familiar acquaintance. He looked for signs of blood, wounds, or blows on his brother's body. Yusuf stared at him with a glazed look of accusation now. Nessim was repulsed. He had, after all, brought him in to all this. He reached up and closed his brother's eyes.

His feelings weren't all that clear yet. After the surprise and shock came the indifference built in him for experiencing death so often in the recent past. Slowly, that was followed by a great sense of indignation and anger. His brother had been murdered by the madman, the same man who might yet steal the glory of his work. He wanted to yell, to swing about wildly, to pound something, but he could only sit and stare at the body of his brother.

Then his mood changed radically. The sadness and the sorrow seized him. He had to mourn for everyone, do the mourning for his parents as well as for himself. He felt Yusuf's deep embrace again, and even though he hadn't done much of it for a long time, he heard the sound of his laughter. He thought of the quickness in his eyes, the moodiness of his temperament. All the small things about him paraded through Nessim's mind, but most of all Nessim remembered how much Yusuf had idolized him.

He swallowed hard and sat limply for a while, fighting back tears. There was no time to cry now. Later, in the quietude of respite, he would do his crying. As much as he hated the idea, he would have to leave Yusuf's body just where it was. There would be no burial. His remains would be lost in the rubble, and suddenly he longed for that. *Bring on the explosions and the death*, he thought. *Let it come.*

Keeping track of his mission, he deadened the final switch and then sat his brother's body up straight again. He looked at him once more. "I'll see you one more time, my brother; when I return to activate the switches, I'll say our final good-bye then." He turned away and crawled to where he could listen for voices and footsteps. Then he moved out and dusted himself off. He got back to the corridor quickly and for a fleeting moment he thought about going after Tandem right then, searching the basement completely until he found him and killed him. But then he realized he couldn't risk the battle. First he had to consider his mission. The secondary bomb must be planted. When that was done, he would have his time and he would have his revenge.

Barry Wintraub woke with a start. Shirley was still asleep beside him. Some part of his brain, working like an alarm clock, signaled the morning. As he sat up, he realized this wasn't just another morning. This was the day Chaim Eban was to arrive. This was the third day. They were into the countdown. Things had to be done quickly and efficiently.

As usual, the boys were up arguing with each other. Their verbal battle built and built until one struck the other and the sound of crying began the symphony of noise Barry called "Family Togetherness." A little more impatient than usual, Barry seized them both by the backs of their necks and shook them a lot more fiercely than they were used to. They grew silent immediately.

"I don't want any of this today, understand. I want a good day out of both of you."

"But he hit me," Jason said.

"He poked me first."

"I'm not interested in how the fight started. The fight is over. All fights for the day are over."

They both looked down, totally disappointed. Barry stared at them a moment longer and then went into the bathroom to shave. Afterward, when they were all dressed and walking across the grounds to go to breakfast, Barry described to Shirley what he was going to ask her to do.

"Remember I told you I would need your help on this case?"

"Oh yeah."

"Well, after breakfast, I'm gonna want you to accuse a woman of stealing your wallet out of your pocketbook."

"You're what?"

"You heard me. All you'll do is point to her and say, 'That's her.' I'll take it from there."

"But . . ."

"Can you do that?"

"Sure I can do it, but what's it all about?"

"I'll explain the whole thing afterward."

They dropped the kids off in the children's dining room and joined Karl Trustman in the lobby.

"Chaim Eban will be here at three o'clock," he said.

"Uh-huh. Right after breakfast we'll have a short meeting in Oberman's office. Then we'll work on this Casewell woman."

"Can you point her out to me in the dining room?"

"Sure."

After they entered, Barry showed Trustman Brenda Casewell's table and indicated which woman she was. He studied her for a moment and then nodded.

"You know her?"

"No," he said quickly, but after they sat at their table, Barry noticed that Trustman continually looked across the dining room to study the Casewell woman.

Nessim had decided that he wouldn't tell Clea about Yusuf until everything was over. It was much too disturbing, and he knew there would be trouble if she found out about his death.

"Did you find Yusuf?"

"I did," he said. "Just as I thought. Stubborn. Stayed behind."

"Won't he be hungry down there all day?"

"I'll get something to him later."

"What about Tandem?"

"No sign of him."

"But you made it impossible for him to do the explosion?"

"Yes."

She breathed relief. It was a partial victory. She was conniving. After he had planted the bomb under Eban's table, she intended to try her hardest to get him to leave the hotel and not reactivate the other explosives. She'd give it her best effort. She began now, by being warm to him.

"Will you want me to help you later, when you do the other bomb?"

"No, I don't want you involved at all."

"But I am involved."

"Only in a very slight way," he said. He was trying to give her the gift of a free conscience, but she refused it.

"If I'm part of you, I'm part of what you do."

"Think whatever you wish," he said. He seemed harder, even more resigned than before. "You'll stay in the room while I'm doing it. When it's finished, I'll . . ."

"What?"

"I'll come up," he said. He didn't want her to know that he intended to hunt for Tandem, all day if necessary.

"Nessim."

"Yes?"

"You still . . . I mean, we still . . ."

"Yes," he said, but he didn't look at her. He took her arm and they went to breakfast. He pushed all thoughts of Yusuf out of his mind, fighting them back by thinking only of the work that had to be done. When they got to their table, he looked up. There was a chandelier above them. It could have been disastrous.

"Everyone knows my wife?" Barry asked when they were all seated in David Oberman's office.

"All but me," Tom Boggs said. He smiled. "I'm Tom Boggs."

"I'm nervous," Shirley said.

David laughed anxiously.

"That's because we're going to use her," Barry explained. "To accuse Brenda Casewell."

"Oh," David said. "For a moment there I thought she knew more than we did."

"Tom's man is on her right now," Barry began. "As soon as we leave here, we'll go to wherever she is and Shirley will say that's the woman who took her wallet out of her purse while they were both in the ladies' room."

"She's gone back to her room," Boggs said. "As of now."

"That's perfect. Then we'll search the room and naturally find the pistol."

"Then what?" David said. "Arrest her and get her out of the building?"

"Not right away. We'll put a man outside her door and tell her we're going to investigate the gun. It's my hope that she'll panic and, in that time when we leave her alone, call someone in this hotel. That someone is our other party."

"And if she doesn't?" Trustman said.

"At least we'll have taken care of one potential source of danger."

"Okay," David said. "Get to it. The faster this is all over, the better. Everyone's starting to get jumpy around here. Even my father. Claims he saw people on the fire escape late at night."

"Fire escape?" Trustman said, his eyes narrowing.

"Yeah. We checked it out, but security found nothing."

"Okay," Barry said, standing. "Let's get the switchboard operator set then. We've got to know everything Brenda Casewell does and everything she says."

"Some Passover," Shirley muttered, but no one but Barry heard her.

27

Lillian Rothberg and the Obermans had a little surprise for the guests. They kept it secret until about an hour after breakfast. Most activities in the hotel didn't begin until ten—the health club not opening, nor the pool, skating rink, or field house. Many people milled around in the lobby, just outside the dining room door.

Nessim and Clea sat on a love seat that was against the wall just to the right of the main desk. He eyed the doors to the dining room. The packet of plastique and the detonator, all set to be planted, were in his jacket pocket. At this moment he was wondering how he would get the opportunity to do it. Then the Rothberg-Oberman surprise began. It was perfect for him.

A group of the hotel's regular stage musicians set up in the rear of the lobby, and without any previous announcement or warning, suddenly began to play Israeli and Jewish music. They went right into the hora, and groups of guests formed small circles, laughing and shouting, to dance. It was all designed to get the people into the right mood for Chaim Eban's arrival. The lobby became a banquet hall. Bellhops joined in. Some of the receptionists were pulled away from their desks to hold hands in the circles. A security guard at the door was scooped up by a passing group. Everyone participated. It became a spontaneous outburst of joy.

"This is my opportunity," Nessim said to Clea. "You go up to the room or they'll pull you into the dancing too."

"Be careful," she said, touching his arm. He patted her on the hand and got up. She went to the elevator, looking back only once. When she was gone, he made his way gradually and unobtrusively toward the dining room door. Three women, seated on a nearby couch, got up with their arms entwined and began laughing and kicking their way into a circle of people. The end woman reached out for him, but he smiled and backed away.

"No, no, thank you. I have a bad leg."

She didn't want to argue. They were off. Relieved, he inched farther toward the door. The attention of just about everyone was turned to the music and the dancing now. Mrs. Adelman came out of her back office, looked over the scene, and then went back to her work. Nessim halted his advance when the doorway to David Oberman's office opened and a group of people came out. Three men and a woman made their way across the lobby to the elevators and paid little attention to the festivities. One of the men looked very familiar to him. He studied his face a little while longer. He had seen his picture somewhere—in a briefing once. That was it. He was a member of Israeli security. Nessim turned his back and paused. When that group entered the elevator, he waited no longer. He slipped into the dining room.

The tables were all set for lunch. He heard some voices coming out of the kitchen, but other than that, the dining room was apparently deserted. He waited to be sure no one was lingering down the other side, no one who would see him go to his knees at the Oberman-Eban table. Then he hurried across the dining room, stopping at their table. When he was sure it was clear, he went down and crawled underneath. He worked quickly, placing the packet where it was sure to catch its best advantage. Most likely, the table would splinter into hundreds of sharp wooden and plastic projectiles anyway, he thought. If the impact of the explosion didn't kill Eban, that would. Of course, it would kill everyone else around the table too, and possibly a number of people at nearby tables. All that synchronized with the major explosions and the collapse of the building was sure to get rid of some of the Hezbollah's worst enemies.

When he was finished, he came up slowly. A busboy had come out of the kitchen and was changing some arrangements at his table, located near the center of the room. Nessim, on all fours, waited and watched. The busboy stepped back and inspected his own work.

When he turned and left the room, Nessim did not wait for another staff member to appear. He shot up quickly and began walking toward the door. He was nearly there when a voice cried out. It was the maître d'. Incredibly, the man had been sitting behind his desk all the time. He was so involved in his work that he hadn't spotted Nessim until just then and Nessim had not seen him there, crouched over his papers.

"Can I help you, sir?"

"Er . . . no. I'm afraid not. My wife thought she left her shawl here at the table, but apparently . . ."

"No, no one's reported any garments left."

"Yes, well, she probably never brought it down with her."

The maître d' just nodded, smiling stupidly. Nessim walked out. The other man looked after him and shook his head. Some of the guests were weirdos all right. Wouldn't he have known if his wife had worn her shawl into the dining room? Who could figure it? He went back to his work.

"Shirley will stand back," Barry said, "until we make entry into the room." Boggs nodded. Trustman just stared at the closed door. Boggs, who had seen the pistol inside, was the most nervous of all. His fingers fidgeted against the weapon in his jacket. He had only shot it half a dozen times on the shooting range. He never really handled a gun before he took the job. The Obermans got him a permit. As head of security, he was the only one to carry a gun. It was the way they wanted it.

Shirley, a half smile on her face, stood back to observe her husband in action. She had seen detectives and policemen make entry into suspects' apartments and houses on television and she was now going to find out if it was done that way in real life. Barry unbuttoned his jacket and knocked firmly on the door. He stepped back. She was proud of his professional posture. *My mother should see him now*, she thought.

Brenda Casewell opened the door slowly and looked out. She was clothed in a dress and had her hair pinned up neatly, but she wore no shoes. When Barry was satisfied as to the safety of the situation, he nodded gently to Boggs.

"Yes?" Brenda said. Boggs stepped in front of Barry.

"Mrs. Casewell. I'm Tom Boggs, head of hotel security."

"Yes?"

"We've got a rather sticky situation here," he went on, taking the deepest, most authoritative voice he could. "An accusation has been made against you."

"Accusation?"

"Yes. By Mrs. Bagglesdorf." They had decided to change names, and Shirley took on another character. Boggs turned and pointed to her. Shirley stepped forward.

"That's her," she said. She had stuck a wad of Jason's bubble gum into her mouth and chewed on it rather ostentatiously.

"Huh?" Brenda said.

"I'm afraid we'll have to come in," Boggs said and stepped past her. Everyone but Trustman followed. He remained outside, waiting and watching in the hallway.

"What the hell is this?"

"Did you use the ladies' room in the lobby today?" Boggs asked.

Barry moved so that he stood between Brenda and the closet.

"I did not."

"This lady says you did."

"She certainly did," Shirley said. "I'd remember that face anywhere." Brenda looked at her. "And those hips."

"Now just a moment. Who the hell . . ."

"Mrs. Bagglesdorf claims you took her wallet out of her purse."

"While I was indisposed in the toilet," Shirley said. She looked at Barry to see how well she was doing. He nodded.

"What?"

"Since an accusation has been made, we'll just have to search your room quickly. I'm sorry," Tom said. He nodded to Barry. Barry opened the closet.

"You can't do this; I want to see regular police."

"I am regular police," Barry said. He took out his wallet and flashed his badge. Brenda's eyes went wide in disbelief.

"This is ridiculous. I tell you I never saw this woman and I didn't go into the ladies' room."

"Just a quick search, Mrs. Casewell," Boggs said.

"She's afraid because she took it," Shirley said.

Barry slid the garments toward him on the clothes rack. Brenda started for the closet.

"You have no right . . ."

Barry had the raincoat in hand. He reached into the pocket and pulled out the revolver. Brenda stopped in her tracks and backed up.

"What's this?"

"Mrs. Casewell . . ." Boggs looked at her with exaggerated surprise. "You carry a weapon?"

"I knew she was some kind of thief," Shirley said, happy to go on in her role. She was really beginning to enjoy it now, although the sight of the pistol did take her breath away for the moment.

"I . . ."

"Do you carry a permit for this?" Barry said.

Brenda stared at him a moment.

"I have one, but I left it home, in the city. Now listen, this woman . . ."

"Well, I'm afraid we'll need to take the gun," Barry said and dropped it into his pocket. "This is a very serious thing, even more serious than stealing a wallet."

"I tell you I didn't steal any wallet. She's crazy."

"Now just a moment," Shirley said. "Who the hell . . ."

"Hold on," Barry said, pulling his wife back a little more roughly than she expected. "We'll just go down to the office and check out your registration of this weapon. I'll make a New York call. If that's on the up-and-up, we'll take care of this other matter later. Until we return, Mrs. Casewell, we would appreciate your remaining in your room." He looked at Boggs.

"Right," Boggs said. "That's standard hotel procedure."

"What about my wallet?" Shirley said.

Barry looked at her. "We'll get that back, I promise. Let's go." He turned her around bodily.

Shirley glared at Brenda as they left the room.

When they closed the door behind them, they walked quickly to the elevator. Trustman had its door open and waiting. They left Cooper guarding Casewell's door.

"Keep your fingers crossed," Barry said. "I think we've got her fooled. Let's hope she starts using that phone."

When they got down to the office, the switchboard operator had already written information on her pad.

"She's calling this number," she said. Mrs. Adelman, now standing behind Barry, looked over his shoulder. "That's the Monroe, New York, exchange. I know it."

"You do?"

"I'm familiar with most of the area codes in a hundred-mile vicinity," she said pedantically. "We have guests coming from all over."

The switchboard operator, now listening in on Brenda's call, began to repeat everything she heard.

"Hello. (It's a woman.)"

"I must speak to Hamid."

"Hamid? Oh, I don't remember which one was Hamid, but he's not here."

"Who is this?"

"Mrs. Tandem. Beatrice. My husband's not here either. No one's here. Is someone supposed to be coming here for lunch?"

Brenda Casewell just hung up.

"We'll wait a few minutes," Barry said.

"I know that name," Mrs. Adelman said. "Tandem."

"You do?" Barry was beginning to find Mrs. Adelman fascinating.

"Beatrice Tandem's husband, Paul Tandem, was once head of security at this hotel."

Brenda Casewell's phone light went on again.

"Yes? 215? Just a moment."

"Check it out, please," Barry asked Mrs. Adelman. She flipped a sheet on her clipboard.

"Mr. and Mrs. Martin Jaffe."

The switchboard operator raised her hand to indicate contact.

"Hello."

"I must speak to . . . to your husband."

"He's not here right now. Who is this?"

"Where is he?"

"Who is this?"

"My name's Brenda. Tell him . . . tell him I'm in the hotel, but I'm in trouble. Tell him to pass it on. He'll know."

"She hung up," the switchboard operator said.

"Thank you. Boggs," Barry said, "get up to room 215 and keep your eye on the door. I want to speak to Mr. Oberman and find out some more about this Tandem. If the woman leaves, follow her. We'll be on the walkie-talkie."

"Right."

"Whaddaya think?" Barry said as Trustman and he headed into David's office.

"I think we're going to be very grateful to you, Lieutenant Wintraub."

David stood up as they entered.

"Well?"

"It worked. She made two calls. One to a Tandem in Monroe. Mrs. Adelman said he worked here."

"Paul Tandem? We had to fire him more than five years ago. He was drinking on the job, and he was pitifully drunk the night his son died."

"Son died?"

"As stubborn and as pigheaded as his father. He had been very sick for days and kept it to himself because he wanted to finish the holiday and make his money. Walked around with a very high fever, walking pneumonia, they called it. He finally collapsed in the dining room. The staff helped him into the kitchen, but he insisted he'd be all right. Refused to leave. They called me and I called Paul, but he didn't answer at the booth, so I sent a bellhop to find him. He was drunk and shacked up with a chambermaid in the help's quarters. To make a long story short, by the time we got him and his son to the hospital, and the kid got attention, he was already in serious trouble. He was critical for a while and then he died. It was just too late. Naturally, I had to let Tandem go. It was a very bitter affair. Doesn't surprise me that he's in on any plot to do harm to people in the hotel."

"Well," Barry said, "that explains their understanding of this place. It's time to move in on them and clean this all up. We're heading to room 215. She contacted a party there. They must be the ones."

"Jesus, be careful. Should I call the local police?"

"In a while. We'll have to turn them over once we apprehend them. Raise Boggs on the walkie-talkie."

David leaned over and pressed the talk button on the one on his desk.

"Boggs."

"I'm here."

He handed it to Barry.

"Any activity at the room?"

"Nothing."

"We're coming up." He handed the walkie-talkie back to David. "I'll have Boggs keep Brenda Casewell in her room until we send for the locals. They can book her on an unlicensed weapon's charge until we have further information here."

"Okay. It's only a matter of hours until Chaim Eban arrives."

"We'd better move fast," Trustman said.

The music in the lobby continued as the hotel and its guests went on, oblivious to the frantic activity in their midst.

28

Nessim came down a side stairway into the basement. It let him out below the area where the girders were located. He was closer to the laundry. A group of custodial people were unloading the carts of linen and stuffing the material into great washing machines as quickly as they could. It was as if the metallic monsters demanded feeding. He watched them for a moment to be sure he had drawn no special attention to himself and then turned left to walk up the corridor.

It was true that Tandem had many places to hide. He might not even be in the basement and only had said it to throw Nessim off if he did come looking for him. Perhaps he had been in the area of the deep girders and had been watching Nessim when he found his brother. Maybe he sat in the shadows enjoying Nessim's grief. The thought infuriated him. He felt for his pistol. He'd use it, if he had to. He'd use it, damn it. But he'd rather kill this man with his bare hands, strangle him if he could.

More chambermaids came walking through the corridor. A bellhop followed. All of them looked at Nessim, but he didn't return the gaze and none stopped to speak to him. It was risky being here, but he had to do it. He had to. He stopped at the first storage room, but before he could walk in, the door swung open. Nessim paused and got into a posture to strike out. An elderly custodian backed out of the room, pulling a cart loaded down with cartons of canned goods. He grunted with the effort to roll the wheels over the little rise in the floor. Nessim relaxed and then went over and pulled the cart to help him.

"Thanks," he said. "These damn things weigh a helluva lot more 'n people think."

Nessim nodded and smiled and then continued down the corridor. The old man rolled the cart in the opposite direction. The next door Nessim came to was closed. He looked behind him, and when he was satisfied that it was safe to do so, he went over and turned the knob. The door opened and he stepped into a room housing electrical equipment. It buzzed with ominous warning. There was nothing else in the room and no real place for anyone to hide. He stepped out again. Two men were coming down the hall, carrying a large stage flat between them. He waited for them to pass and then walked on.

He knew that the girder area was just a little ways ahead now, so he slowed his pace and thought. Even if he didn't get Tandem today, he'd search for him afterward. He'd refuse all other missions and live to hunt the man down. It would only be a matter of time. Perhaps the command would help him, just to speed up his utilization to them. In any case, Tandem could not escape. There was no way he could escape. The conclusion made Nessim feel a bit more relaxed. He came to another door and stopped again. This one was slightly open.

Gazing through the opening, he could see that it was filled with cartons too. From the labels he understood that the cartons contained all sorts of paper supplies. A hotel as big as the New Prospect required so much, he thought. Quite a drain on natural resources. He laughed to himself, thinking what a great deed he was going to do for nature by blowing this monster to bits. He opened the door farther and peered in. There was no one visible, but someone could easily be hiding behind one of the cartons, he thought. Maybe he made a place for himself there. He stepped inside.

Paul Tandem had slept deeply for hours, but his body ached when he awoke. He seriously wondered whether or not he could remain up on the shelf all day and had come to the conclusion that he would detonate the explosives in the middle of the hotel lunch.

In the Catskills, three meals a day was traditional hotel fare. All the guests usually took advantage of it. He was sure he'd get just about every one of them in the dining room then. So he didn't get the one Israeli, so what? What the hell was one Israeli compared to just about three thousand Jew bastards upstairs? It was after eleven. He'd only have to wait a little more than two hours. He closed his eyes and tried resting again.

Not long afterward, he heard footsteps just outside the storage room door. He opened his eyes and listened closely. It wasn't a custodian because whoever it was approached very slowly.

He backed himself farther against the wall and watched, nearly holding his breath. Then Nessim appeared. He had really hoped that Nessim wouldn't come looking for him, that he would simply accept his control and be satisfied. But obviously that wasn't to be the case.

Then Tandem thought, if Nessim was going to spend the afternoon searching the basement for him, he'd eventually find Yusuf's body. There'd be no way to avoid conflict then. He had to kill Nessim too. If he could only get at him in this room, away from the activity outside in the basement.

He moved his arms up slowly and pressed his face against the floor of the shelf. Nessim walked farther in, crouched, and began looking behind the big cartons. *If he comes over to this side*, Tandem thought. *If he gets close enough.* Nessim crossed the room, expecting Tandem to come out at him any moment. He was poised to ward off blows. When he covered the width and satisfied himself that Tandem wasn't hiding behind anything, he stopped and straightened up. He was just under the shelf. Tandem inched toward the edge of it. *When he steps out*, he thought. *When he steps out.*

Another disappointment, Nessim thought. *I probably won't find him. This is his home ground. He knows it too well to permit himself to be discovered. I'll have to smoke him out another way.*

He shook his head and stepped forward to walk out of the room. At that moment, Tandem, hovering above him and waiting, scooped down with his hands clenched and caught Nessim just under the chin. Tandem's intention was to literally hang him to death on his arms. He pulled upward with all his might.

The blow to his Adam's apple stunned Nessim. Tandem had come at him from nowhere. Nessim hadn't even considered the shelves in the room, and now he might die because of that error. He raised his hands and tugged downward, but Tandem, on his knees now, had much better leverage. Both men, aware of the danger if they attracted attention to this struggle, were caught up in a nearly comical silent effort, permitting themselves only grunts as they strained against each other.

Nessim's feet began to leave the ground. He felt the blood rushing to the top of his head. His heartbeat quickened, and the feel of it in his chest cavity, pounding out emergency oxygen and blood to all parts of his body, frightened him. All his life systems were on red; every part of him was screaming warnings. Sirens sounded in his ears. Tandem's grip closed even tighter. Nessim's attempts at breaking the hold were futile.

In a moment, the strategy came to him. Instead of pressing down against Tandem's force, he should somehow go with it and then slip free. He released his grip on Tandem's wrists and reached up for the shelf, dangling dangerously near death for an instant. The move caught Tandem by surprise and he hesitated a second. Nessim pulled himself upward, toward the shelf, faster and harder than Tandem had expected. The effect was a total release from Tandem's grasp. When Nessim had that, he let go of the shelf and fell backward to the floor, just under the shelf, free of Tandem's death clasp.

Tandem knew his best advantage lay in quick reaction. Nessim must not have the time to recuperate. The moment Nessim broke free and fell to the floor, Tandem jumped off the shelf. When he landed, he kicked the door of the storage room closed. This had to be a private fight to the death or the victor would get none of the spoils.

Nessim had time for one quick breath. Tandem spun and drove his left foot at him, aiming squarely for Nessim's face. He missed, and Nessim caught his foot with his hands and prevented Tandem's return. He twisted the foot hard and Tandem fell. Nessim was up and drove his own foot into Tandem's abdomen. He caught him well near the groin, and Tandem brought his legs up in pain. Nessim went behind him quickly and took out his knife. He flipped out the blade and grasped Tandem by the hair, pulling his head back. Tandem reached up to rip away Nessim's arm, but Nessim did not go for his throat.

He drove the knife into the corner of Tandem's left eye and with a flick of his wrist, sent the eyeball splattering against the nearby wall. Tandem's scream was the scream of a wild animal caged and crushed to death. Nessim drove the knife into his mouth, pressing the blade through Tandem's tongue and pinning the organ like a piece of meat on a skewer. It ended his scream quickly. He began to choke on his own blood.

Then Nessim carefully wrapped his forearm around Tandem's throat, catching him expertly under the Adam's apple, and tugged upward. It was only a matter of moments. Tandem's body jerked about in spasms like a fish onshore. Then he stopped and fell limp. Nessim dropped him and stepped back. He kicked him over on his back, so the blood wouldn't drip out of his mouth. He stared at him and struggled to catch his breath.

His first thought was to wait and be sure that no one had heard the fight or Tandem's aborted scream. The silence outside cheered him. He wiped his face with his handkerchief and knelt down to search for the transmitter. All he found was the battery. He looked over the floor, but it wasn't there. Then he thought of the shelf. When he boosted himself up and looked, he found the device resting there safely. Tandem had the forethought to leave it so it would not be damaged in the fight.

Good for him, Nessim thought.

He hopped down again and considered the body. He couldn't drag it out of the room now, and he could never put it back up on that shelf. Hiding it behind one of the big cartons would have to do. He made a space and dragged it deeper into the room and then placed a couple of the large cartons in front of it. Before he left the body, Nessim reached down and pulled his knife out of Tandem's mouth. He wiped the blood on Tandem's shirt. Then he looked for the splattered eye. He found it and kicked it back behind some cartons.

After that he broke open a carton of toilet tissue and used some to wipe up the blood. When he was sure he had done the best he could in clearing away traces of the fight, he straightened out his own clothes and opened the door slowly. He peered out first and then stepped into the empty corridor. With the transmitter and its battery once again safely in his possession, he had to go back and reactivate the switches. Then, finally, he would be able to leave this damnable basement, perhaps for good.

As he walked back toward the girders, he smiled to himself, thinking of the good news he could bring to his dead brother.

"No one's gone in or out of the room," Boggs said. Barry nodded. He opened his jacket. Trustman stepped out to the left. They waited for a couple coming down the hall to go into the elevator. Trustman peered out the hall window.

"Ah, a fire escape," he said, but Barry wasn't listening.

"This could be hairy," Barry said. Boggs nodded and stepped even farther back. He swallowed hard and watched as Barry knocked. There was nothing. He knocked harder. They heard a woman's voice. Apparently, she was up against the door.

"Nessim?"

Barry's eyes widened, and Trustman smiled with satisfaction.

"Hotel security, ma'am. We'd like to speak to you."

"Who?"

"Hotel security." There was a pause and a long silence. "Ma'am?" He knocked again. Then he beckoned to Boggs. "Use your key."

Reluctantly, Boggs approached the door and inserted his master key in the lock. Barry indicated that he would turn it and did so. When the door opened, both Trustman and he drew their pistols, crouched, and entered—Barry to the right, Trustman to the left. Clea was sitting on the bed. They searched the room quickly and determined no one else was there.

"What do you want?" she said.

"Why didn't you open up?" Barry asked. Boggs appeared in the doorway.

"I don't know you."

"Where is your husband?" Trustman asked quickly.

"Downstairs. He went downstairs."

"Where?"

"Shopping. To do some shopping. Who are you?"

"We're hotel security," Boggs said. He took out his identification and showed it to her. She looked at it a moment and then looked away.

"Where is your husband?" Trustman demanded again. Barry stepped in between, pulling up the chair from the dresser. He sat down.

"We're looking for a man named Paul Tandem," Barry said slowly. Clea looked up at him, her eyes wide with fear. "Can you help us?"

"I . . . I don't know him."

"You know Nessim, though, don't you?" Trustman said.

"We know who you are," Barry said, still speaking softly. "There's no sense pretending anymore. We have the Casewell woman too."

"Casewell woman?"

"She called you only a short while ago and asked for Nessim. It's all over," Barry said.

"I don't know what you're talking about."

"NOW YOU LISTEN!" Trustman shouted, waving the gun in his hand. Barry stood up and took him by the arm.

"Just a minute," he said. He steered Trustman back outside the room. Boggs remained inside. "You're not going to get anything out of her by shouting and threatening. Can't you see she's half scared to death? I know this type. Let me handle it calmly."

"There's no time to be calm. Do you know the time? Give me ten minutes alone in there with her and I'll . . ."

"Are you crazy? Where the hell do you think you are? You're in the Catskills, in a hotel. It isn't the Sinai Desert. Just relax and let me work on her. Or else go back downstairs and wait," Barry said sternly. Trustman didn't respond. They went back inside.

"Clea. We know your name's Clea and we know you're with two men, Nessim and Yusuf." She didn't look up. "If you keep quiet and let things go on this way, it'll only be terrible for them. We have men all over the building now." He waited. She was still silent. "Will you tell us where Tandem is?"

"I don't know where he is."

"But you know him?"

She nodded slowly.

"Is he in the hotel somewhere?"

"I don't know."

"We know why you are all here. It's useless now, Clea. The best thing for everyone would be to bring it all to a halt, before it gets too involved." He spoke so softly and so reasonably that Clea was put off balance. She looked at him. He was a calm man, even gentle despite his size. She thought of her father.

"I know very little," she said, shaking her head.

"Is Nessim really downstairs?"

"Well, he's not here," Trustman said with impatience. "That's obvious." Barry gave him a look.

"Start searching the room," Barry ordered. "Boggs, you'd better stay out in the hall. Let us know if anyone approaches."

Trustman began opening suitcases and drawers, treating everything roughly. He threw clothes about and scattered shoes across the floor. He stopped when he opened Nessim's special suitcase. There were wires and batteries and some extra switches and detonators within.

"Look here," he said. Barry walked over and observed. "Explosives." Barry whistled and turned back to Clea. She had her hands folded in her lap. Her body was tight, and she stared at the floor.

"They planted a bomb somewhere, is that it?" he asked her. "In Chaim Eban's rooms? If it goes off, it'll only kill innocent people because we've changed his suite. Do you want to be responsible for the deaths of innocent people?"

"There are no longer any innocent people," she said, recalling Nessim's words. She couldn't betray him—disapprove of what he was doing, yes, but betray him, never.

"Then you won't help us?"

"You see what I mean?" Trustman said. "And you're playing nice guy cop."

"I don't know any other way," Barry said.

Trustman just shook his head.

Barry walked over to the dresser and opened Clea's pocket-book. He turned it over and poured out the contents. Then he sifted through them until he found what he hoped for—pictures. There was one with the woman and a man standing on a dock, near some ships in the background. He took it to her.

"Is this Nessim?" She didn't reply. "Okay," he said. "We'll hunt him down and what happens from now on is all your fault." Clea looked up for a moment. Barry waited. Then she looked down again. "You'll remain in the room," he said. "There'll be a man outside all the time." He turned to Trustman and said, "C'mon." The Israeli security man looked at Clea with disgust. He hesitated and then reluctantly walked out of the room.

Barry was talking to Tom Boggs. "You'd better stay here, Boggs. Keep her in the room and call down the moment you see any man approach it, especially if he looks something like this guy." He showed him the picture. "Don't try to deal with him. He's got to be dangerous."

"Maybe I should have some help."

"We don't want to scare him away, but you can put someone way down at the other end of the corridor. We'll check with you continu-ally."

"Where to now, Mr. Nice Guy?" Trustman asked.

"It's lunch. Let's go to their table and show this picture to the others at it to confirm this is the man. Then, it'll be a hotel-wide search for him."

"It'd be much easier if I just went back into the room for ten minutes."

"Maybe. I don't think you'd get what you want, though. And I think your results would make us all wonder if we're on the right side."

It was like a slap in the face. Trustman shut up and simply followed Barry to the elevator.

"It looks like him," Seymour Kleinman said. His wife nodded. "That's definitely her. Why aren't they at lunch? Something happen?"

"We're trying to find out," Barry said, smiling to hide the intensity of his concern. The other couples at the table were even less positive about him. All the men recognized the woman, though.

"I'm glad of that. I was beginning to think we were at the wrong table," Barry said. Trustman shook his head.

"They didn't talk much and we . . . well, we don't like to push ourselves on people," Seymour said.

"Do you think, after you're finished with lunch that is, that you might come out to the lobby and look around for him some?" Barry asked casually. "Mr. Trustman here will accompany you."

"Well, I don't know. What's this all about?" he asked, now getting suspicious.

Barry laughed.

"I guess we can tell you," he said, leaning over. "We think he did some shoplifting earlier today."

"Really? My God!"

"You see," Amy Kleinman said. "You don't really know who you're eating with at these hotel tables."

"I don't like getting involved in that."

"All you have to do is point him out," Barry said. "Then walk away. Mr. Trustman will take it from there."

"That's all?"

"That's all."

"Okay," he said, "but just for an hour. I got a tennis court reserved for this afternoon."

"Understood. We'll be in the lobby. Oh, keep this all to yourself," Barry whispered and looked at the other couples.

"Don't worry. They don't even know we exist."

29

Nessim decided to take the elevator up from the basement. There was no one around at the time. He stepped out quickly when the door opened on the second floor. He was eager to get into the room and shower. He wanted to get out of his clothes. The sweat of the battle now made him feel dirty. He didn't want to tell Clea about Tandem, and it suddenly occurred to him that it would be best to let her believe the plastique was still inoperable. She'd be easier to get along with. He'd tell her they had to remain to be sure the explosion occurred under Chaim Eban's table. It was the best story he could come up with quickly.

He turned and started toward the room and immediately saw the man standing near the window at the end of the hall. Although something about him seemed very suspicious, Nessim didn't slow down his gait. When he could see the door to his room clearly, however, he noted that it was opened. It confirmed his instinctive feeling that something was wrong. It would be better to go downstairs and try to call Clea on one of the house phones. He stopped at an ashtray and casually took out his cigarettes, pounding one from the pack. He could see that the man was studying him intently. He turned a little and noticed another man all the way down the corridor, standing in the same fashion.

Boggs reached up to his jacket pocket to take his walkie-talkie out slowly. This looked like it just might be the man. He was coming down the corridor, in the direction of the room, and he was about the same build of the man in the picture Wintraub showed him. *I'll just signal*, he thought, *to play it safe*.

Nessim caught his movement out of the corner of his eye. He did not see the walkie-talkie clearly, but he saw that the man was reaching for something metallic. The man also unbuttoned his jacket. Everything he did was ominous. Nessim lit his cigarette and threw the match into the ashtray. The man down at the other end of the corridor suddenly broke his stance and began walking toward him. This was a trap. How? Why? There wasn't time to wonder about it. There was only time to act. He had to know if Clea was still in their room. But these men might stop him if he went back toward the elevator. It would reveal that he was afraid of something. On the other hand, all his instincts told him not to go to the room. Nevertheless, he turned again in that direction and this time saw that the man was talking into a walkie-talkie. He was definitely some kind of police or security.

Boggs was shocked. The man was just standing there, looking at him. They said he was deadly. Hardik was coming down the hall, but he was unarmed. Why did they leave him alone up here? He wasn't a real policeman. This was too much. The man wasn't too big. He could tackle him, do physical battle, even ward off kicks and blows, but if he was armed . . .

Nessim felt for his pistol. As he drew closer and saw the man's facial features clearly, he recognized that he was one of the men with the Israeli security agent. He was cornered and Clea was either trapped or taken. He was sure of it now. The man was gazing at him in a most peculiar way. He was just waiting to set up the move against him, waiting for the other one to get into position. With the decisiveness and the firmness that came from being in the thick of things so long, Nessim moved to the right, hugging the wall.

Boggs shifted his position. The approaching man had his hand in his pocket. There was a gun for sure. He had to do something. If he just stood there, the man might shoot first. If he just tried walking away, the man might feel threatened and shoot even faster. There was no time to wait for support. He was like a quarterback with all his defensive tackles down. It was pass or run. He optioned to pass and drew the revolver out of the holster.

Nessim saw the move almost before it occurred. He dropped to the floor, his pistol in hand.

"CLEA!" he shouted.

She heard him and got up from the bed. Outside her door, Boggs froze with the gun in his hand. Hardik yelled, "HOLY SHIT!" and hit the floor himself. In a moment, Clea was at the door. She pulled it all the way open and stepped forward. The abruptness of her move seemed threatening to Boggs, who thought it was part of their plan. He imagined she had a weapon too. He spun and fired, without even looking. The bullet caught Clea in the neck, ripping an artery as it passed through her. The impact slammed her back into the room.

"CLEA!" Nessim shouted again and then fired. He hit Boggs smack in the middle of his forehead. Boggs felt his head jerk back. For a split second, he was conscious and alive. He raised his hand to touch the spot and actually went "Ow!" Then he crumpled to the floor. Nessim spun on his shoulder to avoid whatever gunfire the man behind him would have. For a moment, he didn't see him on his stomach. The man started crawling frantically toward the opened elevator. Nessim shot twice as the man reached the elevator door.

He stopped crawling and the door closed against his body. Because it didn't close all the way, it would not obey the command of whoever was calling for it below.

Moments later, Nessim was at Clea's side. He couldn't believe the amount of blood that had already spilled from the wound in her neck. Frantically, he dabbed at it with his handkerchief. He ripped the pillowcase off a pillow to use that as well. Then he lifted her head. Her eyes opened and she smiled.

"It's very bad."

"No."

"They . . . know about us . . . somehow. But I told them nothing, Nessim. I . . . remained your little front fighter."

"Clea."

"Give it up," she whispered. Her voice got lower. "I feel so . . ."

He felt her body go limp in his hands.

"Clea. Oh, God no. Clea." He pressed her head against him, feeling the blood soak through his shirt. It felt warm, then cool. He kissed her face and stroked the beautiful long hair he had loved so. He lifted her body off the floor and placed her on the bed. For a long moment, he just stood there staring at her. Then he turned to the door of the room. The man who had killed her lay crumpled in the hall, his face in the rug. Nessim wished the man had a hundred lives so he could kill him again and again. He saw the walkie-talkie at his side and remembered that he had sent a message. There'd be more of them in moments. He looked back at Clea; her face was turned away from him. And then he stepped out of the room quickly to go out the hall window and down the fire escape. Nothing would stop him now.

Barry Wintraub and Karl Trustman were still in the dining room when the message came down from Boggs. Shirley was waving at him madly across the room. He waved back and indicated he'd be with her in a while. A security man was at the doorway. They saw him searching for them and caught his attention. Then they moved to his side, got the message, and hurried to the elevator. The one servicing the section of the second floor that contained room 215 seemed stuck. Barry pressed the button again and again.

"Better take the stairs," he said, and turned quickly.

"Over there," Trustman pointed. They walked to it and ran up the two flights. The stairway came out near the end of the corridor. Before they stepped into the hallway, Barry grabbed Trustman's arm and indicated that they should try to appear as casual as possible, just in case the man was still in the hall. But when they stepped around the corner, they were shocked by the sight. Hardik's body lay at the elevator and Boggs was on the floor.

"Oh my God," Barry said. He started to jog. Trustman followed, gun drawn. When he got to Hardik's body, he went down and examined him.

"He's dead," Trustman said. "Hit on the top of the head."

"Christ, don't let that elevator close. We've got to keep people off this corridor." Barry drew out his pistol.

They moved to the room slowly. When they got to the doorway, they hit the floor. Trustman, crawling on his stomach, reached Boggs. He felt for pulse, and then mouthed the word *dead*. Barry shook his head in disbelief. He hesitated and then stood up. The door of the room was wide open. He looked to Trustman, who peered in and then indicated, nothing. Barry pressed against the wall, turned into the room, and crouched quickly to avoid any gunshot. It was quiet. He saw Clea's body on the bed and studied the scene.

"He's not here," he said.

"I know," Trustman said, standing in the doorway. "The window to the fire escape's opened."

Barry walked to the bed and looked at Clea. He saw the wound in her neck.

"My God, how in hell . . . Boggs must've shot her," he thought aloud. "What the hell happened? Why did he try to take him?" He felt for her pulse. Then he turned her head and saw the pool of blood. It sickened him and he turned away. "Listen," he said, walking toward the doorway, but when he looked out, Trustman wasn't there. He had gone out the window to the fire escape and disappeared to chase after Nessim.

Barry dragged Boggs's body into the room quickly and then went down the corridor to get Hardik. He lifted him off the floor and carried him back to the room as well. The elevator door closed. *Fortunately, it's lunchtime*, he thought, *so no one was on this floor*. Except for the bloodstains, there was now no evidence of the battle. He knew what a scene like this could do to a hotel full of people, but the sight of all three bodies in the room disgusted him. It looked like a room in the city morgue. He lifted the phone and called David Oberman.

"All hell's broken loose," he told him. "We can keep it from your people a while longer, but you're going to have to call the local police now. Immediately."

"What . . . What happened?"

"Tom Boggs and his man Hardik are both dead. Shot. Their bodies are in room 215 and so is the body of the woman terrorist, if she was actually a terrorist," he said, looking at her. Incredibly, her face, soft and reposed in death, still maintained its beauty.

"Oh my God . . ."

"Karl Trustman's gone after the man."

"Where?"

"I don't know. Down the fire escape."

"Fire escape?"

"Yeah. I'll talk to you later. I'd better follow."

"Is there anything special I should do . . . with the people, that is?"

"I don't think so. We could do more damage by panicking them."

"Chaim Eban's going to land on that lawn out there in less than an hour. Should I try to turn him away?"

"Sure."

"What if he insists on coming?"

"Have him land on the roof, if possible. Can he do that?"

"On the section above the dining room. We've landed there on occasion. It's flat and it's open and there's an entranceway down the five floors."

"Talk to you later then," Barry said and hung up. He looked at the carnage once more and then went out in the hall to go through the window and down the fire escape.

Nessim was in a frenzy. When he dropped to the side of the building and tried going into the basement, he found that the door had been locked. He looked about frantically and saw some men walking toward him, coming from the direction of the golf driving range. Of course, to his right he could see cars going and coming down the driveway. He looked up the fire escape. In a matter of moments they might be coming down it after him. He tried to collect his wits, and in doing so, he realized he had a terribly large bloodstain on his shirt. The jacket closed over it well enough, but the feel of Clea's blood against his skin almost brought him to tears. Impulsively, he started around to the front of the building.

He hesitated when he came to the door. A security guard was standing there talking to a bellhop. Had the hotel been put on a full alert? Nessim joined a group of guests talking and walking into the front entrance. They all entered and he found himself in the lobby. He had to lose himself in the hotel, kill time until he could detonate the explosives. It was two thirty. That meant five hours more. His first thought was to go back to the basement, but then he wondered if that was the reason the side door had been locked. Did they expect him to do that? Had they expected him there? Were they waiting? Maybe Clea had said something without even realizing it, something that would lead them to believe he would go to the basement. No, he was better off losing himself in the hotel among the guests. He hurried through the lobby and headed for the health club. There was a place he could hide for hours, a place no one would think to look in.

As Nessim walked past the front desk, Seymour Kleinman turned and saw him. He had been waiting patiently for the policemen who had come to his table. He had only forty-five minutes now to give them. Nessim didn't see him there, nor did Seymour try to communicate with him. He watched him go up the small stairway to the left and down the corridor that led to the health club and indoor pool.

If he's wanted for a crime, how come he's just casually walking through the hotel? Kleinman thought. *Although he did look kinda upset.*

"Pardon me," Kleinman said, turning to Mrs. Adelman, "but I was supposed to meet some hotel policeman here about fifteen minutes ago. Do you know anything about it?"

"Mr. Boggs?"

"I don't know his name. He's a big guy, wide shoulders," he said, holding his hands out. "He was with a much shorter man."

"Oh. You probably mean Lieutenant Wintraub and Mr. Trustman. What's your name again, sir?"

"Kleinman. Seymour Kleinman." He watched her jot it down. Her officious manner frightened him. "I didn't even want to do—"

"Is that the short man?" she interrupted, indicating the front entrance. Trustman had come into the hotel quickly. He stood there looking around the lobby.

"Yeah. Thanks." He headed for him. "Hey," he said, approaching the secuity man. Trustman turned and for a moment couldn't remember who the man was. "Wasn't I suppose to meet you out there?" he asked in a loud whisper.

"Oh, yes, yes. You're from the table."

"I just saw him."

"Where?" Trustman's enthusiasm was frightening. "Down there," he said, stepping back and pointing. "Toward the health club."

"Thanks."

Trustman rushed off. Kleinman stood looking after him for a moment. Then he shook his head and walked away.

30

The men's health club was situated on two floors. Men entered on the upper floor and received locker keys, towels, soap, razor blades, shaving cream, whatever they needed, from a staff member at the desk. The carpeted locker room was right behind Nessim. It consisted of wall-to-wall lockers. There was a universal gym in the middle of the room. When Nessim entered, a half-dozen young boys were exercising on it. Two men were making arrangements for massages later that day.

A small stairway led downstairs to the four sweat rooms, two dry heat and two steam. There was a cold-water plunge, about the size of a small swimming pool, in the middle. There were sinks and needle showers, as well as bathrooms, on the lower floor. Another hallway led off the sweat room area to the indoor pool.

Nessim got his locker key quickly and went to a far corner to undress. He turned his body so no one would be able to see the bloodstain. When he stripped off his shirt, he stared down at the blood that had seeped through. He was repulsed by it now and wanted to wash his body. He took off all his clothes and followed the stairway down to the sweat rooms, a place he considered perfect for hiding. The room filled with the steam heat was foggy. When he looked through the window in the door, he couldn't tell if there was more than one man in it. All he saw was one man near the door. He opened it and stepped inside, making his way to the wooden benches.

The room had a small rock formation in the left corner. He heard the thin stream of water running over it. Clouds of steam rose from the floor. He used the towel to wipe his chest and then sat back, his face in his hands. When he peered around, he saw that three men were sitting across from him, all with their eyes closed. They and the man near the door were the only ones in the room.

He looked at his watch. The face of it was covered by beads of condensation and when he wiped it, he noted that the condensation was forming on the inside as well. Two of the three men across from him got up suddenly and left the room. The one at the door soon followed. Except for the man now across from him, Nessim was alone. He started to think about the terrible series of events that had taken place. He had hoped he wouldn't, but the quiet of the steam room encouraged it.

Upstairs, Trustman stopped at the desk and asked about Nessim. The attendant nodded, recalling him.

"About ten, fifteen minutes ago. Don't recall him wearing a bathing suit though. Must've gone into the sauna."

"Thanks." Trustman started for the stairway.

"Sir. You're not supposed to go down there in clothes, especially wearing shoes."

"I just want to locate him."

"I could call down for you."

A number of men dressing and undressing turned to look at him. *Damn*, he thought. He didn't want to attract any more attention than necessary now. He slipped off his shoes.

"I'll just be a moment," he said. The attendant shrugged.

Trustman walked down the stairway slowly. He stopped at the bottom and studied the area. Some men were in the cold plunge, and a few had come out of the shower area. The door to one of the dry heat rooms across the way opened. He peered through the doorway. It looked crowded. Another attendant came out of the massage room.

"Can I help you?"

"No," he said roughly.

"Well, you're not supposed to be . . ."

Trustman started away from him.

"Sir?"

"I'm just looking for a friend," he said. He went to the dry heat room and opened the door. A room full of naked men looked his way. He stood there studying them.

"Close the fuckin' door," someone shouted. The rest laughed. He shut it and went across the way to the other dry heat room. Fewer men were there, and he was quick to determine Nessim wasn't one of them. When he turned around, he saw two men come out of a wet steam room, shortly followed by a third. The attendant, with his hands on his hips, stared at Trustman a moment. Then he shook his head and went back to the massage area. Trustman started across to the wet steam room.

The man sitting opposite Nessim looked asleep. Nessim wondered how someone could do that in the steam heat. The intensity of the temperature had brought a redness to his body. A wet film of the condensed steam and his own sweat covered him. The man looked as though he was melting. Suddenly, the door opened. Nessim recognized Trustman immediately. Quickly, he buried his face in his towel and leaned over.

Trustman could see nothing clearly, and the steam annoyed him. He dropped his shoes to the floor and stepped into the room. Two men were on the far side, but one was older looking. The other . . . *It was possible*, he thought. He felt for his pistol and started across the tile floor.

Nessim waited until Trustman was right beside him; then he slid his right leg out and swung it behind his ankles. The blow sat the Israeli security man down with a thud. Instantly, Nessim flipped his towel over Trustman's head and wrapped it tightly around his throat. Trustman, momentarily dazed by the fall, first struggled against the material choking him, trying to tear it away from his neck. Then he attempted to turn on his stomach. He reached back for Nessim's arm, but Nessim evaded his grasp. When Trustman, a much more powerful man, did succeed in twisting his body over, Nessim simply moved with him, still maintaining his tension on the towel.

Trustman coughed and sputtered. The cutoff of air, combined with the terrible heat, weakened him quickly now. He slipped on the slimy tile. Any attempt to take hold of the man's body failed because he couldn't swing his arms around far enough, and the man was agile. Why had he come so close to him? What an error. What a stupid error. He made an effort to stand, but he had to pull against the towel to do that, and the effort only aided Nessim.

Trustman began to swing out wildly, desperate to make contact with the man behind him. He stumbled to his knees and then fell forward, hitting the top of his head on the wooden bench. He felt his eyes bulge and the muscles in his face strain with his efforts. Suddenly his tongue seemed to be crowding his mouth and he opened it to let his tongue rush out. It got caught between his teeth, now clenching, and he tasted his own blood. His head began spinning and spinning. He was blacking out. It was all over. *What an ignominious way to die* was his final thought.

Bill Marcus woke with a start. What the hell was going on? It looked like one man humping another fully dressed man right in the steam room. He wiped his face quickly. The dressed man was waving wildly. He heard the sound of choking and then he saw the towel.

"Hey," he said. "Hey, what the . . ." He stood up. The dressed man went down on the floor. "What the hell's going—"

The naked man spun around and hit him right in the Adam's apple. It was the most shocking, painful thing Marcus had ever experienced, and he crumpled quickly, grabbing at his own throat. He raised his left arm in an effort to keep the maniac away.

Nessim found Trustman's gun quickly and stood up again. It was miraculous that no one else had come into the room, but this man he had just hit . . . He pointed the gun at him. *No,* he thought, *the noise.* He leaned over and hit him hard on the back of the head. The man slumped into silence. Nessim took his towel, wrapped it around himself, threw the pistol into the rocks in the corner, and quickly left the room. No one paid any particular attention to him as he went up the stairs.

*   *   *

Barry had come into the lobby, hoping to find Trustman at the main desk, but only a few guests were gathered there. Mrs. Adelman was explaining something to them in her characteristically patient, but pedantic manner. He approached, looking this way and that for signs of the Israeli security man.

"Yes," Mrs. Adelman told him, when Barry asked about Trustman, "he was here a while ago. A Mr. Kleinman had been waiting for him."

"Kleinman, yes. Which way did they go?"

"I didn't see, I'm sorry."

"Get me Mr. Kleinman's room," he demanded, picking up the house phone on the counter. Mrs. Adelman looked at him and then told the switchboard operator. When he got Kleinman on the phone, he told him where he had sent Karl Trustman.

The health club was a scene of bedlam by the time Barry got there. Dozens of naked men stood around the wet steam room entrance. Barry pushed his way through. An attendant stood blocking the door.

"What happened?" Barry asked. He flashed his badge. "I'm working for the hotel now."

"A few guys went in there and found this dude, all dressed yet, mind you, out cold on the floor. He looks dead. Another guy was rapped pretty hard on the back of his head."

Barry entered. Bill Marcus was sitting up on the bench, holding a towel behind his head. He looked dazed and confused. One of the attendants, a short, thin black man, sat beside him holding his arm. Karl Trustman lay crumpled on the floor; Barry felt for his pulse.

"What happened here?" he asked, turning.

"He says two men was fighting," the attendant replied, acting now like a translator, "the guy on the floor and a naked guy. He saw him gettin' choked wit' a towel. The naked guy hits him in his throat and den raps him wit' somethin' hard. He thinks it was a pipe. We called hotel security. You wit' hotel security?"

Barry nodded, then ordered, "You'd better take this man into one of your back rooms and let him lie down. Then close this room off and cut the steam."

"Sure. What the hell's goin' on?"

Barry didn't reply. He looked at Trustman again. The security man's face revealed his great struggle for life. It was ugly—the features distorted and exaggerated by the effort. His lips looked swollen, his nostrils wide, his eyes bulged. Barry searched Trustman's body for his pistol and couldn't find it.

"Don't let anyone else enter," he told the attendant at the door. "The local police will be here to investigate. I gave the other man some instructions."

"Sure."

"What went on in there?" a plump man with a towel wrapped around himself asked.

"A murder," Barry said. "Some grudge fight," he added. "Anybody see a tall, well-built, dark-complexioned guy leave the room? See which way he went?" There were no replies. He looked about for a moment and then hurried back up the stairs.

Lillian Rothberg and a contingent of her followers, including Toby Marcus, had gathered on the lawn outside to greet Chaim Eban as soon as his helicopter landed. She had gotten the musicians who had played in the lobby out there as well. Other guests, seeing the gathering from the windows of the hotel, began coming out. The music began again.

It was a beautiful spring day. There was only a slight breeze in the air, and the cloudless sky had a rich blue hue. Lillian brushed down her daughter Lori's dress and looked about her. Her other daughter, Denise, hadn't been where she told her to meet them. *Just like her to miss the important moments,* Lillian thought. She couldn't worry about it now. Her time was about to begin. From this moment on, she'd be at the center of things. A few photographers from the newspapers were here to take pictures of Eban's arrival. *They'll be in the New York papers tomorrow,* she thought. She was anxious to be one of the first at Chaim Eban's side.

Suddenly, however, David Oberman was calling to her. He came walking across the lawn rather quickly. She turned and met him halfway.

"He won't land here," he said. She noted the deep seriousness in his face. "For security reasons."

"Where then?"

"On the roof."

"On the roof? But . . ." She turned and looked at the crowd, the musicians, the photographers. "It's all set . . ."

David shook his head.

"We have a serious security problem," he repeated. "I don't even know whether or not he'll be staying. I advised him not to come."

"What!"

"We'll contact you later."

David walked past her and went to the band to quiet them down. Then he announced that Chaim Eban would land on the roof. There were groans of disappointment. He didn't answer any of the questions thrown at him. Instead he hurried back to the hotel. Lillian looked after him. Her heart sank. It all had the appearance of a disaster.

31

Nessim was tired of running and tired of doing battle. A feeling of hysteria had been building inside him. Normally a stoic man, he was now being ripped apart by his emotions. Kept in check and under strict control for so much of his past few years, the feelings tore loose with a raging intensity. Yusuf and Clea, the two people he loved most in the world, the *only* people he loved in the world, were dead. He had no one but himself, and he had long ago come to hate himself. He saw at once that his brother and Clea had been two conflicting parts of his own personality. Each had demanded full attention. Now they were both gone, and he was overcome with a great sense of emptiness.

On top of this, he had been thrown into desperate battles for his life. The animal in him had clawed successfully out of danger each time, and despite his feeling of gloom, he had clung to life with as great a tenacity as a young man with everything in the world going for him. But it had all drained and fatigued him. He moved like a man in a daze. His eyes were red from the strain. His muscles ached with the efforts.

When the mission had been explained to him and he had contemplated it in all its aspects, he rejoiced in the fact that it was a hit-and-run job. He was to go on. There were things yet to do. His time with Clea had encouraged future imaginings. He had undergone a significant change in the sense that he permitted himself the luxury of hope. Most of the other men he knew who served the organization were men of bleak hearts. They thought of themselves as the walking dead. He had spoken with men who willingly tied bombs to their bodies and walked onto airplanes to detonate and explode, envisioning their bodies, and thus their lives, as extensions of the weapons they threw at the enemy. These people had no personal hope. They didn't see themselves as having a future. Until he had met Clea, he had begun to move in that direction and have a similar image of himself. She changed it, and now she was dead. The old image was back again.

He would go downstairs into the darkness of that hotel basement and he would crawl in beside his brother's body. He would wait in the dark and when the time came, he would detonate the explosives with his arm around Yusuf. His brother had wanted to be beside him when he did it. Now he would be. Nessim was determined that this would be the final scene.

After he battled Trustman, he went to the locker upstairs quickly and dressed. He heard the voices of shouting, hysterical men downstairs as some of them discovered the bodies. It took everyone's attention and he walked out unnoticed. He headed for the nearest stairway and went down to the basement. He heard voices all the way down at the end, but other than that, no one was around. Quickly he made his way back to the girders and disappeared under the hotel. No one saw him go there. No one knew what he carried.

Chaim Eban's helicopter appeared suddenly over a rim of trectops on the horizon. Guests who were outside saw it approaching and shaded their eyes to watch its descent to the hotel roof. Those guests who had gathered to greet him on the lawn walked about in the hotel in confusion. There were all sorts of rumors and stories. He would be in the lobby in twenty minutes; he would come out to address people on the lawn; he would be secluded in his rooms until dinner. Consequently, groups gathered everywhere.

Barry was on his way back to David's office when the helicopter landed. A patrol car from the sheriff's office had pulled up just outside the front entrance of the hotel, but everyone thought that was all part of the preparations for Chaim Eban's arrival. Sheriff Balberri and his deputy went directly into the hotel and David's office and were there only a few moments before Barry arrived. David was on the phone with the security man on the roof.

"The 'copter's touched down," he said. "They'll bring him directly here."

"Then he refused to turn back?" Barry asked.

"Absolutely. I think he wants to take charge of things personally."

"What things?" Balberri asked. He took off his hat and brushed back his long, thin graying hair. A man in his early fifties, Balberri was a man who had devoted all his life to local law enforcement. He began as a village traffic cop, became an active member of the Democratic Party, first as a committeeman and then as its candidate for county sheriff. He was a personable man who became a natural campaigner and had been virtually ensconced in the office. The last few elections found him up against simply names on the ballot. No one bothered to actively campaign against him anymore. He was a phenomenon not unusual in local politics—an unbeatable candidate.

"Karl Trustman was just murdered in the steam room," Barry said. David's face dropped with the shock.

"No."

"What the hell's going on here?" Balberri looked to his own deputy as if he could see something he missed. The young man just shrugged. "Who was murdered?"

"Ralph, this is going to be very complicated, but to make things short—you know Chaim Eban, an Israeli military hero, has just landed at the hotel for a night of fund-raising and speeches."

"Sure."

"Apparently some Arab terrorist organization has plotted his death."

"Why weren't we informed immediately?"

"We weren't sure about anything. Then things just started happening quickly. Thanks to Lieutenant Wintraub here, a New York detective, we've uncovered them."

"But not apprehended them," Barry said.

"There was a gun battle on the second floor during lunch and . . ." David swallowed and shook his head, still unable to believe it. "Tom Boggs and his man, and another security man, were both shot to death."

"Tom Boggs!"

"And now, Lieutenant Wintraub has reported an advance man from Israeli security was killed."

"He chased the terrorist to the steam room," Barry said. "Confronted him there." Turning to David, Barry added, "One of your guests was hurt too. Hit on the head."

"That might be the ball game," David said. "We've been trying to keep the lid on this so as not to panic the people."

"No one heard the gunfight?" the sheriff asked.

"Everyone was at lunch and Barry put the dead bodies in the room. A female terrorist was shot too."

Balberri sat down. "Is that it?"

"No," Barry said. "The terrorist or terrorists are still somewhere on the grounds or in the building. I haven't uncovered their sabotage."

"Paul Tandem is with them, helping."

"Tandem? That degenerate?"

The phone rang.

"It's the health club," David said, picking up the handset. "Who? Bill Marcus. Did you call for Dr. Bloom? The sheriff's on his way. Just keep everyone out of that area. All right." He hung up and turned to the sheriff. "Where do you want to begin, Ralph?"

"Jesus." The sheriff wiped his face. "I'd better call in the BCI, for one." He paused, knowing the delicacy and the import of his next statement. His mind rushed ahead of him as he envisioned what the impact could be on the entire hotel industry, the county's major source of revenue. This was the most politically dangerous situation he had ever confronted. It could cost him his career. "If we don't apprehend these people and uncover their sabotage," he said, looking at his watch, "within the next two hours, you'll have to empty this hotel, David."

David turned in his chair, his hand on his chin. He nodded slowly. His voice cracked with emotion.

"You're right. Okay," he said. He looked at Barry. "Any suggestions? You're the man who's been in on this from the start."

"Keep Eban secluded as much as possible. Tighten your security on the grounds and keep all outsiders away." He turned to the sheriff. "Have the suite originally reserved for Chaim Eban searched thoroughly."

"I'll get some more of my men around the grounds too," the sheriff said.

"Damn," David said. "If I have to tell these people to leave, there will be pandemonium."

"Don't I know it," Sheriff Balberri said. "Let's get started."

After Bill Marcus had been examined by the doctor, they had him dressed and took him out a side entrance to place him in an ambulance. Although his head ached and his throat was still sore, he was conscious and aware of everything now. Toby had been called to his side and stood by staring in disbelief. She was at the entranceway when the stretcher was rolled out.

"I believe he's got a concussion," the doctor explained. "We'll take X-rays and see how bad it is."

"I don't understand. What happened?" She looked down at him. "Why'd you get involved in someone else's fight?"

"Who got involved? The guy just turned and hit me."

"We'd better let him take it easy now," the doctor said. He signaled to the ambulance attendants so they would lift him into the ambulance.

"Listen," Bill said. Toby leaned in after him. "I want to go back to

New York. I don't want to stay up here in some country hospital. Get me to New York."

"But . . ."

"They'll take me in an ambulance," he said. The attendants closed the door.

"Of course," the doctor said as Toby backed away. "After I get an X-ray reading, if that's what he wants . . . If he'll be more comfortable with his personal physician . . ."

"But isn't it bad to move him? I mean . . ."

"We'll see, but I don't think so." He squeezed her arm. "He'll be all right."

Toby stood there as he walked to his car.

"Oh," he said, turning around. "You can look into ambulance services by going to the main desk. Mrs. Adelman will help you."

"But . . ." She watched the ambulance go down the driveway and then turned to look up at the hotel. "Damn it," she said and stamped her foot.

Barry walked out of David's office slowly and went outside to think. Tandem was a man who would be recognized on the hotel grounds. He wouldn't be somewhere they could see him. Perhaps he wasn't even here and was just used for the information he could give the terrorists. And now the extremist knew he was also recognizable. Where would he go to hide? Why would he hide? Why was he still here if the purpose was simply sabotage? . . . Unless they hadn't yet planted their bomb or had to stay to detonate it.

He walked out to the driveway and stared at the old main house. He wondered what Shirley and the kids were doing and if they were anywhere in the building or on the grounds that presented danger to them. Then he turned and looked back, studying the fire escape he had come down earlier. The window to the second floor was still open. He looked back at the old house. Something was trying to come back to him, something said, something—David's father. The old man had seen people on the fire escape late at night. They said teenagers, but was it? He hurried across the grounds to the old main house.

Solomon Oberman got up from his easy chair to answer the door. He lowered his glasses on the bridge of his nose and closed his copy of *Catskill Quarterly*. He had been studying an article on the resorts, underlining everything he thought was poppycock.

"Mr. Oberman?"

"Yes?"

"I'm Lieutenant Barry Wintraub, sir," he said, showing his identification. "Can you tell me about the figures you saw on the fire escape these past two nights?"

"What was it, robbery? I knew it, damn it." He slapped his thigh with the magazine. "C'mon in."

When Barry came out of the old house, he studied the basement door by the fire escape. *Logical place to hide*, he thought, *but why had they gone down there at night?* Their sabotage work must have been done in the basement. But what? Could they reach Chaim Eban's suite through the basement? Maybe through the heating system. Does that mean poison gas? The thought terrified him.

He went back into the hotel and got Mrs. Adelman's attention.

"I don't know if it's possible for you to answer this," he started—

he thought he'd start off with a note of challenge—"but that party we traced on the phone, the Jaffes, do you know if they specifically asked for that room, 215?" She just looked at him and then her eyes lit up.

"Why, yes, they did. And I was wondering about that."

"Thanks," Barry said quickly. He looked for the nearest stairway to the basement and hurried over to it. He came out near the stage-craft area. Two men were painting flats and another was cutting out huge styrofoam stars. They looked up at him.

"Hi," he said. "Happen to see any guests come this way today?"

"Guests?" They looked at one another and all shook their heads. He continued down the corridor. An elderly custodian was push-ing a cart that held a tall carton. He was coming toward Barry so he stopped and waited for him.

"Excuse me," he said. The old man paused, letting the cart back against his foot. "Have you seen any guests down here, males?" The old man wiped his face with a gray handkerchief.

"Guests, huh? When?"

"Today."

"Nope."

"You're not here at night, are you?"

"Hell no. Get off at five. That's enough for me."

"Yeah, well . . ."

"Wait a minute," he said. "There was someone earlier. He came out of nowhere it seemed. Helped me get the cart out of that storage room there."

"Did he look like this?" Barry showed him the picture.

"Can't say for sure. Might have. Didn't look at him much."

"Which way did he go?"

"Well, he didn't follow me. He went back up the corridor."

"Thanks. Thanks a lot."

Barry hurried on. He stopped at an electrical room and examined it. *Could they be doing something with electricity?* he wondered and studied the wires. Not finding anything suspicious there, he went on. *There are so many possibilities*, he thought. When he came to the first girder, he paused to look around and envision where he was in relation to the hotel above him. The elevator all the way at the end of the corridor helped him get his perspective. The dining room and the five floors above it were all to his right. He turned and looked off into the depth of the basement beyond. It was a very poorly lit area since there weren't any storage rooms located in it. Then he heard the squeak of wheels and turned to see the old man pushing his car back up the corridor.

"Excuse me," he said, as the man got close. "But aside from the electricity and the heat, is there anything else that goes upstairs from the basement?"

"Huh? Goes up?"

Barry nodded.

"Well, water does."

Water? Yeah, water, he thought.

"And that girder you leanin' against," the old man said, smiling.

"Girder?" Barry stood up and looked at it.

"All of 'em do," the man said, gesturing farther in, "to support the damn building. What are ya tryin' to figure out?" he asked, but Barry was lost in thought. The elderly custodian shrugged and went on to the storage room just down from them to get another carton. Barry started in a few feet, still thinking. Suddenly he heard the old man shout. He turned and ran into the room. The old man stood back and pointed. Tandem's dead body rested exposed since the old man had moved another one of the big cartons. A stream of blood and mucus ran down his cheek from the gouged-out eye socket.

"Sorry end for a sorry fella," the old man said.

"You know him?"

"Yeah, sure. Used to work here. That's Paul Tandem," he said.

32

Barry didn't go back upstairs. He sent the old man up and told him to report what he found to Sheriff Balberri. Then he went back to the dark area across the way. He stood there thinking again. *That woman's husband is down here*, he thought. Perhaps both terrorists were. They were certainly ruthless people. Before continuing on with his search, he was going to wait for support, figuring the sheriff or his deputy would be down soon; then he looked to his right and saw the plastique.

The impact of total recognition and discovery sent an electric chill down his spine. He approached the footing of the girder and knelt down. He was by no means a bomb expert, but he had seen plastique and he had seen some detonators. This looked different in its construction and design, but he understood that the penlight battery provided the needed impulse. With careful fingers, he worked the battery out. Then he saw the small picture inked in beside the detonator—a hawk with a sword through it. He remembered the picture in the Mandel apartment. He had tracked down the killers of the JDL member, followed his instincts and leads, and come to the end of the trail.

A series of contradictory feelings overcame him. He was elated that he had been right, but he was suddenly alarmed and terrorized by what it could have meant and still could mean if he didn't disarm all the other detonators. These girders supported the structure and the dining room was directly above him. His own wife and children would be in there tonight. He had brought them to it.

He moved across the basement quickly to the other girder and worked out the battery from the detonator. Carefully and cautiously, he went farther into the basement, disarming each packet of plastique as he came to it. Each time he did one, he felt that much more relieved and yet with each girder he approached, he expected some opposition. They were here somewhere. They had to be. They were just waiting for all the people to move into the dining room and then they'd detonate—wanton killing to get Chaim Eban? Or was it their main intention to kill everyone else, too?

He despised them as any law enforcement agent despises the criminal element, always threatening, out there, dangerous. Yet he hated them for even deeper, more personal reasons. Rabbi Kaufman had seen it in him, had known it lay dormant there, waiting to exert itself. *I am a Jew*, he thought, *and these people have come here to kill me and my family and people like us because we are Jews. No battle in the Sinai Desert, no attack on the Golan Heights, no embattled kibbutz smacks more of the ancient rivalry than does the conflict in this basement now. A battle for Israel is being waged here.*

Nessim had been sitting next to his dead brother and delivering one of the longest monologues of his life. He wasn't even aware himself of just how much he had been talking. He described all that had transpired upstairs and, for the first time, permitted tears when he came to the part about Clea.

"They killed her, but it was partly my fault. I should have never agreed to bring her into this. I should have either come with you or by myself. Maybe with that Casewell woman. It was my mistake. I didn't even think about it."

As he continued talking, he began to behave more and more irrationally. He was no longer talking to himself by bouncing his words off his dead brother; he was treating his brother as though he were alive. As if he knew it mattered, he didn't look directly at him when he spoke. When he pounded out a cigarette from his pack, he offered the pack to the corpse and then put it back into his pocket.

"Well, Yusuf," he said, "you wanted so much to be beside me when I detonated the plastique. You're going to have your wish. That's right. We'll do it together." He paused and leaned back against the wall. Yusuf's body was now in the same position, only his head was forward, chin to chest. "She was . . . was really so brave at the last moments. You should have seen her. If only we had left her in Athens, huh. If only . . ." His voice trailed off, his thoughts lost in the smoke that traveled into the darkness. He sat staring at memories.

Not long after, he heard Wintraub walking on the other side. He crushed his cigarette out and leaned out to see who it was. Barry disappeared behind the next-to-last girder. He had understood from the structure of things that there were these two left. With the same great care, he worked out the battery and put it with the others in his jacket pocket. Still expecting to meet up with the terrorists, however, he waited in the shadows and looked out. Now that he was in the most secluded spot, the chances were that much greater.

Nessim, on his knees, took out his pistol and waited. Perhaps it was just a custodian doing a routine assignment. Perhaps not. He would take no more chances. If there was the slightest suspicion, just the slightest now, he would risk the gunshot. If they found him, he'd detonate everything and take his chances on getting as many as possible in the building above.

Barry waited a moment more and then began to cross to the other girder. Nessim saw his shadow first and then the clear outline of his body. Whoever it was, he was coming straight at him. He crouched, held his revolver braced against the girder to steady his aim, and waited to take his best shot. A little more than halfway across, Barry hesitated. It was the odor of cigarette smoke. He was sure of it. They were nearby. He listened for voices. Instinctively, he went to his knees.

The moment he did so, Nessim fired. He thought the action indicated that the man had seen him. He was sure this man had come hunting for him. The bullet whizzed past Barry's ear, and the report of the pistol carried in tinlike echoes back down the basement, seeking a way out. Voices of shouting men could be heard coming from the main corridor.

"HEY," Barry yelled. "IT'S NO USE. IT'S ALL OVER FOR YOU."

"No, you are wrong," Nessim called back. "It's all over for you. In fact, it's over for all of us."

"STAY BACK," Barry shouted to the oncoming men. "STAY BACK."

Nessim put his gun down and slowly took the transmitter out of his pocket. He unscrewed the back of it and slipped in the tiny battery. *It would have been a great feat,* he thought. *Command detonation at its best. At least the organization will salvage something from all this. They'll still remember the Seder Project.*

Barry went to his stomach and began crawling over the basement floor. He got to a point where he was sure he could make out the dark shadows of a man standing and another sitting with his back to the wall.

"Hey," Barry called. "You're surrounded. There's no way out. Give it up."

"But there is a way out," Nessim said, half laughing. "We're going up, or rather, the up is coming down."

"What's going on up there?" a voice cried from behind Barry. He turned.

"Stay back. They're in here."

"It no longer matters how far back *they* stay," Nessim said. He enjoyed talking like this at the moment. His thumb rested on the transmitter switch.

"You're wrong," Barry said. He crouched quickly, expecting to be shot at, but they weren't shooting. He reached into the jacket pocket and grasped all the batteries he had taken from the detonators. Then, leaning on one arm, he heaved them toward the shadows and the voice as if he were heaving a hand grenade. The batteries bounced and rolled around Nessim. "Your plastique explosives can no longer be detonated."

Nessim leaned over and picked up one of the batteries. His heart sank. He felt anger like he had never felt it before. A shout built itself up from the pit of his stomach and climbed through his throat. When it came out, it was the raging of a wild animal. It was shrill and long. Barry had rarely heard anything like it. He inched back in anticipation. Nessim stood up and shot his pistol wildly. The bullets ripped into the basement walls and pinged with reverberations everywhere. When the gun had been emptied, he threw it into the darkness. Barry heard it bounce near him. He got to his knees and struggled for a clear view so he could take an effective shot.

"You were very clever," Nessim said. "Very clever. But you have yet to disarm one."

Barry understood his meaning and frantically rolled over to get as far back as he could. Nessim smiled to himself, knelt down and took his brother's hand in his, and then flicked the switch looking directly into the detonator. He wanted the satisfaction of watching his system at work. The pleasure barely registered in his brain.

Chunks of cement were thrown about like spitballs. They smashed into tiny bits against the walls and over the floor. The steel girder was shoved out to its right. The metal screamed as it bent. Ceiling plaster and installation materials fell in pieces all around Barry. He buried his head in his arms and rolled himself into a tight ball. Dust clouds rose up from the floor. Ominous cracks broke out along the side of the basement wall nearest to the blown girder. They ran like spiders' legs, tearing the cement. The floor of the basement vibrated, and slabs of cement around the girder's footing tore up and shattered, exploding in every direction. Barry felt his body peppered by pieces of it. It stung through his clothes.

The sound of the detonation was deafening beyond imagination. Because of the closed-in nature of the area, the trapped sound waves were amplified. The belly of the basement became a giant speaker queezing the noise and sending it rushing out. It gave the impression that a series of explosions was going on all along the basement. Custodians, chambermaids, everyone put his hands to his ears and cowered in fear. And this had only been one-sixth of the potential blast.

Directly above the exploded girder was the far right corner of the hotel dining room. The tables had been set for dinner, and only a few staff members were there with the maître d'. The explosion shook the entire floor, however. Tables on that side rose off the floor and slammed down, sending their dishes, glasses, and silverware bouncing and crashing to the floor. The chandeliers above shook violently, smashing their glass teardrops against one another and sending down a rain of fragments. Even though the floor on that side of the building sank only inches, it created a deep incision between the wall and the floor in corners and sides.

Depending on where they were located in the hotel in relation to the area of the explosion, guests and staff members reacted with proportionate intensity. Those just outside the dining room took hold of one another or of furniture, or they pressed their bodies against the nearest wall. Although the vibrations and sounds could be felt and heard throughout the building, people in the health clubs, on tennis courts, in the indoor pool, skating rink, stores, and luncheonettes interrupted their activities for only a few moments. Some people thought jet planes had broken the sound barrier. They waited to see whether the noise would continue or whether someone would tell them something had happened. Apparently, nothing had, so they went on with their recreation.

When the rumbling stopped and the dust began to settle, Barry stood up and looked around him. The floor of the basement was strewn with debris. A water pipe on the right side had busted and a heavy spray was shooting up. The size of some of the chunks of material around him was astounding. He was amazed he hadn't been badly battered or killed.

The ceiling still creaked and strained with the weight of the building on that side. The girder on the left with its supporting ribs was now shouldering the weight of the whole area. He heard shouting and saw custodians and two of the sheriff's men approaching. He brushed down his clothes and walked toward the girder. It dangled from the ceiling, bent away from the floor. Then he scanned the basement and imagined what would have been had all those girders gone together.

"You all right? What happened?" the first deputy asked.

"Someone committed suicide," Barry said and started away. Despite the awesome destruction and wreckage around him, he felt successful.

The terrorists had been stopped. Thousands of people had been saved. He had no notion of, nor did he imagine, any more could be. Yet a small wristwatch continued to tick under the main table in the dining room. Nessim's legacy remained.

33

The compromise between David Oberman and the police was to keep the truth subdued until after Chaim Eban left. That way, the guests would no longer have reason to feel threatened by any further attempts on his life and there would be no panic or mass exodus from the hotel. With the police off the grounds and the terrorists killed, everyone would get the impression it was all over before he knew about it.

The official word given out about the explosion was that a boiler had blown in the basement. The dining room was thoroughly cleaned up and minor repairs were done. Construction men were called in to repair the damaged girder. Those who knew about the murder of Karl Trustman in the steam room and asked more about it were told that it had been a family grudge fight and the police were investigating. The bodies of Boggs, Hardik, and Clea weren't taken out of the hotel until evening. Boggs and Hardik were both bachelors, but their immediate families were notified they were killed in a security matter. Details were held back. There was fear that someone would get to the media, and they didn't want that to happen until Eban departed.

Chaim Eban himself was in David's office getting a briefing when the charge detonated in the basement. Jerry Wilson, the agent from the State Department security; Chaim Eban; and Yael Brand, a tall woman in her forties who served as his personal secretary, sat around David's desk and listened to him relate the chronology of events.

Dressed in Israeli military attire, Chaim Eban sat back with his fingers together in cathedral fashion and listened. He was a little over six feet tall and had dark brown hair and hazel eyes. There was a slight smile on his cleanly shaven, lean face. The corners of his eyes had the deeply worn creases of a man who had spent years under the desert sun squinting. There was a deceptive sense of peacefulness about him. He sat with tight, but not stiff, posture. Added to this correct, military demeanor, however, was a sense of warmth. It was in the softness of his voice—though talking with him only a short while, David got the feeling he was a man who seized command quickly, listened with an analytical ear, and cut right to the heart of things.

The sound of the explosion interrupted them. David called down to the basement immediately, but no one knew what was happening.

"I'd better get down there," he said. Eban rose too. David said to him, "If you go out into that lobby, the people will just mob you again."

"He's right," Jerry Wilson said.

"I'll call you immediately," David added. He waited a moment. Eban nodded and sat down again.

Instead of calling, David did the best thing. He brought Barry Wintraub back upstairs with him to give Chaim Eban the whole story firsthand.

"There's no sense in calling for more security now," Jerry Wilson said after it was all related.

"Oh no, no," Chaim replied. "Our New York detective here has done the job. You have our deepest gratitude."

"I'm only sorry we lost good men in the process."

"We could've lost a helluva lot more," David said. "I shudder to think about it."

Later, Barry went back to his rooms to shower and rest. He intended to call the city and report everything. Shirley and the boys weren't there when he arrived, but they came in while he showered.

"I'll tell you all of it," he told her, "but it's going to take the rest of our holiday."

Lillian Rothberg was ecstatic. All the arrangements for the evening were to be kept. Whatever problem had been brewing was resolved. She rehearsed her introductory remarks for the Eban speech to be given in the nightclub after dinner. Abe was still upset about what had happened to Bill Marcus, but she didn't feel the loss of Toby really would have any significance on the course of events. Toby wasn't doing that much anyway.

After Eban had been settled in his suite, Lillian was called to go over and meet with him. He was as charming as she had expected. Pictures and headlines flashed through her mind. He wanted her by his side as much as possible.

"We are, after all, in debt to your organizational abilities, Mrs. Rothberg."

"Please. Call me Lillian."

"Lillian," he said, smiling.

The dinner was to be one of the most exciting events of the holiday period. A small band had been set up near the front of the dining room, and it played the same Israeli and Jewish music that had been played during the day. A banner had been made by the stagecraft people. Hanging down from the ceiling over the dais, it read SHALOM CHAIM EBAN. People came in dancing, clapping hands, and hooking arm to arm. The dining room staff was thrown off rhythm by the men and women in the aisles, stamping their feet and singing, but there was no anger or annoyance. Everyone was caught up in the joviality.

The public address system was set up. Rabbi Tannenbaum, from the nearby synagogue, was to give a short blessing and welcome to Chaim Eban, but Eban would make no remarks now. He would save his talking for later. He didn't appear until most of the people were seated in the dining room. Then he came through the entrance with David, Gloria, and Pop Oberman; they were followed by Jerry Wilson, and Yael Brand, who held hands with Bobby and Lisa Sue. Abe and Lillian Rothberg with their daughters, looking terribly embarrassed, were in the rear.

People came to their feet and applauded. There was shouting and waving of napkins. Eban lifted his hand in a gentle salute to the crowd. Women leaned forward to kiss him. Men stuck out their hands. He shook as many as he could as he moved quickly to the head table. The band continued to play. It paused, and then three thousand people rose to sing "Hatikvah" in Chaim Eban's honor. The flag of Israel had been raised just under the American flag above the dais.

Barry held Shirley's hand. He felt a special significance when they sang "Hatikvah." Chaim Eban, only a few feet away, looked to him and nodded with meaning. Barry was proud of himself in a new way. When he turned and looked at the crowd and saw all these beautifully dressed people, when he saw the faces of the young and the faces of the old, when he looked into the faces of his own children, he felt a real sense of gratitude that he had been given the opportunity to save them. Certainly God had chosen him, had placed him here so that he could accomplish what he had. It restored his faith. He began to wonder about the order of things. He was touched by his personal memories of Torah and the sound of his own voice singing the bar mitzvah. As funny as it all seemed to him at times, he had tried to run away from who and what he was. How ironic it was that people who battled his heritage had given it back to him.

But it was seven ten. Nessim's watch ticked on, like an organ of his body outliving him. It ticked equally distant from the bodies of Chaim Eban, David and Gloria Oberman, Solomon Oberman, David and Gloria's children, the Rothbergs, and the members of Eban's party. It ticked against the mass of plastique explosives, closing in on indiscriminate death; for as a thing of no consciousness, it did not know or care about the people around it. It would destroy anyone, anywhere. It had been placed there by desperate men who sought to move events on the other side of the world. It encompassed all the conflict, all the bitterness, and all the sorrow of that part of the world. It had come over the oceans and through other countries to get to this spot in the Catskills and no amount of music or singing could drown out its ugly voice.

A lone car moved in the darkness of the road adjacent to the New Prospect. Hamid, by himself in the front seat, pulled over to the side and turned off the lights.

"Okay?" he asked. El Yacoub leaned forward.

"Yes. This should do."

They stared for a few moments in silence.

"There has been nothing in the news, nothing on the radio, nothing to suggest . . ."

"We'll just have to wait and see. It won't be long now. I have seven fifteen."

"Who do you suppose called Tandem's wife? I could make no sense out of anything she said."

"It's not important now. We could do nothing now anyway."

"Still, I wish we knew."

"We'll know all in a matter of minutes."

The Claw leaned back into the darkness of the backseat. He melted in with the shadows. Only his eyes were illuminated, reflecting the lights from the hotel gates across the street. There was also the glow of the small dial on his wristwatch. He touched it with his thumb as if he could stroke the seconds and encourage them.

"When can we start to eat?" Jason asked. Shirley tried to ignore him, but he tugged on her dress. "Huh?"

"When the rabbi is finished," she said, smiling at Mrs. Rosenblatt, who glared.

"I'm hungry."

"Me too," Keith said.

"Relax, boys." Barry nudged Jason gently. Keith began tapping his fork on his lap. Shirley caught the action out of the corner of her eye.

"Put that back on the table," she said. He didn't, so she reached over to take it out of his hand and the fork clattered to the floor. She looked up, smiling. "Children," she said. Lucille smiled back, but the Rosenblatts just stared stone-faced. "Pick it up," she ordered out of the corner of her mouth. Reluctantly, Keith went down on his knees and crawled under the table to get the fork. When he sat back again, Shirley and Barry closed their chairs in on him tighter to keep better control.

"Dad."

"Quiet, Keith. The rabbi's getting ready."

"But I want to ask you something."

"Can't you wait?"

"I guess so," he said, lowering his head. Barry looked at him.

"Okay, quick. What?"

"Why do they have watches under the table?"

"What?"

"Watches. How can people tell time if it's under the table, huh?"

"Where did you see a watch under a table?"

"There," he said, pointing to Chaim Eban's table.

Barry hesitated a moment and then stood up.

"What is it?" Shirley asked. Everyone at the table was looking up at him.

"Nothing." He took a few steps toward the Eban table and then squatted, leaning over and bracing himself on his hand. When he saw it, he felt glued to the floor.

"Vot's he doin'?" Mrs. Rosenblatt asked. Shirley didn't reply. Everyone at the table turned to see. The rabbi began his blessing.

"Excuse me," Barry said, tapping Lillian Rothberg on her leg. She looked down in astonishment. Denise started to laugh. "I think I dropped something and it rolled under your table. I'm sorry." He started to crawl under. Bobby and Lisa Sue watched him, but everyone else's attention turned to the rabbi.

It was seven eighteen. Barry studied the packet frantically. His understanding of these things was obviously limited, but he followed the wire that went into the plastique and decided that had to be the key to disarming it. He gambled and detached it. Nothing happened. He looked at it a moment and then ripped the watch off. When he held it in his hand, he couldn't believe the sweat that had poured out of his body during those moments. His whole body trembled. He felt as though he might faint under the table. Turning, he saw the children peering under at him. He smiled weakly and backed out. Jerry Wilson saw him but didn't say or ask anything. He seemed to understand it was better to wait.

"Barry, what the hell are you doing?" Shirley asked as he returned to the table. They were all looking at him, and people at nearby tables who saw him crawl in and out were staring at him as well.

"I . . . er, thought I saw a valuable piece of jewelry dropped under that table, but it only turned out to be this old watch," he said, opening his palm. They all looked. Mrs. Rosenblatt shook her head and leaned over to her husband.

"Tomorrow," she said, "you make udder arrangements and get us at annuder table." He nodded obediently.

Chaim Eban's name was mentioned and the crowd cheered again. Barry sat back, his arm around his son, who looked at him with satisfaction.

"Does the watch work, Dad?"

"It sure does."

"Can I have it later?"

"You sure can," he said. "You earned it."

After the dinner ended, Barry told Jerry Wilson what he had been doing under the table. Wilson went back and removed the whole packet. When he examined it and the watch, he told Barry how closely it had come to going off.

"I wish you hadn't told me that," he said.

"Apparently this was their backup device if something went wrong. I'll discuss it with Chaim and recommend he leave the hotel tonight. Staying over is a luxury he can no longer afford. Who knows what they'll send in here next."

Later on, Eban agreed. When the festivities and the speeches ended, the Eban party made ready its departure. Barry accompanied David Oberman to the roof of the building to watch the helicopter take off. They stood together in the cool night now filled with stars and watched them load up. Chaim Eban walked over to them as the helicopter was started. He shook David's hand and then held Barry's.

"Once again we owe you a great deal, Lieutenant."

"This time it was my son's inquisitive mind. I'll never stifle him again." Eban laughed.

"We could use a man like you. If you would ever like to take a vacation in Israel," he added smiling, "at our expense . . ."

"These free vacations are gettin' kinda rough."

"Shalom, Barry Wintraub."

"Shalom."

Eban shook his hand firmly and then turned to join the others in the helicopter. They watched it ascend into the night.

"Well," David said. "You've got a full week yet. Now you can really enjoy the hotel."

"I guess so. If I can relax. It'll be more like collapse."

"If you can't, you're welcome to come anytime you can. In fact, you and your family have a standing invitation to a free Passover here from now on."

"My mother-in-law won't be so happy to hear that."

"Bring her, too."

"Now I'm not so happy."

They laughed and then looked out over the hotel grounds. Lights twinkled in the distance, and cars could be seen going and coming on the Quickway, a highway to New York and upstate.

"I see my father's light is still on," David said, looking at the old main house. "I guess I'll go over there and sit with him a while. Maybe I'll try to describe the events of the past three days."

"That'll keep him awake forever."

David nodded and they turned to go back down.

In the distance, Hamid drove off toward New York. He and El Yacoub had been silent ever since the great disappointment. They waited, hoping that things had just been thrown back a few hours, but nothing happened.

"In the morning, we'll try to find out what went wrong," the Claw finally said.

"And then?"

"We'll begin again."

Hamid nodded. He understood the Claw's fanaticism, but he

recalled Nessim and Yusuf vibrantly alive. He thought about the times they spent together in the Middle East, and he mourned the death of their childhoods. He began to feel very old, way beyond his years.

Rabbi Kaufman came out of the synagogue basement with a group of his followers. The young men stood beside him as he hesitated on the walk. He looked out across the road at a dark alley. Many of the men followed his gaze and stared with him, remembering.

"Stay together," he said. "Think only that there is danger and death lurking." Some of them nodded with hate; some nodded with fear.

"Shalom," he said.

"Shalom," they replied.

In the distance, a police siren wailed. They all turned to listen, wondering for whom it cried.

ABOUT THE AUTHOR

Andrew Neiderman is the author of numerous novels of suspense and terror, including *Deficiency, The Baby Squad, Under Abduction, Dead Time, Curse, In Double Jeopardy, The Dark, Surrogate Child,* and *The Devil's Advocate*—which was made into a major motion picture by Warner Bros. For twenty-six years, Neiderman has been the ghostwriter behind the epic series attributed to V. C. Andrews. He lives in Palm Springs, California, with his wife, Diane. Visit his website at www.neiderman.com.

EBOOKS BY
ANDREW NEIDERMAN

FROM OPEN ROAD MEDIA

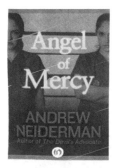

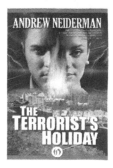

Available wherever ebooks are sold

OPEN ROAD

INTEGRATED MEDIA

Open Road Integrated Media is a digital publisher and multimedia content company. Open Road creates connections between authors and their audiences by marketing its ebooks through a new proprietary online platform, which uses premium video content and social media.